FOREST GHOST

FOREST GHOST

Graham Masterton

This first world edition published 2013
in Great Britain and 2014 in the USA by
SEVERN HOUSE PUBLISHERS LTD of
19 Cedar Road, Sutton, Surrey, England, SM2 5DA.

British Library Cataloguing in Publication Data

Masterton, Graham author.
  Forest Ghost: a novel of horror and suicide in America and
  Poland.
  1. Boy Scouts–Suicidal behavior–United States–
  Fiction. 2. Scout leaders–Suicidal behavior–United
  States–Fiction. 3. Soldiers–Suicidal behavior–
  Poland–Fiction. 4. Forests and forestry–Fiction.
  5. World War, 1939-1945–Poland–Fiction. 6. Horror
  tales.
  I. Title
  823.9'2-dc23

ISBN-13: 978-0-7278-8344-5 (cased)

All Severn House titles are printed on acid-free paper.

Severn House Publishers support the Forest Stewardship Council™ [FSC™],
the leading international forest certification organisation. All our titles that
are printed on FSC certified paper carry the FSC logo.

FSC
www.fsc.org

Typeset by
Falkirk, Sti
Printed and
TJ Internat

Owasippe Scout Reservation, Michigan

B ill's black Labrador, Mack, found the first one as he was snuffling around in the thick brown layers of last fall's leaves. He barked, twice, and then circled around and around, excitedly thrashing his tail.

'What you got there, boy? Not another goddamn quill pig. You remember what happened the last time you chased after one of those? You had a sore snout for days.'

Bill carried on walking through the trees. It was shady here, but up ahead of him Lake Wolverine was sparkling blue in the sunshine. He could see the jetty from which the Scouts dived into the lake, and where they tied up their boats. Unusually, though, he could see no Scouts, only their red-bottomed boats bobbing in the water.

He could hear no shouting or laughter, either. He stopped for a moment, and listened, but all he could hear was the soft subversive rustling of the beech trees and the piercing cries of two blue jays, calling to each other.

Mack barked again. Bill turned to see that he was still circling around the same heap of leaves, and still wagging his tail as if he were trying to wag it right off.

'Come on, Mack! Whatever it is, leave it! We're going to be late, else!'

But Mack wouldn't come. Instead, he buried his nose into the layers of leaves and furiously started digging.

Bill stalked back and seized him by his collar. 'You know what happens to dogs who don't do what they're told? They don't get no bully sticks! Now, leave that, whatever it is, and let's get going!'

As he dragged Mack away, however, he saw a pale hand lying amongst the leaves. It looked like a child's hand, with three or four friendship bracelets knotted around the wrist.

'Oh my Lord,' Bill said. He kept hold of Mack's collar with one hand, but he knelt down and started to clear away the leaves with the other. It didn't take him long, because they were only a superficial covering, just enough to have hidden the body from anybody passing by.

It was a young boy, of about twelve or thirteen years old. He was coppery-haired, with a snub nose and freckles. He was wearing a Camp Wolverine T-shirt and blue shorts, but his feet were bare. Resting in the palm of his right hand was a scouting knife, with a blade that was rusty-colored with blood.

Mack barked again, but Bill said, 'Hush up, will you? Have some respect,' because there was no question that the boy was dead. His throat had been cut from one side to the other, so that it was gaping wide open like a second mouth, with scores of shiny green female blowflies crawling in and out of it.

Bill took his cellphone out of his shirt pocket, but there was no signal out here in the woods. However, he knew that there was a phone in the Camp Wolverine dining hall, so he stood up and pulled Mack away from the boy's body and started to walk as fast as he could toward the lake.

He was still a hundred yards away from the water's edge when Mack started to pull sideways at his leash and bark again.

'For Christ's sake, Mack! What's eating you now?'

Mack began to pull harder and harder, until he was wheezing. In the end, Bill let him have his head. Mack had never been a disobedient dog, and if he sensed that something was wrong, then Bill reckoned he had better let Mack show him what it was.

There was a small clearing in the trees close to the edge of the lake, where the scouts would light fires when it grew dark and toast marshmallows and sing 'Great Green Gobs of Greasy Grimy Gopher Guts' and tell each other horror stories.

This was eleven o'clock in the morning. The sun was shining, and a fresh breeze was blowing off the surface of the lake, but what Bill found there was worse than any horror story that he had ever heard. All around him, at least fifteen boys and seven adult men were lying on the dirt, some of them wearing scout uniforms, some of them wearing T-shirts and shorts, several of them naked. They were all dead. Some of them had their throats cut, in the same way as the coppery-haired boy. Others had their wrists cut – not crosswise, but all the way down the length of their radial arteries so that they would have bled out faster and it would have been almost impossible to save them, even if they had been found while they were still alive. At least three of them had scout knife handles sticking out of their chests. One of the men was lying on his side with his stomach cut open so that his intestines had spilled out on to the leaf-mold beside him. He was still wearing his thick-rimmed glasses.

Even Mack stayed still, and didn't bark. He looked up at Bill and there was something in his expression that Bill had never seen in a dog before, and he had owned dogs all his life. It was fear. Whatever had happened here, Mack was afraid of it. He was actually trembling, and he was pawing the ground as if he couldn't run off fast enough.

Bill had to turn away. He could feel bile rising in his throat and the last thing he wanted to do was puke. He said, 'Come on, boy,' and tugged at Mack's leash, and he began to walk stiff-legged around the perimeter of the lake toward the wooden camp buildings.

When he reached the dining hall he said, 'Stay,' to Mack, and climbed the steps. Inside, the corridor was warm and stuffy and smelled strongly of cedar wood. Before he could reach the phone, Bill had to gallop to the restroom at the end of the corridor, throw open the door, and vomit an acrid orange slush into the washbasin and halfway up the splashback.

Afterward, he raised his head and stared at himself in the mirror. A sweaty, gray-haired man with a beard, and a face that was leathery from years spent in the outdoors. He couldn't understand what he had just witnessed, but he knew that it was probably the worst thing that he would ever see in his entire life.

For the first time in a very long time, he crossed himself.

Nostalgia Restaurant, 5307 North Clark Street, Chicago

Jack was arguing with Mikhail about the sauce for his stuffed cabbage when Sally came into the kitchen.

'You didn't add any tomato catsup, for Christ's sake! You didn't add any crushed tomatoes! You didn't add any *paprika* for that matter! No wonder it tasted so goddamned bland.'

'My mother always cook with just beef stock,' Mikhail protested. 'Salt, pepper, beef stock. That is Polish. With *tomato*, that is Slovak.'

'I don't give a toot how *your* mother cooked it. *My* mother cooked it with tomato sauce and crushed tomatoes and that's how we're going to cook it here.'

'I hate Slovaks.'

'I'm not too crazy about the French but that doesn't stop me cooking with cheese.'

Sally said, 'Sorry to interrupt you, Jack. I need a word.'

'Sure. Be right with you.' He pointed a finger at Mikhail and said, 'You got it? Tomato sauce, crushed tomatoes, and plenty of paprika.'

Mikhail shrugged and pulled a face. 'OK. You want to me to cook like Slovak, I cook like Slovak. Slovaks cook like shit. That's because they don't know shit from food. A Slovak, he will pick up dog turd and eat it because it looks like wiener.'

'*Mikhail* . . .' Jack warned him.

Mikhail raised both hands in surrender, and started taking down saucepans and ladles and colanders from the hooks above his head with as much clatter as he could, like a one-man percussion band.

Jack followed Sally back into the restaurant. It was only four-thirty in the afternoon, and the lunchtime session was over. His two waitresses, Jean and Saskia, were clearing up the tables and relaying them with red-and-white checkered cloths, ready for the evening. It was sunny outside, but inside the restaurant it was quite gloomy. It had dark wood paneling on the walls and an old-fashioned mahogany bar, with scores of bottles of exotic spirits on the shelves behind it. On the walls hung large dark oil paintings of Polish cities like Kraków and Wrocław, with castles and churches under thunderous skies.

'What's the problem, Sal?' Jack asked Sally. 'You want a beer, or are you on duty? How about a soda?'

'No, I don't want a drink, thanks,' said Sally. 'Something terrible's happened.' She paused, and took a deep breath, and then she said, 'Two days ago the local scout troop sent off a party on a camping trip to Michigan. They were supposed to be going for a week.'

'Yes, sure, I knew about that. One of the kids – Malcolm – he's really good friends with Sparky. My God – they haven't had an accident, have they?'

Jack suddenly realized that Sally had tears in her eyes. 'They're all dead, Jack. All of them. Sixteen scouts between the ages of eleven and eighteen and seven adult leaders.'

'Dead? *What? All* of them? How?'

'I've just been talking to one of the deputies from the Muskegon County Sheriff's Department. They still can't work out exactly what happened, or if anybody else was involved, but one thing is absolutely beyond question. They all killed themselves, every one of them. It was a mass suicide.'

'I can't believe it. What did they do? Take poison or something?'

Sally shook her head. 'Some of them cut their own throats, apparently, and some of them slashed their wrists. One of the leaders cut his own stomach open – you know, like hara-kiri.'

'Jesus. When did this happen? I haven't seen anything on the news. Not that I ever watch it. Too goddamned busy running *this* madhouse.'

'One of the reservation forestry workers found them around eleven this morning, when he was out walking his dog. But the CPD didn't want to release any details to the media until the parents had all been informed.'

'All of them dead? So Malcolm must have killed himself, too? Malcolm Cusack?'

'I'm afraid so,' said Sally. 'They sent us a complete list of names, so that we could tell the scout troop and the next of kin.'

'Malcolm was only twelve years old, for Christ's sake. Skinny little kid; wouldn't have stepped on an ant. I don't know how the hell I'm going to break it to Sparky. He's going to be devastated.'

Jack suddenly felt light-headed. He pulled out a chair and sat down at the nearest table. Sally pulled out another chair and sat beside him. She laid her hand on his wrist and said, 'Malcolm is the reason I'm here.'

Jack frowned, not understanding what she meant.

'We're flying all of the victims' families to Muskegon first thing tomorrow morning to identify the bodies and visit the location where they died. We thought that it would help to bring them closure. There's also a possibility that one or two of them might be able to give us some clue as to why they killed themselves. Maybe they all got themselves involved in some kind of online suicide cult.'

'So where do I fit in?'

'Corinne Cusack is a single mother, as you probably know.'

'That's right. Her husband died about a year ago, didn't he?'

Sally nodded. 'Jeff Cusack. Very sudden. Very sad. But they had only just moved here to Edgewater before he passed away, so Corinne doesn't have any family close by. She hasn't really had the chance to make many friends yet, either. Well – grieving widows are not exactly the best company. The thing is, Jack, I asked her if there was anybody she would like to go with her to Muskegon – you know, to give her moral support. Of course I'm going there myself, but I won't have time to give her any one-to-one care. She nominated you, and Sparky.'

'Corinne Cusack wants me to fly with her to Michigan?'

'You and Sparky, both. According to her, Sparky was the only friend that Malcolm had. He used to get bullied at school and Sparky was the only one who ever stood up for him.'

Jack said, 'I would have to take him anyway, if I went. You know that.'

'Of course,' said Sally. She waited for a moment, and then she said, 'So? Do you think you could do it? The CPD will be picking up all of your expenses. You know – flight, and any accommodation if you have to stay overnight. I doubt if it will come to that, though.'

'I don't know, Sally. I'm just trying to think what effect it could have on Sparky.'

'It might be just what he needs, to visit the place where his friend died. It might help him to come to terms with it.'

'Oh, sure. And on the other hand, it might give him screaming nightmares. It took him nearly six months to get over seeing that dog being run over.'

Sally waited a moment longer and then she stood up. 'OK, Jack. I can give you some time to think about it. But you would be doing me such a tremendous favor, believe me. Call me later this afternoon, if you can.'

Jack looked at her. In many ways, she reminded him of Agnieszka. A little shorter, a little bigger-breasted. But she had a similar blonde crop and similar high cheekbones, although her mouth was wider and her lipstick was always redder. He wondered if – in another life – they might have been more than just friends. She was a police detective, however, the most hard-boiled woman he had ever met, and he ran a restaurant and liked to paint watercolors in what little spare time he ever had. Their attitude to life was so different that he couldn't imagine any relationship between them could have lasted.

He checked the antique Polish clock on the opposite wall, with its wearily swinging pendulum. It was twenty minutes of five now, and he had to collect Sparky from school. He didn't know how he was going to break it to him that Malcolm was dead. He went through to his small office at the back of the restaurant to collect his car keys. In the same drawer there were three Oh Henry chocolate bars which were Sparky's favorite. It was a ritual that Jack gave him one every day when he came out of school. What was he going to do today? Say, 'Here's your candy bar and by the way Malcolm's killed himself'?

He looked into the kitchen to see how Mikhail was getting along. Mikhail was stripping the leaves from a head of white cabbage, and looked up at Jack as if he would like to be doing something similar to *his* head, instead.

'I know,' he said. 'Slovak recipe. Tomato. Paprika. *Phaugh!*'

Jack walked out to the narrow yard in back of the restaurant where his black '98 Camaro was squeezed in between the trashcans and the wall. The space was so tight that he could barely open his door wide enough to climb in. He was halfway in and halfway out when a voice called out, 'Jack! Jack! Wait up a second! Jack!'

It was Bindy from the bookstore next door. She was small and excitable, with rimless spectacles and wildly curly brown hair and she always reminded Jack of a hyperactive Disney animal. She was wearing a baggy mustard-colored dress and at least five strings of amber beads.

'Hi, Bindy. Sorry – I'm kind of in a hurry here. I have to pick Sparky up from school.'

'Oh, OK. I just wanted to tell you that we have Tamara Thorne coming to the store on Wednesday.'

Jack was still uncomfortably jammed in the half-open door of his car. 'Tamara Thorne? Is that somebody I should know?'

'Tamara *Thorne*, Jack! The medium! She wrote *How to Talk to the Loved Ones You've Lost.*'

'Oh, yes. You gave me a copy, didn't you?'

'That's right. You can bring it along and she'll sign it for you. But the main thing is, she's going to be holding a séance. She's going to try to get in touch with people who have passed beyond.'

'Bindy, I'm really pushed for time here. I'll come in and talk to you about it later, OK?'

'OK, Jack. Just thought that you'd like to know. Maybe you'd like to try and contact Aggie.'

Jack didn't say anything, but gave Bindy a fixed grin and forced himself down into the driver's seat. Bindy gave him a little wave and went hurrying back to her bookstore. Jack adjusted his rear-view mirror and looked at himself. The last thing he wanted to think about right now was getting in touch with the dead.

Von Steuben High School, 5039 North Kimball Avenue, Chicago

Jack parked outside the school's front entrance. It was unusual for Sparky to be late: he was usually standing on the sidewalk, patiently waiting.

Nearly five minutes went by, during which time Jack kept a sharp lookout for parking attendants. Chicago's parking attendants were notorious for slapping tickets on anything on wheels, even if a meter still had time left to run, or it was two minutes after nine p.m. Eventually, Sparky came down the steps of the red-brick building on his own, carrying in his arms a celestial globe, or what looked like a celestial globe. He was frowning, for some reason. He was blond-haired, like his mother had been, and he always looked pale, even when Jack had taken him on vacation to Florida and he had spent all day in the sun. He was wearing a maroon T-shirt and flappy brown cargo pants, and his shoelaces were undone.

He opened the door, folded the passenger seat forward, and carefully stowed his celestial globe in the back.

'What's that?' Jack asked him, as he climbed into the car and closed the door.

'It's an astrological globe,' said Sparky, pronouncing his words very clearly, as if he were talking to somebody of limited intelligence. 'Mrs Hausmann said I could borrow it for the weekend, so long as I drew her star chart for her.'

'That's what it does, then?' asked Jack, as he pulled away from the curb and headed back up North Kimball Avenue. 'Tells fortunes?'

'It helps an astrologer to work out which astrological houses are going to be affected by which planets, and when.'

'Oh. I see. That's cool.'

'Yes. Mrs Hausmann said I could borrow it because she's

never come across anybody who can accurately tell fortunes like I can.'

'Well, it's just a talent you have. I never believed in it myself until you started doing it.'

Jack turned right at the Shell gas station into West Foster Avenue.

'Apart from that, how was your day?' he asked Sparky. He knew exactly what Sparky was going to say next, and he was trying to put it off.

'It was OK. We had Mr Kaminski for algebra and that was OK. I had a cheeseburger for lunch and that was OK. I took out the tomato.'

'You and Mikhail ought to get together. He hates tomatoes, too. He says they're Slovak.'

'Actually they first came from South America. The first people to eat them were the Aztecs.'

'Oh, right. The Aztecs, huh?'

'Yes. They called them *xitomatl*.' A pause, then, 'Dad . . . where's my Oh Henry bar?'

'I'm sorry, Sparks. I guess I forgot to bring it.'

They were crossing the north channel of the Chicago River, and the afternoon sunlight momentarily flashed from the surface of the water on to Sparky's face, bleaching his skin so that it looked even whiter, and making his hair shine in fine gold filaments.

'You *never* forget to bring it. You always give it to me when we go past Jimmy John's.'

'I know. But I was in kind of a hurry today. I forgot it.'

Jack glanced across at Sparky and saw that Sparky was staring at him with those stonewashed blue eyes as if he didn't believe him for a moment.

Sparky said, 'It's happened, hasn't it?'

'What? What are you talking about? I forgot your candy bar, that's all. I'm sorry. You can have it as soon as we get home.'

'It's Malcolm, isn't it?'

'Malcolm? What about him?'

'He's dead. That's why you didn't bring me my Oh Henry bar.'

'Sparky – how can you possibly know that? Malcolm is away on a scout camping trip in Michigan.'

'I *told* him not to go,' said Sparky, clenching his fist and beating on his knee for emphasis. 'I told him and I told him and I told him and he still wouldn't listen.'

Jack reached across and laid his hand on Sparky's skinny arm.

'He *is* dead, isn't he?' said Sparky.

'Yes, he is. I don't know how the heck you knew about it, but yes.'

Sparky's eyes suddenly filled with tears, and he shook his head from side to side in grief and frustration. 'I *told* him not to go. I could see it in his stars. All the signs pointed to it. I even drew his chart for him, and I showed it to him.'

'I'm really sorry, Sparks. I don't know what to say to you. You guys were so close.'

Sparky sniffed and wiped his eyes with the back of his hand. 'He wanted to prove to everybody that he was tough. I told him it didn't matter what everybody else thought about him. But he said if he went to Owasippe and showed everybody that he could swim and light fires and tie knots and all of that scout stuff, they wouldn't call him a geek any more.'

'But you did his star chart for him, and that showed you that he was going to die?'

Sparky nodded, his mouth puckered in misery.

Jack said, 'I have to tell you that they *all* died, not just Malcolm. The whole troop, fifteen scouts and seven leaders. Sally came round and told me, but it's probably going to be shown on the news, later.'

'All of them? I didn't see that in the stars. Not *all* of them. Only Malcolm. They weren't murdered, were they? What happened to them? It wasn't like *Friday the Thirteenth*, was it?'

Jack hesitated, and then he said, quietly, 'They killed themselves, Sparks. They all committed suicide, including Malcolm. That's what Sally said, anyhow.'

'I saw Castor in his chart,' said Sparky. 'Castor is a fixed star and that usually means a head or a neck injury which could be serious enough to kill you. The Sun was in Aries, and it was squared by Mars and Saturn. That was almost the same chart that Henry the Second of France was given in the year 1554. Five years later, when he was jousting, a lance went right through the eyehole in his helmet and into his brain.'

Jack glanced at Sparky again. Although his voice sounded flat, tears were still rolling down his cheeks. Jack was used to this apparent contradiction. Sparky always spoke as fluently as somebody twice his age, and with very little emphasis in his voice, almost as if he were reading from a prepared script. But Jack knew how emotional he could be. The first time Sparky had witnessed Malcolm being bullied at school, he had come home trembling with rage and frustration.

Jack said, 'Malcolm's mom has asked if we could go with her to Muskegon tomorrow – you and me. She has to identify Malcolm formally and the police are going to take all of the next of kin to the spot where they died. When something like this happens, some people find it pretty hard to get to grips with it, and I guess they think that might help.'

'Does anybody know why they all killed themselves?'

'I'm not sure. They might have left suicide notes, but if they did, Sally didn't mention it.'

'I don't want to go.'

'Are you sure about that? I think Malcolm's mom could really use our support right now.'

'Something made him do it and I don't want to meet that something.'

'I don't get you. He committed suicide, Sparks. They all did. It's not like Jason Voorhees came out of the woods in his hockey mask and killed him.'

'I don't want to go.'

They had reached the Nostalgia Restaurant. Jack stopped outside the front entrance to let Sparky out, because his parking space in the back yard was so tight that Sparky wouldn't have been able to open the Camaro's door wide enough to lift out his astrological globe.

'OK,' said Jack. 'If you really don't want to go, I'll call Sally and tell her we can't do it. I did warn her that it might be too upsetting for you. Listen – you go inside while I park the car. Are you hungry?'

Sparky shook his head. Jack put his arm around him and hugged him. 'I'm so sorry, Sparks. I really am. I know how close you were, you and Malcolm.'

Sparky whispered, 'I told him not to go. I *told* him. He just wouldn't listen.'

Corinne Calls

By the time Jack had parked his car and squeezed out of it, Sparky had taken his astrological globe up to his bedroom.

'What is the matter with young Sparky?' asked Saskia, as Jack came into the restaurant. 'He just go straight upstairs and he don't even say hallo.'

'Looked to *me* like he'd been crying,' put in Jean.

Jack briefly told them what had happened. Jean pressed her hand against her forehead and then said, 'Oh, *no*! My friend Ruby – her son Jimmy belongs to that same scout troop. I hope *he* wasn't one of them!'

'Why don't you call her, just to make sure?' Jack suggested. 'Go ahead – do it now. You don't want to spend the rest of the evening worrying about it.'

Jean went to make her phone call while Jack went through to the kitchen. Mikhail's two sous-chefs had arrived and were busy prepping for the evening. Piotr was furiously chopping up potatoes to make dumplings, while Duane was mixing a thick stuffing of mushrooms, walnuts and horseradish.

Piotr was short and chunky, with buzzcut hair. He had recently come to live in Chicago from Lublin, in Poland, but Duane, a tall young African-American with a bald head and large gold earrings, had lived in Chicago all his life. For some reason, he had a talent for cooking authentic Polish food. Even Jack's mother said that Duane's *zrazy* were to die for.

'What's Sparky having tonight?' asked Duane.

'I don't know. He's kind of upset. I'll tell you why later. Maybe some soup.'

'The soup tonight is *zhurek*. Otherwise there's *borsch*, or cherry soup.'

'Thanks, Duane. Everything OK, Mikhail?'

Mikhail had his back turned but he lifted his hand to show that everything was under control. Jack didn't say anything about tomatoes.

He went up the narrow back stairs to the three-bedroomed apartment over the restaurant. The apartment was large, with high ceilings, although it was mostly furnished with old-fashioned couches and armchairs which Agnieszka had inherited from her parents, and its heavy brown velvet curtains gave it an Eastern European gloom, like the restaurant below.

He went to Sparky's bedroom door and knocked. 'Sparks? You OK? You want anything to eat?'

There was no answer so he opened the door. Sparky was sitting at his desk with the astrological globe in front of him. Through the window, Jack could see the brown brick wall of the building next door. It had a large hoarding on it with a stylized picture of a ram's head, and the words *Capricorn Hardware*. It had always struck Jack as one of life's coincidences that Sparky should have an astrological sign staring into his bedroom window, especially since Sparky *was* a Capricorn.

Jack sat down on the end of the bed and watched Sparky turning the globe around and around – occasionally stopping to jot down figures and symbols on a notepad.

'So what are you doing now?' he asked.

'Looking back,' said Sparky. 'Trying to find out what happened.'

'Looking *back*? I thought astrology looked into the future.'

'Unh-hunh. The stars can show you the past as well. Just because nobody took any notice of their stars at the time, that doesn't mean that the warnings weren't there. I looked back at President Kennedy's stars for November twenty-second, 1963, and if anybody had drawn him a star chart, he would never have driven through Dallas in an open-topped limo. The third degree of Gemini was rising, and the Moon had reached the square of Mercury.'

'Sparky,' said Jack, standing up and laying a hand on his shoulder. 'Maybe you should give this a rest for now. Come down and help me in the restaurant.'

Sparky didn't turn around and look up at him, but Jack could tell that he was silently crying. 'No, Dad,' he said. 'I have to do this. I want to.'

Jack waited for a while, with his hand still on Sparky's shoulder. Sparky was wearing a Chicago Bears T-shirt now, and around his neck hung the greenish-blue metal pendant that his late mother always used to wear, in the shape of a large teardrop. The goat on the brick wall opposite stared at him with yellow-eyed malevolence, more like a demon than a goat.

'OK,' he said at last. 'Come down when you feel like it. Duane's made cherry soup, or *zhurek*, if you'd prefer it.'

He went back downstairs. As he crossed the restaurant, the front door opened and Corinne Cusack walked in. *Oh shit*, he thought. *And I haven't even called Sally yet, to tell her that Sparky and I won't be coming to Muskegon.*

'Jack!' called Corinne. She was quite tall, nearly as tall as he was, and she had a fashion-model figure, flat-chested but with very long legs, although she always seemed to walk in an uncoordinated way, like a new-born foal. Her long reddish hair was tied back with a gray silk scarf, and she wore a loose gray silk sweater and a black knee-length skirt. Her face was long and narrow, with hooded green eyes. She was wearing no make-up.

'Corinne,' said Jack. He came over and embraced her. Underneath her sweater she felt unbelievably thin and bony. 'I don't know what to say to you. I'm so sorry for your loss.'

'He was looking forward to it so much,' said Corinne. 'Especially since it meant that he could take a week off school. Do you know what he said to me?'

'Corinne, please. Why don't you sit down? Can I get you a drink? A cup of tea, maybe?'

They sat on stools at the bar, Corinne awkwardly crossing her legs. She looked up at all the bottles behind the bar and said, 'Maybe a vodka-tonic. No ice.'

Henryk the barman hadn't started his shift yet so Jack poured the drink for her, with Polish vodka, and a Jack Daniel's for himself. Ordinarily, he didn't drink alcohol when he was at work, but today was no ordinary day.

'He said he was going to go to camp like Clark Kent and come back like Superman,' said Corinne. Her green eyes were sparkling with tears. 'He was scared to go. I knew he was scared. But he felt so much that he had to prove that he was tough. I think he wanted to prove it to *me* much more than the boys at school. He wanted to prove that he could take care of me.'

'I'm so sorry,' said Jack.

Corinne took a tissue out of her pocketbook and wiped her eyes. She took a sip of her vodka-tonic, and then she said, 'Detective Faulkner asked me if I knew anybody who could come to Owasippe with me. I hope you don't mind but I said *you*, and Sparky. I couldn't think of anybody else, and Malcolm and Sparky were such good friends.'

'Yes, she told me. The only problem is . . . well, you know that Sparky has Asperger's?'

Corinne nodded. 'That was what made it so amazing, that he helped Malcolm so much.'

'The problem is, Corinne – he doesn't want to go. It's irrational, I know, but he thinks that something killed Malcolm and, whatever it is, he's scared of it. I'm sorry.'

'I just can't make sense out of any of this,' said Corinne. 'I know Malcolm was being bullied at school, and he was grieving for his dad . . . but *why*? I was always there for him. And all of those other scouts killed themselves too. Why did they do it?'

'I really don't know, Corinne. I'm just sorry that we can't come with you. I would, myself, but I can't leave Sparky here on his own. My mother keeps an eye on him, usually, when I have to go away, but she's in Florida right now, visiting my aunt, and she won't be back for a couple of days.'

'It's OK. I understand. It was presumptuous of me to ask, really. It's just that I didn't know who else to turn to.'

Jack said, 'You have family, don't you, back in – where was it?'

'Seattle. Yes. But we never got on too well. Jeff was about the only real friend I ever had.'

She finished her drink while Jack sat and watched her. He didn't know what else to say to her. She seemed to him to have a conflicting personality, needy but remote – lonely, but wary of allowing anybody too close to her. It could be grief, he guessed, for her recently deceased husband. As his mother had once said to him about his father, you don't stop loving somebody just because they're dead.

She climbed off her barstool, in that awkward way of hers, as if she were just about to lose her balance. 'Thanks, anyhow, Jack. I guess this is something I'll have to deal with on my own.'

But at that moment, Sparky came down the stairs. He was carrying a sheet of paper and he looked very serious.

'Sparky!' said Corinne. 'Are you all right, sweetheart?'

Sparky walked up to them and said, 'It's OK, Mrs Cusack. We'll come with you to Owasippe.'

'Sparky?' said Jack.

'No,' said Sparky. 'We will definitely come with you.'

'Are you sure?' asked Corinne. 'Your dad here thought you might get too upset.'

'We have to come with you,' said Sparky. 'It's important.'

'What's that you have there?' Jack asked him.

Sparky held it up. 'It's a star chart. I drew it with Mrs Hausmann's astrological globe.'

'Is it for Malcolm?'

'No, it's for us. There's a connection between what happened to Malcolm, and our family. That's why we have to go to Owasippe.'

'What connection?' asked Jack. 'How can there be a connection?'

Sparky said, 'I don't really know yet, but there is. The stars show it clearly.'

'You're sure you haven't made a mistake?'

Sparky shook his head. 'I've done it three times over. It's always the same. Every time I check today's date, and the way that Malcolm died, the globe comes up with *our* chart, too. They match exactly.'

Jack looked at Corinne, and shrugged. He could tell by the look on Corinne's face that she didn't believe any of this. All the same, she said, 'I would really like it, if you could come with me, you and your dad.'

'We have to,' Sparky repeated.

'In that case, I'll call Sally Faulkner, and tell her. Corinne? You want to stay for something to eat? Sparky? You ready for some soup yet?'

Sparky said, 'That's all my dad ever does. Tries to force food down people's throats.'

Fears of the Forest

I t was warm and sunny when they arrived at Muskegon County Airport, with a soft summer wind blowing and the blue sky streaked with mares' tails. Altogether there were 51 of them, parents and relatives of the scouts and scout leaders who had died, as well as five police officers from District 24.

Their conversation as they had flown over Lake Michigan had been subdued, barely audible over the sound of the engines, with some of the mothers quietly sobbing. Sparky had said nothing at all, but busily continued to scribble astrological signs in his notebook, as well as lists of figures, and geometric diagrams. He had never once looked out of the window to see the sun shining on the lake like hammered glass.

Sally approached Jack and Corinne and Sparky as they came out of the airport building. 'So glad you could help out, Jack,' she said. 'And you, Sparky.'

Jack thought of telling her that Sparky had insisted on it, and why, but then he decided against it. No matter how strong it appeared to be in Sparky's star chart, he didn't think there could really be any astrological connection between Malcolm's death and the Wallace family. Even if there were, how would it help the police to determine how and why these scouts and their leaders had taken their own lives?

'There's a bus here to take you all up to the Owasippe Scout Reservation,' said Sally. She turned to Corinne and added, 'We're so sorry for your loss, Ms Cusack. If there's anything at all that you need, you have only to ask us.'

In a husky voice, Corinne said, 'Thank you, Detective.'

It took them a little over 40 minutes to drive north to Owasippe Scout Reservation. Through the tinted windows of the bus, the woods on either side went by like the landscape in a dream. Again, most of the journey passed in silence, with only the occasional sound of a woman's muted weeping. Outside the reservation buildings, eight or nine squad cars from the Muskegon County

Sheriff's department were parked at all angles, as well as three khaki panel vans from the Medical Examiner's office and satellite trucks from all of the local TV stations. A flag was flying at half-mast, and flapped in the desultory wind like somebody giving a slow hand-clap.

As the relatives disembarked from the bus, sheriff's deputies and staff from the Medical Examiner's office were on hand to direct them through to the main assembly hall. There, the bodies of all those scouts and scout-leaders who had committed suicide were lying on trestle tables, covered with sharply pressed green sheets. The assembly hall was lit by shafts of sunlight, and there were two priests standing in the far corner, one Episcopalian and one Catholic, so it looked more like a church than a morgue. But there was an underlying smell like rotten chicken, which was quite unlike a church, and somebody had obviously tried to mask it with lavender room spray.

As they approached the double doors that led into the assembly hall, Corinne took hold of Jack's hand and said, 'Will you come in with me? I don't think I can face this on my own.'

Jack looked at Sparky, who said, 'That's OK. I'll wait outside. I want to remember him the way he was when he was alive. And I need to see the woods, because that's where it is.'

Jack said, 'OK.' He didn't ask what 'it' was. He was used to Sparky coming out with odd remarks like that and most of time he took no notice. They almost made sense and that was good enough.

Sparky went off toward the back of the building and Jack saw him asking directions from an Eagle Scout. The Eagle Scout had his hand on Sparky's shoulder and was pointing to the glass doors that led outside to the verandah.

'You ready for this?' he asked Corinne.

She nodded, and took hold of his hand, and gripped it tight. Together they pushed their way into the assembly hall, where medical staff were already lifting up several green sheets so that relatives could identify their dead.

Across the end of the hall, Jack saw a banner with the scout rallying cry *Attawaytago!* sewn on to it in bright red cotton letters. *God*, he thought, *you couldn't get any more bitterly appropriate than that. That's the way to go.*

He couldn't stop himself from looking as they made their way between the trestle tables. He saw an African-American boy, no older than thirteen, whose face was completely unblemished, as if he were smiling in his sleep. He saw another boy, white, with tousled brown hair, but this boy looked more bewildered, as if he couldn't understand why he was killing himself. He had a bruise on his cheek and his neck was covered right up to the chin by a thick white crêpe bandage.

'Cusack?' asked a large red-cheeked woman with a frizzy black perm and a clipboard.

'That's right,' said Jack.

The woman folded back the green sheet and there he was: Malcolm Cusack, with his gingery hair and his freckles. He looked ridiculously boyish to be dead, and Jack half-expected him to suddenly open up his eyes and say: 'Surprise!' But he didn't open his eyes, and he wasn't moving, and he wasn't breathing. Like the brown-haired boy, he too had a bandage covering his neck.

'Why does he have that bandage?' asked Connie. She was gripping Jack's hand so tight that his wedding band was digging painfully into his middle finger.

The woman consulted her clipboard. Jack noticed that she had a large brown mole on her upper lip. He tried gently to twist his hand free but Corinne still wouldn't let go.

The woman said, 'Cusack, Malcolm J.? The cause of death was . . . his external carotid artery was severed.'

'What? What does that mean?' asked Corinne. Under normal circumstances, she would have known, or guessed, but here in this makeshift mortuary with all of its green-sheeted bodies and its smell of lavender room spray, she needed to have it spelled out to her.

The woman looked at Jack, raising her thick black eyebrows like two crows taking off from a field. Jack leaned closer to Corinne and said, 'He cut his throat, Corinne. I'm sorry.'

Corinne stared back at him in green-eyed disbelief. 'He cut his throat? He wouldn't! He *couldn't* have. Why would he *do* that?'

'Why did any of these kids kill themselves? And these adults, too. That's for the cops to work out. I can't think of any explanation at all.'

Corinne reached out and touched Malcolm's forehead with her fingertips.

'He's so cold,' she whispered, and then her knees buckled and she almost fell to the floor. Jack managed to catch her around the waist, and hold her upright. She was too heavy for him to lift and carry out of the assembly hall, but he managed to support her as they made their way back between the green-sheeted tables to the doors.

As the doors swung closed behind them, she stared at Jack, and her face was bloodlessly white. 'My God, Jack. He's really, really dead.'

'Come on,' Jack told her. 'Sparky's outside. Let's go join him and get ourselves some fresh air.'

When all the relatives had identified their dead, they boarded the bus again and drove through the trees to Lake Wolverine. The clearing where Bill had found all of the bodies was still cordoned off with yellow tape, and five forensic officers in white Tyvek suits were crawling around it on their hands and knees, sifting through the twigs and the leaf mold.

'How are you feeling now?' Jack asked Corinne, as he helped her down from the bus.

'Oh, much better, thanks, Jack. It was so terrible to see Malcolm like that, but I'm still glad I came here. If I hadn't, I always would have wondered what it was like, where he died.'

They looked around. The sky was beginning to grow more overcast now, and the color of Lake Wolverine was changing from blue to slate-gray. A whippet-thin sheriff's deputy with a bristly little moustache came up to them and said, 'Deputy Jeppersen. OK if I ask you folks some questions?'

'Of course,' said Corinne. 'Whatever I can do to help.'

Deputy Jeppersen made a note of Malcolm's name and Corinne's contact numbers. Then he said, 'Did your boy ever talk about taking his own life, for any reason?'

Corinne shook her head. 'His father died suddenly last year and Malcolm was naturally very upset. He was always talking about seeing him again when he got to heaven, but he never gave me the impression that he would take his own life to do that.'

'Did he ever talk about suicide pacts? Or mass suicides, like Jonestown, that kind of thing?'

'Never. He liked his video games, and I guess some of them were quite violent. What's that one called? Grand Theft Auto? But that was all. He liked building model airplanes, too.'

'Did you supervise his internet activity?'

'No. I didn't see the need for it. He was always real quiet and well-behaved.'

'Those quiet and well-behaved ones, ma'am, sometimes they can turn out to cause the most mayhem.'

'Malcolm was never any trouble, Deputy,' said Jack, sharply. 'I can vouch for that.'

'OK, sir. No offense meant. But you won't object if your local PD takes away your son's PC, just to check his hard drive for anything that might give us a clue?'

'No, I won't object to that.'

'Just one more question, if you don't mind, and I know that this is kind of touchy, to say the least. Did you ever get the feeling that your boy might be engaged in some inappropriate relationship with any of the adult scout leaders or any of the other boys?'

Corinne stared at him hard. 'You're asking me if my twelve-year-old son who committed suicide by cutting his throat only yesterday morning was *gay*?'

'I apologize for having to ask it, ma'am, but if there was something of that nature going on in your boy's scout troop, and it was on the point of being discovered – well, that could have been a motive for mass suicide.'

Corinne said, 'I think you need to get the hell away from me. Right now.'

'Yes, ma'am. Like I say, ma'am, I apologize for having to ask it, but we have to consider every possibility.'

At that moment, Sparky came up to them and said, in that clear, expressionless voice of his, 'It was something very much scarier than that.'

Deputy Jeppersen looked at him, and then at Corinne, and then at Jack. Then back to Sparky again. 'What makes you say that, kid?'

'Because it's true.'

'So – OK – what was it, this something that was so much scarier?'

'I don't know yet.'

'You don't know?'

'No.'

With that, Sparky turned around and walked away toward the edge of the lake. A sudden gust of wind made the trees swish and the surface of the water ruffle, and over in the distance Jack saw lightning flicker.

Deputy Jeppersen stood there, confused, with his pencil poised.

'My son has Asperger's,' Jack explained.

'Oh, yeah?' Deputy Jeppersen obviously had no idea what that meant, but he tucked away his pencil and folded his notebook and said, 'Thanks for your help, anyhow. And I'm sorry if some of my questions offended you.'

He walked off to question some of the other bereaved relatives. Jack and Corinne followed Sparky to the edge of the lake, where he was standing with his face tilted toward the wind and his arms held stiffly down by his sides.

'What was that about?' Jack asked him.

'There's something here,' said Sparky. 'I told you there was.'

'There's something here but you don't have any idea exactly what it is?'

Sparky looked around. 'It's in the woods,' he said, at last.

'Do you think it's still here?'

Sparky nodded. 'It's watching us. Can't you feel it watching us?'

'I can't say that I can, no.'

Sparky pointed toward the trees. 'It's over there somewhere. It's watching us.'

Corinne said, 'Is it a person? Or what? Don't you have *any* idea?'

'I don't know,' said Sparky. 'But I can feel it.'

'You're scaring me now,' said Corinne.

Jack said, 'Maybe we should go take a look. I mean, whatever it is, how can it hurt us? None of us are in the mood for committing suicide, are we? We don't even have any knives, do we, that we could kill ourselves with?'

'I think we should tell the police,' said Corinne.

'The police won't believe us,' said Sparky.

Jack said, 'OK. You can feel that it's watching us. Where from, exactly?'

'Over there.'

'Can't you be more specific?'

Sparky shielded his eyes with both hands and peered toward the woods. After a long pause, he pointed again, and said, '*There*. Between those two big trees. That's where it's watching us from.'

'Well, come on then,' said Jack. 'Let's see if we can flush it out.'

He didn't really think that there was anything there. This was just Sparky's autistic imagination inventing an explanation for something that was inexplicable. Sparky always believed that there had to be a logical reason for everything, no matter how trivial it was, and if he couldn't work out what it was, he would become highly agitated and start biting his lips and twisting his hair around the end of his finger.

They circled around the clearing where the CSIs were still hunched over like a family of large white bears. Corinne was hesitant at first, but Jack took hold of her hand and said, 'Listen – it's going to be fine. There's nothing here, but if I don't give Sparky the chance to look for whatever it is, he's going to be upset for hours. Days, even.'

Sparky led them through the woods, between the beech trees. There was no wind in here, and no birds singing. Even the blue jays had stopped calling to each other. They could hear their own footsteps, and every now and then they heard a sudden furtive scamper, as squirrels ran across the dry leaves in between the trees. Apart from that, though, the woods were unnaturally hushed.

As they walked further, Jack began to experience the strangest feeling. There was nothing in the woods to give him any idea of scale. The trees could have been enormous, or they could have been little more than saplings. He looked up and saw the blue sky through their branches, but there was no way of telling how tall they were. For all he knew, he and Corinne and Sparky could have been giants, or as small as action figures.

Sparky kept about six or seven paces ahead of them, although every now and then he stopped, and listened, and looked around.

'I don't think there's anything here, Sparks,' said Jack. 'Not now, anyhow.'

Sparky stood perfectly still, with one finger raised, as if he were saying *wait*.

The silence was overwhelming. They waited – and as they waited, Jack began to feel that something was rushing toward them through the woods, something invisible and noiseless and still some distance away from them, but something tempestuous. He was seized by a sudden urge to snatch at Corinne's hand and turn around and start running back to the lake. The woods seemed claustrophobic, as if it were impossible to breathe in here.

Corinne said, 'What is it? What's happening?' while Sparky spun around and around, as if he couldn't make up his mind what direction the threat was coming from.

Jack saw something flickering behind the trees, something white. It could have been an animal leaping or a man running or . . . *what*? He couldn't tell. All he knew was that it filled him with panic, and that they had to get out of those woods, and fast.

'Come on!' he shouted. His voice sounded strangely flat, as if he were shouting in a locked, empty room. 'Sparks! Let's get out of here!'

Neither Sparky nor Corinne needed any further urging. Jack took hold of Corinne's hand again and the three of them began to run back toward the lake. Jack's vision was blurred as he ran, and he was deafened by the sound of their feet hurtling through the leaves. But there was another sound, too – a whistling sound, like a strong wind gusting through the woods behind them, and catching up with them, fast. He felt dry leaves pattering against his back, and even the leaves on the ground ahead of them began to dance.

They came bursting out of the woods and into the clearing around the edge of the lake, all three of them gasping for breath. They turned around, to look behind them, but the wind had already died down, and the last few leaves had fluttered to the ground. Two of the CSIs raised their hooded heads to stare at them, but then they went back to their sifting.

'Did you see it?' asked Sparky. His eyes were wide and his face was as white as paper.

Jack said, 'I don't know. I saw something. I don't have any idea what it was. Corinne? How about you? Did you see it?'

Corinne shook her head. 'I didn't see anything, but I *heard* something, for sure, and I *felt* something. I don't know . . . it was like a tsunami coming, only air instead of water.'

'I'm going to talk to the cops,' said Jack. 'There *is* something out there, and they really need to find it, and fast.'

A Grim Discovery

Jack could tell that Deputy Jeppersen thought they were simply being hysterical. As they tried to explain to him what they had seen and felt in the woods, however, a beefy gray-haired man in uniform came across to them and said, 'What's the problem here, Deputy?'

'These folks think they saw somebody lurking in the woods over yonder.'

'Not necessarily some *body*,' Jack corrected him. 'Some *body* or some *thing*.'

The beefy man had steel-gray eyes like nail-heads and a double chin which bulged over his collar. He held out his hand and said, 'Undersheriff Dan Porter. And you are?'

'Jack Wallace. This is my son, Sparky. Well, his real name's Alexis. This is Mrs Corinne Cusack. Her son Malcolm is one of the victims. We came up here to give some moral support.'

'And you saw somebody or something in the woods?'

'That's right. Only glimpsed it. Something white; or somebody all dressed up in white. And we heard a kind of a wind blowing.'

Undersheriff Porter glanced sideways at Deputy Jeppersen as if to say, *time-wasters*. But all the same he said, 'OK. You saw something white or somebody all dressed up in white, and you heard a kind of a wind blowing. If that something in white wasn't a somebody, any ideas what it could have been?'

'I don't know,' said Jack. 'Maybe a deer, something like that. But it didn't look like any deer that I've ever seen.'

'And the wind? It's pretty gusty today, on and off.'

'Well, yes.'

'So what were you folks doing in the woods? I presume you've already visited the main assembly hall, ma'am, to identify your late son's remains?'

Corinne nodded, and whispered, 'Yes. Yes, I have.'

'I'm very sorry for your loss, ma'am. It's going to take us

some time to establish exactly why they did it, but it seems pretty certain that all of the victims took their own lives.'

'That's what we were doing in the woods, sir,' Sparky piped up. 'We were looking for the why.'

Deputy Jeppersen leaned close to the undersheriff and muttered, just loud enough for Jack to be able to hear him, 'The kid has asparagus.'

'Asperger's,' Jack corrected him. 'It's a form of autism. It means he has some difficulties with social communication, but he has a very high IQ and he's very sensitive to the world around him.'

The undersheriff looked around the lake, frowning, as if he had been expecting some miracle to occur, like the Second Coming, but it was running behind schedule. Eventually he turned back to Deputy Jeppersen and said, 'OK. Since we have the K-9 Unit here we might as well make use of it. Ask Deputy Ridout to bring out Barrett and search the woods where these folks think they saw what they saw. You can take four men with you. We're almost through with identifying the victims, anyhow.'

To Jack, he said, 'You won't mind showing us the location, will you, sir? I'd prefer it if your son and this good lady remained here, though, please.'

'Sparky?' asked Jack. 'Can you stay here with Malcolm's mom for a while?'

Sparky said, 'OK. But you should be very careful, Dad. That thing in the woods, it's really scary.'

Undersheriff Porter said, 'Don't you worry, kid. We'll look after your dad. You can give Barrett a dog-choc when he's through searching the woods. He's a really great tracker, believe me.'

After a few minutes, a young deputy arrived from the parking lot with K-9 Barrett, a black-and-tan German Shepherd. K-9 Barrett looked around alertly and intelligently as Undersheriff Porter explained to his handler and four other deputies what he wanted them to do. In fact he looked more alert and intelligent than the humans.

'I have to confess that I don't believe there's anybody in the woods to be found, or if there is, that he or she is in any way connected with this incident,' said Undersheriff Porter. 'However, we have a reputation in the Muskegon County Sheriff's Department for being thorough, and thorough is what we're going to be. OK, then. This gentleman will show you where to start searching.'

Corinne put her arm around Sparky's shoulders and led him back to the main buildings, where the rest of the relatives and scout leaders were gathered out on the verandah. The dog-handler said to Jack, 'I'm Deputy Ridout, sir, and this wonder-dog here is called Barrett. If you want to lead on, please, we'll follow you. Don't worry. Once Barrett picks up a scent, he'll be off like a space shuttle.'

Jack led the deputies back into the trees. The woods were not as silent as they had been before. The rising wind was making the leaves rustle, and there were plenty of birds whistling and whooping, and all of this was punctuated by the crackle of broken twigs beneath their feet and Barrett's persistent panting. They could even hear a distant airplane passing high overhead.

'I guess we saw it about here,' said Jack, when they reached the place where Sparky had been spinning around and around.

Deputy Jeppersen raised his hand and called out, 'OK, everybody! This is the spot where this gentleman saw something white, maybe an animal, or maybe an individual dressed up in white. Barrett here is going to try to find a trail, if there is one. The rest of you split up and fan out, and look for footprints or any other disturbances.

'If you do happen to see anything resembling what this gentleman saw, do your best to apprehend it, if you can. Or at least try to find out what it is. Or *who* it is.'

As the rest of the deputies spread out and started combing the woods, Jack and Deputy Jeppersen and the dog-handler started to search the immediate area, moving gradually outward in a clockwise spiral. K-9 Barrett buried his snout into the leaves and the leaf mold and inhaled deeply, but he still didn't seem to be able to pick up any distinctive scents.

'This is one hell of a tragedy,' said Deputy Jeppersen, picking up a thick branch which he could use to poke into some of the layers of leaf mold. 'You can't even begin to think how it happened, can you? All of those moms and dads back there – they all keep asking me why, and I just don't know what to say to them.'

He bent down to pick up something shiny, then dropped it again when he realized that it was only the discarded end of a Pringles tube.

'There has to be a reason for it,' he said, 'even if it's crazy. Remember that UFO cult, in San Diego? Heaven's Gate or something like that. They thought that if they committed suicide, they were all going to be taken away by an alien spaceship. More than thirty of them, if my memory serves me. But at least they explained why they were doing it, and they all left farewell messages. These scouts . . . nothing. Zilch. No explanation whatsoever.'

They circled around a little further, but Jack had the feeling that it had gone now – whatever it was that he had seen flickering white behind the trees and whatever had caused that eerie, blustery wind.

He stopped and looked around and listened, but because of the approaching electric storm the woods were becoming restless, and all he could hear was leaves stirring and birds twittering and the distant rumbling of thunder.

'I'm sorry,' he told Deputy Jeppersen. 'I don't think we're going to find anything. There *was* something here, I swear it, or else I wouldn't have wasted your time. Maybe the dog scared it off.'

At that moment, however, K-9 Barrett barked loudly, and started to tug at his leash. Deputy Ridout said, 'What is it, Barrett? Come on, boy, what have you picked up there?'

'Raccoon, probably, knowing that dog,' said Deputy Jeppersen. But as Barrett pulled Deputy Ridout sharply off to the right, he reluctantly followed. 'Might as well see what he's so fired up about. He does occasionally make himself useful, sniffing out narcotics, and lost children, and decomposing hoboes.'

Barrett led them down a slope. It became steeper and steeper with almost every step they took, until they were leaping and bounding from one tree trunk to the next in order to slow themselves down. At last the ground began to level out, but the woods were thick with briars here, which snagged their clothes and scratched at their arms. Jack began to feel that he was caught up in some surrealistic fairy story, fighting his way through an enchanted forest. They battled their way through the briars, however, and found themselves in a dark, shady hollow, surrounded by overhanging oaks.

It was quite cold in this hollow, because it never received any sunlight. In the center of it there was a pool of water, tainted sepia-brown by leaf mold, and utterly stagnant. It was the smell that hit them first. They didn't need a tracker dog to tell them that they had found dead human bodies.

Barrett scrabbled his way right down to the very edge of the pool, and then waited there, with his front paws together and both ears pricked up, guarding his discovery.

'Holy shit,' said Deputy Jeppersen.

Deputy Ridout was standing beside Barrett, his right hand holding his leash, and his left hand clamped over his nose and mouth. The sweet brown stench was appalling, and once he had breathed it in once, Jack felt that he would never be able to get rid of it. He could even *taste* it, as well as smell it.

Standing up to her waist in the middle of the pool was a woman with no head. She was wearing a white sleeveless T-shirt, the front of which was heavily stained with blood and with the green and black juices of putrescence. Her arms hung by her sides, both yellowish and peeling and hugely inflated. The three-inch stump of her neck was like a volcano erupting – not with lava, but with maggots, scores of them, which kept wriggling out of her neck and dropping down into the water. Above her, a cloud of blowflies waited their opportunity to lay even more eggs.

K-9 Barrett made a whining sound in the back of his throat, and Deputy Ridout said, 'OK, boy. Good boy. Let's get you out of here.'

He allowed Barrett to pull him out through the overhanging branches, and a few seconds later Jack and Deputy Jeppersen heard a splattering sound as he vomited into the briars.

'How about you, sir?' Deputy Jeppersen asked Jack. 'You can light out of here if you want to, because I'm not sticking around for long, neither. I'm just going to call it in, and that's it.'

'I'm OK,' Jack told him, although 'OK' wasn't really the word for it. He felt unreal, and revolted, but at the same time he felt the need to understand what had happened here. He approached the edge of the pool and looked down into the water. Although it was stained brown, it was transparent, and quite clear, and he could see that the woman's bare legs were buried deep in the mud and leaves at the bottom of it, right up to her pale mid-thighs. There was something else in the pool, too, which was more difficult to see, because it was deep in the shadows behind her. It looked like a body, curled up into a fetal position; and when he carefully made his way around to the left-hand side of the pool, he saw that it was. A man, it looked like. Naked, white, blotchy and bloated. He had a tattoo of a pawprint on his shoulder, maybe a cougar or a mountain lion.

'Here,' said Jack, beckoning to Deputy Jeppersen, who was vainly trying to get an answer on his r/t from his fellow deputies.

'What is it? I can't get a goddamn signal for nothing. Listen.' He held up his mike and all Jack could hear was a thick crackling noise.

He came over and Jack pointed down into the pool. All they could see from this angle was the man's back, with his head bent forward and his knees folded up.

'This is so goddamn gross,' said Deputy Jeppersen. 'What in the name of Jesus went down here?'

He circled right around to the opposite side of the pool. The sides were very steep and slippery, and he had to clutch at the overhanging trees to stop himself from sliding right in. With one hand tightly gripping one of the branches, he used the stick that he had picked up earlier to prod at the body in the water.

At first the body did nothing but sway slightly. Deputy Jeppersen prodded it even harder, and it started to wallow in the water. He prodded it again and again, and suddenly, filled with gas, it rolled right over. It was a man all right, although his face was so puffed up that Jack doubted if even his mother could have recognized him. His arms flopped apart and out of his grasp floated the woman's head, as puffed-up as he was, with milky, wide-open eyes. It bobbed to the surface and floated there, staring at Jack as if she were angry with him for having found her far too late.

Jack pushed his way back out of the hollow. The sky was

dark now, and it was beginning to rain, heavy spots that pattered into the undergrowth. Deputy Ridout was standing there with Barrett, looking pale and drawn. A few seconds later Deputy Jeppersen came out, too.

'I got through to Undersheriff Porter,' he said. 'They're sending a forensic team out here right now.'

Lightning cracked, over by Blue Lake. Then it began to rain in earnest, so that after a few minutes the three of them were drenched, and Barrett had to keep shaking himself. None of them wanted to go back into the hollow, however, and seek shelter under the trees. They just stood there with the rain trickling down their faces and soaking their clothes as if they felt that they needed to be cleansed.

Ghost Story

By the time Jack had trudged back to the main reservation buildings, the rain was hammering down so hard that the gutters over the verandah could no longer cope, and water was cascading down the outside walls. Rainwater was dripping from his nose and every few seconds he was deafened by a multiple barrage of thunder, as if there was a war going on nearby.

He climbed the steps back up to the verandah and went inside. The relatives of the dead scouts and scout leaders were milling around in the hallway, uncertain what to do. They must have been told that another incident had occurred, but not what it was.

He found Sparky and Corinne sitting on chairs in a recess on the left-hand side, underneath a noticeboard of all of Owasippe's summer activities. Corinne was holding a Styrofoam cup of coffee, but he could see by the skin floating on its surface that she had allowed it to grow cold.

'What's happening, Jack?' she asked him. 'The cops have been running around like headless chickens. I saw some TV people, too, and they were all going crazy.'

'You found some more dead people, didn't you?' said Sparky, in a high-pitched monotone.

Jack hadn't wanted to tell Sparky straight out, but there was no point in trying to prevaricate if he had guessed already.

He nodded. 'Yes, we did, Sparks. A man and a woman. We found them in a pool of water. The cops don't know what happened to them yet.'

'Oh, God,' said Corinne. 'Are you OK?'

'Little bit shaky, to tell you the truth. It wasn't very pretty.'

'A man and a woman? Had they committed suicide, too?'

'The woman certainly hadn't. But, like I say, the cops don't know what happened to them yet, and I'm not too sure I want to talk about it just yet.'

'You're *soaking*,' she told him. 'You need to get out of those wet clothes before you catch pneumonia or something.'

Jack looked around for any members of the scouting staff. Sparky tugged at his sleeve and said, 'We *did* see something, didn't we, Dad? We weren't just making it up?'

'No, Sparks, we weren't just making it up. But we still don't know what it was, and we don't know for sure that it had anything to do with what happened here.'

'Did she have a head injury? The woman?'

'You could say that.'

'I thought so. That's Castor again. Castor is the evil star.'

An office door opened on the opposite side of the hallway and a khaki-uniformed scout leader came out, with a sheaf of papers under his arm. Jack manoeuvered his way through the crowd of relatives toward him and called out to him, 'pardon me!' as the scout leader started to walk away.

'Talking to *me,* sir?' blinked the scout leader. 'Something I can help you with?'

'I sure hope so. I was wondering if there were any dry clothes anywhere around that you could lend me?'

The scout leader was plump and bespectacled with a dented bald head that had been burnished by outdoor activity to the color of a shiny brass doorknob. He stared at Jack as if he had asked him a question in Swahili.

'I was outside, in the rain,' Jack explained. 'I was helping the sheriff's deputies to search the woods.'

The scout leader shook his head and tutted. 'I *warned* them something like this would happen! I warned them so many times!' He dropped his papers on the floor and bent down to pick them up.

'Anything would do,' Jack told him. 'Maybe a tracksuit, or a sweater and a pair of jogging pants.'

'Don't sell off any more acreage, I said!' the scout leader went on, gathering up his papers. 'You'll regret it if you do! In its heyday, this camp covered more than eleven thousand acres, did you know that? Eleven thousand! Now it's down to less than five, and the Chicago Scout Council wants to sell the rest of it off, for development! You're playing with fire, that's what I told them! Playing with fire! It won't be just the local community you're up against, or the scouts, or the staff alumni! No, sir! There are things in these woods that will fight you back, too!'

'Some – ah – dry clothes?' Jack prompted him.

'Oh. Yes. For sure. By cracky, you *are* wet, aren't you? You see that door at the end of the corridor, on the right? That's the storeroom, for the shop. You should find some Owasippe sweatshirts in there, and some sweatpants. Leave them a note to say you've taken them, and your address, so they can bill you.'

'Thanks,' said Jack. But before he turned away, he said, 'What "things in the woods", exactly?'

'What?' The scout leader blinked at him. Tucking his papers back under his arm, he took off his spectacles and used one of the pointed ends of his boy-scout scarf to wipe the fingerprints off them.

'You said that "things in the woods" would fight back, too.'

'Well . . .' said the scout leader. 'Anybody who knows anything about woods will tell you the same.'

Jack was just about to ask him what 'the same' actually meant when Sally appeared. She looked tired and harassed and her hair was all messed up.

'My God, Jack, have you been swimming?'

'Oh, very funny. I got caught in the rain. Did they tell you what we found?'

'Yes,' she said, with a grimace. 'I've just been talking to the undersheriff. He wants me to keep these poor people in Muskegon overnight so he can ask them some more questions tomorrow morning about their children. Most of them just want to go back home.'

'Why does he need to talk to them again? The bodies we found in that pool must have been there for *days*, long before any of us got here.'

'He's just being an overzealous a-hole, I'm afraid. What exactly was their condition, these bodies, if you don't mind my asking you? All the undersheriff told me was that they were a male and a female and it appeared to be a murder-suicide.'

'Well, he's probably right. The woman's head had been cut clean off, and the guy was curled up under the water clutching it, like a goddamned football. *He* may have committed suicide but *she* sure didn't.'

Then he said, 'Just a second, Sal,' and turned around to apologize to the scout leader for interrupting their conversation, but the scout leader had gone. Jack could just see his coppery doorknob head bobbing away through the crowd. 'Shit,' he said.

'What's wrong?' asked Sally.

'I'm not sure. I was talking to that scout leader and he said something about "things in the woods". He said that the scout council wanted to sell off all of this land for redevelopment, but that there were "things in the woods" which would fight back, if they tried. He shot off before I could ask him what he meant.'

Sally patted the front of Jack's soaking-wet shirt. 'I expect he meant the wildlife. Nothing more aggressive than a pissed-off raccoon, and I can tell you *that* from experience. Right now, though, I have to persuade fifty-one tired, grieving and impatient people that they would be better off staying the night at the Holiday Inn in Muskegon rather than their own much more comfortable beds. And *you* need to get yourself out of these clothes.'

'OK. You're right. Maybe I can catch up with that scout leader again before we leave.'

'What time are you going?'

Jack checked his watch. 'We have a flight at seven-twelve. Which means we have to be out of here in less than forty-five minutes.'

'Jack,' said Sally, as he turned to go. 'I just want to thank you for coming today, and for everything you've done. You and Sparky, both of you. It was over and above the call of duty, and I really appreciate it.'

Jack said, 'Thanks, Sal.' He felt again that there could be something between them, but that was probably because she reminded him so much of Agnieszka, and because he was feeling tired, and it would have been so comforting just to have some-body hold him close. Apart from that, he knew that if they became lovers, their relationship couldn't possibly last, and then he would lose her as a friend.

He went along to the storeroom, which was a small, stifling room stacked with Owasippe T-shirts and Owasippe sweatpants and other souvenirs, like Owasippe mugs and Owasippe tote bags, all of them marked with the head of Chief Owasippe, in his full-feathered war bonnet.

He quickly changed into a baggy green-and-white tracksuit, bundled his wet shirt and pants into a plastic Owasippe shopping sack, and went back outside. As he came out, he almost collided with Undersheriff Porter.

'Oh – I was looking for you, sir,' said Undersheriff Porter. 'I wanted to tell you how much we appreciate your help in locating those cadavers. Also to ask you for your contact details. The medical examiner in Lansing will be carrying out autopsies on both of them and she may need to ask you a few additional questions.'

'Jack Wallace,' said Jack, shaking the undersheriff's hand. It was dry and horny, as if he spent as much time chopping up firewood as he did undersheriffing.

'Interested to know exactly what it was you saw in those woods,' he remarked.

'Like I said before, something white, running behind the trees. It could have been anything.'

'Maybe it was a cougar. We do have cougars in the woods around here, but you hardly ever see them. You can go your whole life and never catch sight of one. Ghost cats, they call them. On the other hand, maybe it was the ghosts of Chief Owasippe and his two sons. There's plenty of people who swear they've heard *them*, on a really quiet night.'

'You're not serious.'

'It's a local legend. Back in the eighteen-somethings, Chief Owasippe gave his sons a canoe and sent them off into the unknown to prove their manhood. They made it all the way to Chicago, and they made friends with the settlers at Fort Dearborn. But they were away for so long that Chief Owasippe went and sat under a pine and waited for them to come back, and he wouldn't touch food or drink until they did.'

'And *did* they come back?'

'Nope. They were only two nights short of home when they sheltered their canoe under a riverside bluff, and while they were sleeping the bluff collapsed on them and buried them. And that's a true story, because years later some trappers found their canoe, and their cooking-pots, and their two skeletons.'

'So what happened to Chief Owasippe?'

'He fasted himself to death. And that's why you can hear

him and his sons walking through the woods here at night, and some say that if you call out to them, they'll answer you.'

Jack looked at Undersheriff Porter narrow-eyed. Maybe the undersheriff was shooting him a line, but he didn't detect the slightest flicker on his face that might have given that away.

'Well, it's a good story,' he said. 'But I don't believe that what we saw was a ghost – or *ghosts*, plural.'

'Neither do I,' said Undersheriff Porter, still expressionless. 'Personally, I don't believe in ghosts. But some pretty unaccountable things happen in these woods from time to time. One of my deputies took his boys camping out here once and he says that in the middle of the night they all got the willies so bad that they packed up their tent without even waiting until first light, and hightailed it home. He said he couldn't understand what made them feel that way, but whatever it was it frightened two shades of shit out of all of them.'

He sniffed, and then he said, 'What I'm trying to tell you, Mr Wallace, is that I'm a skeptic. I don't think there's any such thing as the supernatural, or ghosts, or even life after death. But I do believe that there are things on this earth that we don't yet know about, or understand, and that they deserve to be thoroughly investigated to find out what they really are. Either we'll laugh at ourselves for having been so scared of them, or else we'll run for the hills, screaming.'

Premonition

They arrived back at the restaurant at a quarter of ten, in the middle of the evening sitting. Every table was taken, and there were several customers sitting at the bar waiting. A five-piece Polish band was playing a noisy folk song, 'Ja Tu I Ty Tu', accompanied by a drum and two fiddles, and the conversation was so loud that Jack had to shout when his manager Tomasz came up to greet them.

'Glad you are back!' bellowed Tomasz, in his ear. 'Very, very busy tonight!'

'I'm not complaining!' Jack told him. 'Can you take care of things for the rest of the night? I'm bushed!'

'No problem!' Tomasz replied. He was a big man, with prickly gray hair and a big bovine face. He wore a scarlet coat with the restaurant's signature letter *N* embroidered on the pocket, a black shirt and a red bow tie. He had worked for the Wallaces ever since the restaurant opened seven years ago, and he was unceasingly cheery, always telling jokes and slapping his customers on the back as if he had known them all his life.

Two months ago, however, Jack had come out of the restaurant into the yard at the back to get some fresh air and found Tomasz standing by the wall, silently crying. Tomasz had wiped his eyes and gone back inside without saying a word, and Jack had never asked him what had upset him so much, but ever since then he had suspected that there was much more to Tomasz than back-slapping and humorous banter.

'Sparks – you go up to bed now,' said Jack. 'I'll be up in a couple of minutes. Don't forget to brush your teeth!'

Sparky plodded tiredly up the stairs while Jack went behind the bar and opened a cold bottle of Żywiec beer.

'Long day, huh?' asked Tomasz.

'Long, and horrendous, believe me.' Jack didn't really want to talk about it, or even think about it. He looked around the restaurant and said, 'How's the new *gołąbki* recipe going down?'

'From Mikhail, nothing but complaint. From diners, nothing but compliment. We sold maybe eight or nine, and every time people say how much they like it. More tasty than before, they say.'

'OK. I'll just have a word with Mikhail and then I think I'll call it a day.'

'By the way,' said Tomasz, 'you have visitor.'

Jack looked around. 'What – here, now?'

'No, no. She come here maybe eight o'clock, eight-thirty. When I tell her that you will not be back until much later, she leave. But she leave address and contact number. Here.'

Tomasz took a dog-eared visiting card out of his breast pocket and handed it to Jack. It was printed in italics, and the address had been corrected in purple ink. The name on it was *Maria Wiktoria Koczerska* and the amended address was in *Belmont Gardens*, which was a little over five miles away, to the south-west, a quiet residential area on the outer limits of the Polish district of Avondale.

'Did she say what she wanted?'

Tomasz shook his head. 'No. But she did say that it was important. She said to call her as soon as you can.'

'What was she like? Young? Pretty?'

Again Tomasz shook his head. 'Once, maybe. But not now.'

'OK, Tomek, thank you. I'll give her a call in the morning. You're sure you can manage down here tonight?'

'Don't you worry, Boss. Everything is under control.'

Jack went through to the kitchen to see how Mikhail was coping with tonight's crowds. He was shouting and swearing at Piotr and Duane, as usual, but the food was coming out fast and it was looking good.

'One borsch with meat roll! Two Polish plates with *pierogi*! One Silesian dumplings! *Where is fucking Silesian dumplings*? One *bigos*!'

'Tomasz tells me the new *gołąbki* recipe is going down well,' Jack told him.

Mikhail flipped over a veal cutlet in his skillet, with a burst of flame. 'So . . . must all be Slovaks in tonight,' he said, violently shaking a pan of sauerkraut with his other hand.

Jack gave him a reassuring pat on his fat, sweaty shoulder.

'So long as they like the food and they pay for it, I don't care what they are.'

'No Russian though,' said Mikhail. 'All I feed to Russian is cyanide.'

Jack went upstairs to the landing, unlocked his apartment door and went inside. He could still hear the clatter and the hubbub from the restaurant downstairs, with an occasional burst of laughter, but up here it was very muted.

Sparky's bedroom door was ajar and his bedside lamp was still on, but Sparky was fast asleep, wearing his Star Trek pajamas. His hair was tousled and he was breathing through his mouth. Jack stood over him for a while, watching him, feeling even more sorry for him than he did for himself. Jack had lost his wife, and his lover, and his best friend, but Sparky had lost his mother.

He went over to the window and tugged the drapes closer together. Outside, on the brick wall facing him, the yellow-eyed face of Capricorn grinned at him maliciously. *Saw death today, did you, Jack? Saw it again, in all its ghastly glory?*

He looked around the room, at all the star maps that Sparky had pinned on the wall, and on the photograph of Agnieszka that he had stuck over the head of his bed. Agnieszka, smiling under a summer tree, in her orange dress. That picture had been taken less than three years ago.

If only we knew what was coming, thought Jack. He was sure that Sparky's interest in astrology had been inspired by Agnieszka's death. *I don't want anything like that to happen to me again, not without my knowing in advance. Not without my doing everything I can to stop it.*

He switched off Sparky's lamp and closed his bedroom door, and then he went into the kitchen and took another bottle of Żywiec out of the icebox. The living room was silent and stuffy. He switched on the wide-screen TV but he kept it on mute because he wanted to think about what had happened today at the scout reservation, and what he had seen there. He couldn't begin to imagine how that woman had been buried up to her knees in the bottom of that pool, or had her head cut off. God – in his mind's eye he could still see those maggots writhing.

Had the man decapitated her, and then drowned himself, or had somebody else killed both of them? And if so, why?

Two and a Half Men flickered on the screen in front of him. It must have been a repeat because it still had Charlie Sheen in it. On the side table next to the couch there was another photograph of Agnieszka, in a silver frame, looking at him almost coyly. He remembered the day he had taken that picture, and he wished now that he could have said, *Don't look at me like that, Aggie; one day that look is going to make me miss you more than you can know.*

He took the visiting card that Tomasz had given him out of his pocket. He didn't recognize the name and he couldn't think what anybody could have to tell him that was so important. Then, however, he turned it over, and saw that a name was handwritten on the back. *Grzegorz Walach.*

Now, that *did* mean something. Grzegorz Walach had been his great-grandfather. His grandfather had always been telling him colorful stories about him. He had been a famous violinist in Poland before World War Two, and played for the Warsaw Philharmonic Orchestra. The great conductor Leopold Stokowski had heard him playing and been so impressed that he had invited him to join the Chicago Philharmonic, and that was why in 1937 the family had emigrated to America.

When Germany had invaded Poland on September 1, 1939, however, Grzegorz Walach had been playing for a season in Warsaw, and he had sent a telegram saying that he had decided to stay and fight in the defense of his country. The family had never heard from him again.

Jack turned the card over and over. For some reason he couldn't understand, it unsettled him, a message from a past that may be better if it stayed forgotten. He looked at the clock on the table next to Agnieszka's picture. It was nearly ten-thirty now, and he wondered if it was too late to give this mysterious Maria Wiktoria Koczerska a call.

He heard more laughter from the restaurant, and the band striking up with 'Hej Sokoły' – 'Hey, Falcons' – which was still popular in Poland not only today, but had been sung by Home Army guerrillas during the war. That decided him. He reached over and picked up the phone.

As he did so, however, the living-room door opened wider and Sparky came in, his hair sticking up at the back and his eyes bleary.

'Hey, Sparks, what's wrong?'

Sparky came over and sat down close to him.

'I'm going to bed myself in a minute,' said Jack. 'Come on, it's been a very long day.'

'I had a nightmare,' said Sparky, his eyes roaming around the room as if he were worried that something out of his nightmare might have followed him in here.

'Well, I'm not surprised,' said Jack. 'But it's only your brain trying to make sense of things. Losing Malcolm like that – that's really so tragic. And nobody even knows why.'

'I didn't have a nightmare about Malcolm. I had a nightmare about the woods.'

Jack put his arm around him and gave him a reassuring squeeze. 'That doesn't surprise me, either. They were pretty scary those woods, weren't they? And what we saw there – even if it was a cougar, which it probably was – they can attack people, too. Like, not very often, I don't think. But they do. Especially young kids.'

'It wasn't *those* woods. It was some different woods.'

'In your nightmare, you mean? What woods were they, then?'

'I don't know. But they were different. They had different trees and they smelled different.'

'You can *smell* things, in your nightmares?'

Sparky nodded. 'I smelled a campfire, too. And there were some men, talking.'

'Oh, yes? What were they saying?'

'*Był biały. Wglądał jak duch.*'

'It was white and it looked like a ghost?'

'Yes. Over and over.'

Jack gave Sparky another squeeze. 'Listen, Sparks, you're overtired and all stressed out, that's all. How about some warm milk to help you sleep?'

'But it wasn't a nightmare like I usually get.'

'Well, all nightmares aren't the same. It depends what things have been worrying you during the day. Today it was obviously woods, and spooky-looking white things. I don't blame you for having nightmares about that. I was pretty freaked out myself.'

'But it was *real.*'

Jack sat up and looked at him. He had said it with such conviction that Jack almost believed him.

'What do you mean, it was real? A nightmare is just a dream, Sparks. That's the definition of a nightmare.'

'But this really happened.'

'Men in the woods saying "it was white and it looked like a ghost", in Polish?'

'Yes.'

Jack stood up. 'Come on, Sparks. I think you need to go back to bed, I really do. Just try and think of something else. Count sheep or something. It won't be even half as scary in the morning. Look – I'll leave the light on for you, OK? And you can leave your door open, too.'

Sparky reluctantly went back to his bedroom. Jack stood in the middle of the living room for a few moments, not quite sure what to do. He knew that he should go to bed, too, but the visiting card was lying on the table and the phone was lying next to it, and somehow Sparky's nightmare had made him feel that he needed to call this Maria Wiktoria Koczerska, whoever she was.

He punched out the number and waited. The phone rang and rang with an old-fashioned burring noise. He was about to hang up when a woman's voice said, querulously, *'Halo? Słucham. Tak?'*

'Dobry wieczór. Is this Ms Koczerska?'

'Mrs Koczerska, yes. Who is calling?'

'Jack Wallace, from the Nostalgia Restaurant on North Clark Street. My manager tells me you came around earlier when I was away.'

'Ah yes, Mr Wallace, I did. But thank you anyhow for calling. There is something I very much wanted to show you.'

'You wrote the name of my great-grandfather on the back of your card. Grzegorz Walach.'

'Tak. I did. Your great-grandfather is disappearing in the war, is that right?'

'That's right, yes. He volunteered to help fight the German invasion in 1939, but his family never heard from him again.'

'Of course. There were many tens of thousands like that, Mr Wallace, who disappeared without trace, and who do not even have a grave marker that their relatives can visit to lay a few flowers. My own great-uncles, the same happened to them.'

'So what's this about my great-grandfather?'

'It is better if I show you, Mr Wallace. Maybe you can come to my apartment?'

'I'm a very busy man, Mrs Koczerska. I have a restaurant to run, as you know.'

'*Tak*, yes, of course. But if I can explain to you the fate that befell Grzegorz Walach – if I can *prove* to you what happened to him—'

'You can do that?'

'Why would I lie to you? *Dlaczego miałabym cię okłamywać? What would be the point of it?'

'OK. I guess I could come tomorrow, around eleven in the morning, if that's convenient.'

'That would suit me very well, Mr Wallace. I look forward to it. *Dobranoc.*'

'Goodnight, Mrs Koczerska.'

Jack put down the phone. He thought he ought to feel excited but instead he felt strangely apprehensive. Maybe he was just exhausted, and upset by the day's events. There was something else that unsettled him, though. Something that Sparky had said. *'There's a connection between what happened to Malcolm, and our family. That's why we have to go to Owasippe.'*

Jack didn't know why this should make him feel disturbed, but it was the earnest way that Sparky had said it, and the fact that Mrs Koczerska had turned up at the restaurant on the same day they had gone to the scout reservation to see Malcolm lying dead in that makeshift morgue. He had never believed in fate, and coincidence. He believed that life was what you made of it yourself. It made him feel distinctly uncomfortable to think that Sparky might be right, and that the stars and the planets determine our destiny, whether we like it or not.

Box of Memories

When he drew up outside 4125 West Wellington Avenue in Belmont Gardens it was hammering down with rain. He sat in his car for a short while, to see if it would ease off, but if anything it began to pour down even more heavily. A young woman in a red hooded raincoat scuttled across the road pushing a baby buggy, with a wet, bedraggled spaniel trying to keep up with her.

Jack looked at the detached house in which Mrs Koczerska lived. It was one of several brown brick houses along Wellington Avenue, all with crenellated facades like castles. The windows were covered with ivory lace drapes, although he could see a red-and-green table lamp alight in the second-floor window, and he guessed that was Mrs Koczerska's living room.

At last, when the rain showed no signs of relenting, he climbed out of his car and hurried up the concrete pathway to Mrs Koczerska's front porch. He pressed the bell marked Apt #2 and waited. Eventually, Mrs Koczerska's voice said, 'Mr Wallace? Is that you?'

'It's me all right.'

She pressed the buzzer and he stepped into a gloomy, marble-floored hallway that smelled of disinfectant and burned cheese. On the left-hand side stood a tall mahogany coat and umbrella stand with a small dark mirror in it. He saw his own face in the mirror as he passed it, and he thought he looked like a sepia photograph of somebody from the 1930s.

'Up here, Mr Wallace!' called Mrs Koczerska, leaning over the banister at the top of the stairs. 'Is it still raining? I wanted to hang out my sheets!'

'Yes, still raining, and I don't think it's going to be stopping any time soon.'

Jack reached the landing and Mrs Koczerska held out her hands to him, as if he were an old friend she hadn't seen in years. He gave her three pecks on the cheek, and said, 'Pleasure to meet you.'

His manager Tomasz had been right. Once upon a time Mrs Koczerska must have been very pretty. He would have guessed her age around mid- to late-seventies, with steel-gray hair cut into a sharp five-point bob. She had high cheekbones, with a short, straight nose, and a clearly defined chin. She was very small, not much more than five feet two, and her shoulders stooped slightly, but she was immaculately dressed in a long gray cardigan and a white blouse and a pleated gray skirt. Around her neck she wore a triple-stranded necklace of Polish amber beads.

Jack recognized her perfume at once: the distinctive jasmine and orange-blossom fragrance of Chanel No. 5.

'Come in,' she said, and Jack followed her into her apartment.

In many ways, it reminded him of his own apartment. The four armchairs and the couch were heavy and old-fashioned, with lion's-claw feet, like those he had inherited from his grandparents. The drapes on either side of the window were thick brown velvet, with braided silk cords and tassels to tie them back. The side tables were covered with brown velveteen tablecloths, which themselves were covered with elaborate lace overlays. And on every wall, there was a collection of faded photographs of long-dead relatives, some in their wedding finery, some standing in groups in front of houses that had been probably been bombed, in gardens which must have gone to seed decades ago.

'Please, sit down,' said Mrs Koczerska. 'And you must call me Maria, because our families knew each other very well, back in Poland before the war. For all I know, you and I could be related!'

'I can't say I ever heard my grandparents mention any Raczkowskis,' said Jack, sitting down beside the window.

'My family name is Kusociński. Originally from Lublin.'

Jack said, 'No. They never mentioned any Kusocińkis, either. But then they never liked to talk about the old days very much. It used to get my grandma too upset. She would start to cry and you could never get her to stop.'

Maria went through to the kitchenette and came back with a plate of *pierniki* gingerbread cookies covered with dark bitter chocolate.

'I can get you coffee, maybe?' she asked him. 'Is it too early in the day for vodka?'

'I'm good, thanks,' Jack told her. 'I spent over an hour this morning tasting rum babas.'

'Ah, yes,' said Maria. 'I have never tried your restaurant but I have heard good things about it. My neighbors have eaten there.'

'Well, you're welcome to come try it, any time, my treat. Just give me a call and I'll reserve you a table.'

Maria turned to the side table beside her and picked up a black metal box. It was scratched and dented and the lid didn't fit properly. Although a small brass padlock still dangled from the hasp, it was thickly corroded and somebody had sawed right through the shackle – recently, by the look of it, because the cut was still bright.

'This box was sent to me last week by a friend of mine. Her name is Krystyna Zawadka and she is an assistant professor at the Institute of History at Warsaw University.'

Jack said nothing, but watched as Maria opened the lid of the box and took out a bundle of yellowed paper and a small book bound in maroon leather.

'The box was found about a year ago by a team of historical archeologists who were combing through the Kampinos Forest. They were looking for any traces of human remains that earlier exhumation parties might have missed.'

Jack knew all about the Kampinos Forest. It lay about fourteen kilometers northwest of Warsaw. In the spring and summer of 1940, a special squad of German soldiers known as AB-Aktion had arrested at least seven thousand Polish aristocrats, politicians, journalists, teachers, judges, priests and social workers – anybody who might be capable of organizing resistance to German rule. They had been interned, tortured, and then driven out blindfold to a clearing at Palmiry, most of them thinking that they were being transported to another camp. They had then been lined up and machine-gunned. Over two thousand of them, maybe more.

Jack said, 'There's a museum there, isn't there, as well as a cemetery? My mother and father went there once, but I never had the time.'

'You should make time, on your next visit to Poland,' said Maria. 'It is a very moving place. All of those crosses . . . and the tall trees . . . and the wind blowing through the forest.'

'So what did they find in this box?' asked Jack, nodding toward it. 'Something about my great-grandfather?'

'Yes, Mr Wallace, they did. They found my great-uncle Andrzej's diary, with many mentions of his friend Grzegorz Walach, your great-grandfather, and it explains how both of them died. It was not the Germans who killed them, according to him. Your great-grandfather was never captured by the Germans, and as far as we know the Germans did not have him on their list for what they called their *Intelligenzaktion* – eliminating all of the Polish intelligentsia. It appears that they were not aware that your great-grandfather was in Poland at all, otherwise he certainly would have been.'

'Go on,' said Jack, frowning. 'If the Germans didn't kill him, who did?

Maria leaned forward and offered Jack a gingerbread cookie. 'No – no thanks,' he told her. That was so Polish – never letting your guests go hungry.

'You probably know that it was not only the Germans who used the Kampinos Forest,' said Maria. 'Many refugees fled from Warsaw to hide there, and the guerrillas of the Home Army went into the forest to regroup.

'My great-uncle Andrzej and your great-grandfather were two of those guerrillas. They went deep into the forest with maybe thirty or forty other men. That was in August of 1940. They had a very daring plan to assassinate Hans Frank, the German commander of the General Government.'

'So what happened? How did they die?'

'The Germans of course were hunting through the forest for them, but several times they managed to escape and once they ambushed a German patrol and killed at least twelve of them.

She turned the pages of the little diary. Jack could see that the pages were crowded with tiny, crabbed writing, some of it blotchy with damp.

'How is your Polish?' she asked him.

'Pretty rusty, to tell you the truth.'

'OK. In that case, I translate for you. "Now we have been in the forest for nearly two months, we are beginning to become aware that there is something else here which is much more frightening than the Germans. It appears that even the Germans are frightened of it, too, because we have heard them shouting to each other to watch out for what they called *Der Waldgeist*, the Forest Ghost. Also we have sometimes seen them spitting on their fingertips three times, which is supposed to be a way to defend yourself against evil spirits."

'This entry is dated October seventeenth, 1940,' Maria went on. 'But now listen to this, from November eleventh. "Now we are sure that we are being watched and followed by something terrible. Very early in the morning, even before the sun comes up, we have seen it behind the trees. Also when it begins to grow dark. We are not sure what it is. Some of the men believe that it might be a wild animal – an albino elk, maybe. But we all are agreed that it is white, and that it gives us a feeling of dread much worse than any of us have ever experienced before, although we find it hard to explain why. I think that it could be inspired by us being alone in this vast forest, but maybe it is more than that. I believe that I have glimpsed it myself. It is white, and it looks like a ghost."'

Jack felt a prickling sensation on the backs of his hands. 'Read that to me in Polish,' he said. 'Read it to me the way it's written down there.'

Maria frowned at the diary and said, '"*Był bialy. Wyglądał jak duch.*"'

'Have you ever read that out loud to anybody else, apart from me?'

Maria looked puzzled. 'Of course not. Why should I? You are the first.'

'My son said those exact words, only last night. He said he had a nightmare that he was in a forest, and he could smell a campfire, and that a man said "*Był bialy. Wyglądał jak duch.*"'

'Your son speaks Polish?'

'He used to be fluent. His mother always spoke Polish to him, when he was little. Now – well, I'm afraid I don't bother so much as she did, and like I say, I've gotten pretty rusty myself.'

'Your wife is no longer with you?'

Jack gave her a quick grimace. 'She, ah . . . she passed away two years ago. Cancer.'

'Oh, I apologize. I was wondering why she did not come today. I did not know. I am so sorry for your loss. There is never a way to fill the space which a person we loved used to occupy. The world is crowded with empty shapes, where people once were. But – your son spoke those very same words? How do you think he could have known them? It could hardly be a coincidence, could it? "It is white, and it looks like a ghost." Who else would say such words?'

'I don't know, Maria. I can't even guess. My son is into star charts and astrology and all that kind of thing, and he's told quite a few fortunes for people which have turned out pretty accurate.'

He told her about the suicides at Owasippe, and what he and Sparky thought they had seen there, flickering behind the trees. He also told her that Sparky thought there was a connection between the Wallace family and Owasippe, although he hadn't been able to explain what it was.

'Perhaps the white thing that haunts the woods at this scout camp is the same as the white thing that haunts the Kampinos Forest,' Maria suggested. 'Perhaps *that* is the connection.'

'But Owasippe and Palmiry are thousands of miles apart. They're in totally different countries, in completely different cultures. I think that what we saw at Owasippe was probably an animal, like a cougar, and you don't find too many cougars in Poland.'

Maria held up the diary. 'On the other hand, Mr Wallace, there is another similarity which is very hard to explain.'

'Oh yes, and what's that?'

'The way in which those boy scouts died, and the way in which your great-grandfather died. Listen to this – November nineteenth, 1940. "We are all now feeling such terror that some of us can barely speak. The Germans must be feeling it, too, because a patrol came within fifty meters of our hiding place, stopped for a while, and then suddenly rushed away. We could hear three or four of them screaming out loud. Then we heard several shots.

'"Grzegorz and I ventured out as it began to grow dark, even though we were still gripped by such inexplicable fear that we could barely speak. We found the bodies of five young German soldiers lying amongst the trees. Three of them had been shot in the head, but all three of these were clutching their own pistols. The other two had obviously faced each other and shot each other in the mouth with their respective rifles. One of them was still holding to his lips the muzzle of his fellow's Gewehr 98. We could only conclude that this had been a suicide pact between the two of them. They had all killed themselves, rather than face whatever it is that haunts this forest.'"

Jack said nothing, but waited for Maria to finish. She turned over three more pages in the diary, and then she read, 'November twenty-fourth, 1940. "It is no use. It is no use fighting this panic any longer. We have seen the white thing again and again, behind the trees. Yesterday we tried to get away and after five hours of walking we almost managed to reach the village of Truskaw. Somehow, however, the dread was so strong that I could hardly breathe, and Grzegorz was so terrified that he could speak no sense whatsoever, gibbering like a lunatic.'"

Maria paused, and then she said, 'This, on the same page, is the very last entry. "It is hopeless. We no longer fear that the Germans will find us. In fact, we almost wish that they would, to bring a swift end to this indescribable terror. However now it seems that the Germans are too frightened themselves to come into the forest this far. There is no escape from the white thing, whatever it is – a human being, an animal, or a Forest Ghost. Grzegorz and I have talked and we have decided that there is only one course of action that we can take. We will follow the example of those two German soldiers, and together seek the most honorable death that we can. May God save those we have abandoned, and may Our Lady treat us with compassion and forgiveness.'"

Maria closed the diary and placed it back in the metal box.

'That is all,' she said, simply. 'The diary ends there. All the rest of these papers are letters from various members of the resistance – orders to go into hiding, mostly, and what targets they might consider striking against. Krystyna said that the Institute of History has made copies of all of them, including this diary, but they believed that as the last surviving member of my family I ought to have the originals.

She lifted the box up and held it close to her face and deeply inhaled. 'It smells,' she said. 'After all these years, it still smells of forest.'

Jack said nothing for a long time. The rain kept up a soft, persistent pattering, and through the ivory net curtains he could see the drops shuddering down the window pane. Maria closed the box with a squeak and put it back on the side table.

'So that was how they died?' Jack asked her, at last. 'Your great-uncle Andrzej and my great-grandfather Grzegorz?'

Maria nodded. 'As far as we can tell, because their bodies have never been found. They did not want to kill themselves, because they thought that was cowardly, so they planned to kill each other. In effect, though, like your poor little boy scouts, it seems more than likely that they committed suicide.'

Forensics of Fear

Next day, Sparky went back to school, although Jack did offer him another day off, if he wanted it. Jack guessed that he was eager to tell his classmates about how they had gone to Owasippe to identify Malcolm's body, and what they had found in the woods. After all, the scouts' suicides had been headline news on almost every TV station.

He was sitting in his office going through the previous night's takings when Sally knocked at his open door. It was warm outside and she was wearing a sleeveless white blouse and khaki slacks and very shiny scarlet lip gloss.

'Hey, Jack the Polack,' she said. 'How's it going in *gołąbki* world?'

'Pretty damn good, as a matter of fact,' he told her. 'We've been turning people away almost every night this week. So when did you get back from Muskegon?'

'About two hours ago. I'm bushed, to tell you the truth.'

He pointed to the chair on the other side of his desk. 'Take a load off,' he told her. 'How about a soda? Mountain Dew? Fanta?'

Sally unslung her beige leather purse and opened it up. She took out several folded sheets of paper and said, 'Those two people you found in the pool. The Headless Woman and her Tattooed Companion. We identified them.'

'Really? Who are they? Or who *were* they, rather?'

'Researchers, both of them, for Michigan Wildlife Conservancy. Apparently some of the forestry contractors had seen what they thought was cougar scat around that part of the Owasippe Scout Reservation. The two of them were up there to collect samples.'

'Scat? What's that?'

'In wildlife circles, it's what they call animal feces. It's shit, Jack. They scoop it up and send it back to be tested for DNA.'

'Do they know what happened to them yet? Tell me as much as you know.'

'They're trying to piece it all together but it isn't easy. The woman's name was Sandra Greene, with an "e". She was twenty-eight years old and specialized in human/cougar interactions, especially in urban areas and subdivisions where human development has begun to encroach on cougar territory. The guy's name was Weldon Farmer. He was thirty-five years old, married with two kids. He was Sandra Greene's immediate boss. They were both based at the Michigan Wildlife Conservancy Center in Bath, just outside of Lansing.

'Undersheriff Porter told me there was no question that Mr Farmer buried Ms Greene up to her thighs and then severed her head. At the time he buried her, that pool wouldn't have been very much more than a depression in the ground with little or no water in it, because it only filled up after heavy rain. Underneath Mr Farmer's body they found a machete, which he almost certainly used to decapitate her.

'He didn't drown, because there wasn't enough water in the pool at the time he killed himself. It hadn't rained until about eighteen hours before you found them. He cut the femoral artery in his groin, probably with the same machete that he had used to kill Ms Greene, and he bled to death.'

Jack said, 'Was she unconscious when he buried her? I mean, if she hadn't *wanted* him to bury her in the dirt that deep—'

'No, you're right,' said Sally. 'The odds are that she was conscious. There was no sign of concussive bruising on her head, and the autopsy hasn't shown any trace of any kind of knockout drugs in her blood or in her urine – although she must have been there for at least two days before you found her, so any chemicals in her blood would have degenerated long before then. It didn't help the coroner that she was decapitated, so any drugs like diphenhydramine wouldn't have had time to penetrate through to her hair, which is where we usually find the most conclusive traces.'

'So what you're saying is that this could have been a suicide pact?'

Sally nodded. 'That's one of the theories they're working on, yes. So far, though, the Lansing PD haven't found any suicide notes at either of their homes or at their place of work, nor any indications that the relationship between Mr Farmer and Ms Greene was anything but purely professional.

'Undersheriff Porter says he's very wary of jumping to conclu-
sions. Just because all of those scouts and scout leaders
committed suicide so close by, that doesn't necessarily mean
that *this* was suicide, too. Maybe some psychopath forced them
to do it.'

'I don't know,' said Jack. 'I wouldn't cut a woman's head
off, even if somebody was pointing a gun at me. I'd rather
die.'

Sally said, 'I wouldn't say no to that soda now. A Diet
Coke would be great.'

Jack went to the fridge and took out a cold bottle of Coke.
'Any more news on the scouts?' he asked her.

'That's the other reason I'm here. Corinne Cusack called me
this morning. She received a letter in the mail from Malcolm.'

'Oh, Jesus. That must have upset her.'

'Well, it came as quite a shock, I can tell you. I took it
straight to forensics but not before I'd taken a picture of it.'
She rummaged in her purse and produced her iPad. She flicked
through it and then she passed it over to Jack so that he could
read it.

Malcolm had written his letter on lined paper, roughly torn
out of a notebook. His handwriting, however, was very small
and neat and round, in blue ballpen.

Dear Mom,
We went into the forest today to do tracking. At first it was
good but then we got frightend even the leaders were
frightend. We didn't know why but it was the forest. We
are supposd to go tomorrow to do wilderness survival but
I don't want to go it is so frightning. But they say we have
to go for our merit badge.
Love Malcolm.

Jack handed Sally's iPad back. 'Poor little guy. Do you know
if any of the other parents had letters like that?'

'We're checking, but so far Malcolm is the only one. The
trouble is, he doesn't say what they're all so scared of.'

'Maybe it was the Forest Ghost.'

'The Forest Ghost? What's that?'

Jack said, 'I don't know . . . probably this has no connection with those boy scouts at all.'

He told Sally all about his visit to Maria, and what Maria's great-uncle Andrzej had written in his diary.

'Sounds similar, doesn't it?' said Jack. 'I mean, I don't know how it could be, but it does. A white thing, like an animal. Me and Sparky, we saw it for ourselves. And Sparky's absolutely convinced that there's a connection.'

Sally grimaced and massaged the back of her neck. 'This isn't really something I can tell my captain, Jack. He'll either laugh in my face or he'll send me off for psych evaluation. Besides, this isn't really my case. I'm just giving the Muskegon Sheriff's Department some friendly back-up.'

'I don't know what more we can do,' said Jack. 'There's something scary in the forest at Owasippe, just like there was something scary in the Kampinos Forest in Poland, but whether it's the same kind of scary something, I don't see how we can ever find out. Not unless the sheriff's deputies in Muskegon actually *catch* it.'

Sally finished her bottle of Diet Coke and stood up. 'How is young Sparky?' she asked.

'Not too bad, considering. But you know what he's like. I always feel he's got something on his mind that he's not telling me.'

'How about you? How are you feeling?'

'Fine. The restaurant's doing fantastic. I hardly have a moment to myself.'

Sally laid a hand on his arm. 'What I meant was, how are you feeling about Aggie? It's two years ago next week, isn't it?'

Jack suddenly found that it was difficult to speak. 'There's nothing I *can* do, is there? My brain still won't accept that I'm never going to see her again.'

Sally kissed his cheek. 'Just remember, you'll always have a friend in me. Any time you feel low, you just call me.'

Jack nodded. 'OK, Sal. You're an angel.'

Message from Beyond

That Saturday, Jack took Sparky up to see his mother in Highland Park, thirty minutes due north of Edgewater. She lived in a secluded loop, in a detached stone-fronted house with a view through the trees of Lake Michigan. It was gusty that morning, and the clouds were tumbling helter-skelter over the lake as if they were being chased by something that was threatening to tear them apart.

Nina Wallace was waiting for them in the porch when they came up the front steps. She was short, plump and round-faced, with ruddy cheeks and a curly perm which was suspiciously dark brown for a woman of sixty-one. She was wearing a bright summer dress with red-and-yellow flowers on it, and red Minnie Mouse shoes. Jack always thought that you can take the woman out of the Ukraine, where Nina's family had originally come from, but you can never take the Ukraine out of the woman. Her parents had brought her up speaking Ukrainian, and with Jack's father she had always spoken Polish, so even though she had been born and been brought up in Chicago, she spoke English like an immigrant. She was always coming out with sayings like, 'A woman is not harmonica, for a man to toss aside when he finish play!'

'Jack! Alexis!' she called out, lifting up both of her arms. She never called her grandson 'Sparky'. He had been christened Alexis after her father, whose somber mustachioed photograph hung in her hallway, and she never allowed him to forget it.

'Hallo, *mamo*,' said Jack. 'How have you been?'

'Oh . . . no so bad. Nobody come to see me. But no so bad.'

'I came to see you only a couple of weeks ago.'

'Your sister no come.'

'Anya lives in California now, *mamo*. Apart from that she's very busy.'

'All the same she could call. What is wrong her finger, can't call?'

They went inside, to the open-plan living room. Considering how traditional her dress was, his mother's house was furnished in a very sparse, modern style, with plain white walls and white carpets and glass and chrome furniture. The only concession to tradition was an icon of Our Lady hanging by the fireplace. Jack walked through to the dining area, and looked out at the garden. He could see the lake glittering behind the trees, in the same way that the white thing had flickered behind the trees at Owasippe.

'So, how you?' his mother asked him.

'I'm OK,' he told her. 'On Thursday I met this really interesting Polish lady. Maria Wiktoria Koczerska, that was her name. I thought about phoning you and telling you about her, but then I thought, no, it would be better if I told you in person.'

Sparky had already sat down on his grandmother's large white leather couch, and had opened up his iPad. He had told Jack that he was drawing up a new star chart for him.

'You want beer? How about you, Alex? Dr Pepper? I fetch cake.'

'It's okay, *mamo*, we had breakfast only a half-hour ago. Let me tell you about this Maria Koczerska.'

'You're sure you don't want beer? Let me fetch cake anyhow.'

'*Mamo*, she found out what happened to great-grandfather Grzegorz, during the war. She found out how he died.'

Nina Wallace promptly pulled out one of the chrome and white-leather dining chairs, and sat down. 'How she know that? Agnieszka's family never knew. Her mother always say to me, my grandfather Grzegorz was very famous musician, but he stay in Poland when the Germans come, and disappear. Nobody *ever* know what happened to him. So how this Koczerska woman know? I don't believe her!'

'*Mamo*, why are you always so suspicious? I haven't even told you what she said yet.'

'Because you good-looking, widower, got plenty of money, run restaurant. She get her hooks into you with some bull-cock story!'

'She's older than you are, *mamo*, by a mile!'

'So? Old women like money, too, and men! That Mrs Lucas,

across the street, she is seventy-five! But every week the fellow
who mow her grass, he goes inside for extra payment!'

'Come on, you don't know that. He probably goes inside just
to wash up.'

'Huh! He always come out with such big smile.'

Jack said, 'Maria Koczerska was sent a diary that used to
belong to her great-uncle during the war. Her great-uncle was
good friends with Grzegorz Walach. It turns out that they were
hiding in the Kampinos Forest, north-west of Warsaw. In
November of 1940, they committed suicide.'

Jack's mother stared at him in disbelief. '*Fwofff!*' she said,
flapping her hand. 'This woman is telling you bull-cock
story!'

'I've seen the diary for myself. She isn't making it up.'

'They kill themself? Why?'

'There was something in the forest that frightened them. Not
the Germans. Something else. They heard the Germans call it
Der Waldgeist.'

Sparky looked up from his iPad for a moment, and stared at
him, but then he went back to his star chart.

Jack's mother, however, was frowning, her thick dark
eyebrows drawn together. '*Waldgeist*? Wood Ghost? Maybe they
mean *nish-gite*?'

'I don't know. She said it was German for "Forest Ghost".
What's a *nish-gite* when it's at home?'

'Same I suppose. When my family live on West Walton Street,
when I am maybe six or seven, there is Polish-Jewish woman
live next door. Mrs Rosen. She is always telling me stories
about ghosts in the forests when she was little. Wherever there
is trees that they can hide in, she says, you have *nish-gite*. Even
when I am older, sixteen maybe, and I have to walk home
through Humboldt Park in the evening after my work at
Greenberg's Store, I always run quick because I remember what
Mrs Rosen tells me about *nish-gite* in trees.'

She paused, her eyes darting from side to side as she remembered what her neighbor had told her all those years ago, and
thought of herself hurrying home across Humboldt Park. But
then she flapped her hand again and said, '*Fwoff!* It is only a
story! Mrs Rosen trying to frighten me, silly woman! You not

think your great-grandfather kill himself because he is scared
of *ghost*?'

'I don't know,' said Jack. 'It doesn't seem too likely, does
it? But who knows what it was like when they were hiding in
that forest? They could have been discovered by the Germans
and shot at any moment. Maybe the stress made them all go
bananas, and they started imagining stuff.'

'But we didn't imagine what *we* saw, did we, Dad?' said
Sparky, without looking up from his iPad.

'*You* saw something?' asked Jack's mother. 'Where you saw
something? What do you mean, Alexis? Like *nish-gite*?'

Sparky shrugged. 'We don't know what it was, Grandma,
not for sure. But it scared us, didn't it, Dad?'

'It was in Michigan, *mamo*, in a scout camp,' said Jack. 'It
could have been a cougar. In fact, it probably *was* a cougar, so
it was just as well that we got the heck out of there.'

Sparky didn't comment on that, but after a pause he said,
flatly, 'Your stars for next week are so-o-o strange.'

'What – *my* stars?' Jack asked him.

'Yes . . . somebody's going to give you a message.'

'A message? Who is? What's it about?'

'A woman. You haven't met her yet. You won't believe the
message when you get it, but then somebody else far away will
tell you that it's true.'

Jack didn't know what to say to that. Just as he didn't
believe that our destiny is predetermined by the planets, he
had never believed that it was possible to tell what was going
to happen in the future, by any means – stars or crystal balls
or tea leaves or Tarot cards. But Sparky's forecasts often
turned out to be startlingly accurate – even if some of them
had been as non-specific as this one. To be fair, any woman
could give him a message about anything. It might be Sally
giving him some more news about the suicides at Owasippe;
or it might turn out to be Mrs Debska from Polish Meat
Supplies telling him that she had just had a new shipment of
swojska sausage.

But Sparky began to elaborate. 'The person who tells you
that it's true . . . she's a woman, too,' said Sparky.

'Oh, yes?'

'You're going to travel a long way, and you're going to meet her.'

'Really?'

Sparky nodded. 'You're going to meet her and you're going to fall in love with her.'

On the way home, Jack said to Sparky, 'You know I still love your mother, don't you?'

'Yes,' said Sparky.

They were just passing Skokie Lagoons when it started to rain, very hard – so hard that the windshield wipers of Jack's Camaro could barely keep up with it, and he found that he was driving blind.

Under The Witch's Head

Early on Wednesday morning, before the restaurant opened, Jack was restocking the shelves behind the bar with spirits when Bindy came in. She was wearing a flouncy green dress, with matching green ribbons in her hair. She smelled strongly of white musk perfume, which Jack guessed she must have sprayed over herself immediately before she came round to see him.

'Jack! *Hi*, Jack!' she called out, as if she were surprised to see him. 'Are we going to be seeing you this evening?'

'I don't know. Why?'

'Don't tell me you forgot already! Tamara Thorne is holding her séance!'

Jack took two more bottles of Wyborowa vodka out of the case on the counter. 'I don't think so, Bindy. We've been so busy lately. I can't leave Tomasz in the lurch – not again.'

'Oh, but you *must* come! Tamara is absolutely ur-*mazing*! She put my friend Caitlin in touch with her twin sister, and her twin sister died over seven years ago! Caitlin just couldn't believe it . . . they talked and talked and Tamara couldn't have been faking it because she knew so many secrets that only Caitlin and her sister had ever shared. Like, when they were little they had a pet snail they called Silver.'

'A pet snail called Silver? They didn't have a pet cat called Tonto, too?'

Bindy climbed up on to one of the barstools and noisily rearranged all of her flounces. 'You *must* come, Jack! Supposing she gets in touch with Aggie for you?'

'Bindy, to tell you the truth, I don't really believe in any of this psychic stuff. Aggie's gone and that's that. There's nothing I can do to bring her back.'

'There's no harm in trying, though, is there? And who knows? Tamara may surprise you. Besides, if you come along this evening, you might meet somebody you like.'

'Just at this moment in time, Bindy, I'm not looking for anybody. I'm just running this restaurant seven days a week and taking care of Sparky and that takes up all of my time, and more.'

Bindy took off her spectacles and blinked at him short-sightedly. 'People get together by accident, Jack. Sometimes your future partner is right in front of your nose and you never realize. Then, one day, for no particular reason – shazam!'

Jack said, 'I'll try, Bindy. If I get time, I'll see if I can drop by.'

'You promise?'

'I'll see what I can do.'

Bindy climbed off the barstool and looked around. 'It must be so hard, running this place on your own.'

'I have a really great team.'

'Yes, but what do you do at the end of the day, after everybody's gone home, and you've closed up, and Sparky's in bed asleep?'

'I open a beer and I sit and watch TV and then *I* usually fall asleep, too.'

Bindy was about to say something else, but then she obviously decided against it. She gave Jack a forced smile and said, 'See you this evening then, hopefully?'

As they passed Jimmy John's gourmet sub shop on their way back from school, Jack handed Sparky his ritual Oh Henry bar.

'Malcolm's mom called me this afternoon,' said Jack. 'They're holding Malcolm's funeral next Friday.'

'OK,' said Sparky. He didn't unwrap his candy bar right away, as he usually did, but sat staring out of the window.

'You OK?' Jack asked him. 'You didn't have any problems at school today?'

'No . . . everything was fine. I got a grade A in algebra.'

'Hey . . . that's fantastic! I was always terrible at algebra. In fact I was terrible at every subject except woodwork. I probably would have been a carpenter if Grandpa and Grandma hadn't needed me to help them in the restaurant.'

Sparky said, 'You should go tonight.'

'What? Go where?'

'To Bindy's bookstore. You really should go.'

'Oh, you mean the séance thing. I don't think so, Sparks. What if this woman pretends that she can put me in touch with your mom? You and I both know that simply isn't possible. It would be an insult to her memory, to say the least.'

But Sparky said, 'I finished your star chart for this month during recess. You really should go and talk to this woman. She's the one with the message that I was telling you about.'

'I'm sorry, Sparks. I really don't believe that we can talk to dead people, no matter how much we may want to. Don't you think that I would give anything just to hear your mom's voice again?'

'But this woman is the one with the *message*,' Sparky insisted. 'And the message will tell us what happened to Malcolm. Why he killed himself. And why all of those other scouts killed themselves, too. It says so, in your stars. Mercury is rising, and Mercury is the messenger, and also the Lord of Wednesday.'

'Sparks – I'm going to be up to my ears in it tonight. We have seventy-three covers booked already and we always have a whole lot of walk-ins midweek.'

Sparky said, 'Please, Dad. I have to know why Malcolm committed suicide, and this is the only way.'

'Well, I don't think it was a Forest Ghost, or a *nish-gite*, or whatever Grandma called it, do you?'

Sparky said nothing, but still didn't unwrap his Oh Henry bar.

Jack said, 'The police are investigating this very thoroughly, you know that, don't you? Sally keeps me up to date on all of their progress.'

'You will go tonight, though, won't you? I can help in the restaurant while you're away.'

'Don't you start getting involved in the restaurant business. I want you to be an atom physicist when you grow up, not a goddamned *pierogi*-slinger.'

All the same, when eight o'clock came, he went up to Tomasz and said, 'I have to go out for a while. Not long.'

The restaurant was not completely full, although Saskia was just seating a party of seven.

'Fine, no problem,' said Tomasz. 'Take so long as you like.'

Jack turned around and saw that Sparky was standing at the top of the stairs. He gave him a wave, but Sparky didn't wave back. He walked out of the front door of the restaurant on to North Clark Street and then turned left into West Berwyn Avenue. Most of West Berwyn was residential, but there were a few upscale little stores and cafés clustered at the intersection with North Clark, of which The Bookworm was one. Over its front door there was a bright yellow awning with a picture of a worm in spectacles reading a large leather-bound volume. Its double frontage was filled with books on nature and conservation and women's health and *feng-shui* – and of course a special display of Tamara Thorne's book *How to Talk to the Loved Ones You've Lost.*

Jack pushed open the door with some difficulty because the store was already crowded. Earnest-looking men and women in chunky hand-knitted sweaters were holding glasses of yellowy white wine or cranberry juice and waving cheese straws and having loud and earnest conversations. It was very hot in there, in spite of the air-conditioning, and it smelled of hessian and lavender and marijuana. Jack almost turned around and walked back out again, but from the rear of the store Bindy caught sight of him and called out, 'Jack! *Jack!* Come and meet Tamara!'

Jack had to use his elbows to force his way through the crowds who were gathered between the bookshelves because none of them seemed to be prepared to step aside for him. From the snatches of conversation he picked up as he passed, they were too involved in discussing macrobiotic diets and invisible art and the best type of birthing pool.

About fifty folding chairs had been arranged in a semi-circle at the rear of the store, with a large throne-like antique armchair in the center. On either side of the throne were two tall candelabras with six white candles burning in each. Behind it, the back wall of the store had been hung with purple velvet drapes, fastened with thumbtacks.

Tamara Thorne was a very tall woman, almost as tall as Jack and at least six inches taller than Bindy. She was also very thin, and severe, with long gray hair that had been braided tightly around her head like a medieval queen. Her eyes were the palest turquoise; while her cheekbones were sharp, and her chin was sharper. She was wearing a shapeless gray gown that reached almost to the floor, and several elaborate silver necklaces.

'Tamara, I'd like you to meet Jack,' Bindy enthused.

Tamara Thorne held out one limp, long-fingered hand as if she expected Jack to kiss her wrist. Jack shook it, and said, 'Pleased to meet you. I have your book.'

'You *have* it,' drawled Tamara Thorne, 'but have you *read* it?'

'Well – I have to confess, not too much of it. In fact none of it. I run a restaurant around the corner so I'm a little too busy to read. But I'll take it with me when I go on vacation.'

'Let me sign it for you.'

'Ah. Sorry. I forgot to bring it with me.'

'Then why did you come here?'

Jack shrugged and smiled. 'Bindy invited me. What else can I tell you? She seemed pretty keen for me to come along, so here I am.'

'You didn't come here to speak to your wife?'

Jack felt a cold crawling sensation all the way down his back. He looked into Tamara Thorne's stone-gray eyes but she was giving nothing away. Then he looked at Bindy and said, 'You told her about Aggie, then?' He didn't add *'thanks a bunch, Bindy,'* but he felt like it.

Bindy said, 'Jack – I swear to you – I haven't said a word.'

'No, she didn't,' said Tamara Thorne. 'Don't you realize how obvious it is? I knew that you were a recent widower as soon as I saw you coming toward me. It's nothing to be ashamed of. The pain on your face is a measure of how much you loved her.'

'Well, good guess,' said Jack. 'Now – if you'll excuse me – I have a very crowded restaurant to run.'

'You *didn't* come here to speak to your wife, did you?' said Tamara Thorne.

'No, as matter of fact, I didn't.'

'Are you not going to stay to hear what you *did* come here for?'

'OK,' Jack challenged her. 'What did I come here for?'

'Enlightenment. That is why most people come to me.'

'Go on, then. Enlighten me.'

Tamara Thorne turned to Bindy. 'Shall we have everybody sitting down now? Then I can give Jack his message properly.' She turned back to Jack and said, 'It takes concentration, you see. I can't just pluck it out of the air in mid-conversation. Especially not with all of this hubbub in the background.'

Jack had rarely felt so much like telling somebody to take their enlightenment and shove it; but then he thought what he would have to say to Sparky when he returned home. Sparky took all this so seriously, and he would probably sulk for about a week – or what, with Sparky, amounted to sulking: turning his face away whenever Jack spoke to him, and answering every question with a monosyllable.

'All right,' Jack agreed, checking his watch. 'But I can't be too long. We have a party of Kiwanis coming in at nine.'

'I can't make you any promises,' said Tamara Thorne. 'It depends on the spirits, not on me. It depends how strongly they feel the need to contact you.'

'I see. OK. Let's do it, then, shall we?'

Bindy and one of her assistants clapped their hands and called all of the guests in the bookstore to come and take a seat. They did so with a great deal of shuffling and chair-scraping and chatter, but eventually they were all settled in their semi-circle with Tamara Thorne sitting on her throne in the middle.

'Please – absolute quiet,' said Tamara Thorne, spreading her arms wide and closing her eyes. 'Please, everybody, *absolute* quiet. The spirits need to hear the thoughts inside your heads. They need to hear your longings and your desires. They need to hear your grief that they are gone.'

Chattering was replaced by coughing, and throat-clearing, and then at last by silence.

Tamara Thorne, with her eyes still closed, said, 'You will all have read in my book that it is not necessary for you to *summon* any particular spirit. Well, *nearly* all of you will have read that in my book. In other words it is not necessary to call on the one you love, or the one to whom you wish to speak.

'All you have to do is empty your mind of noise and clutter and petty arguments and day-to-day concerns. Turn the inside of your head into an echo-chamber, totally dark and totally silent, in which the voice of your loved ones may resonate. They will speak to you, the spirits, if you listen. Not always – and not always the spirits of your choice. But the spirit world is like a social network, it's like a celestial Twitter, and if you converse with *one* spirit, it is almost certain that your words will be conveyed to the spirit with whom you originally wanted to talk.'

She paused for a very long moment, her eyes still closed, her arms swaying from side to side, as if she were floating on a shallow tide. After a while, she said, 'Thelma says that it wasn't your fault, Bruce. She's very faint, but can you hear her?'

A bald middle-aged man in the audience said, '*Thelma?*'

'Can you hear her, Bruce? I know she sounds very far away, but that's because she is.'

'I can hear her! I can hear her! Thelma?'

'Stay calm, Bruce,' said Tamara Thorne, in a flat, soothing voice. 'Stay calm and listen to what she has to say.'

Jack turned to look at the man. His face was scrunched up in concentration and his fists were clenched. Tears were running freely down his cheeks, and the woman sitting next to him had put her arm around his shoulders to comfort him. Every now and then he nodded and said, 'Yes,' and 'yes,' and 'oh, Thelma, I miss you, sweetheart!'

At last he opened his eyes and looked around. The woman gave him a tissue and he dabbed his face, and sniffed. He tried to say something, but he was too overwhelmed to speak, and all he could do was shake his head.

Jack's first thought was that he was a plant. After all, nobody else in the audience had heard Thelma's voice, even if Thelma really had been speaking to him.

One or two people started to murmur to each other, but Tamara Thorne called out, 'Silence, please! Absolute silence! The spirits are not easy to hear at the best of times, and if you want to hear your own loved ones, like Bruce here, then you will have to be totally receptive!'

Again, she sat with her eyes closed, waving her arms. Jack was wondering how long he was going to have to sit here, listening to this charade, when a voice said, with cut-glass clarity, 'Jack – *słyszysz mnie?*'

Jack felt the same cold shrinking sensation down his back that he had experienced when Tamara Thorne had asked him if he had come here to talk to Aggie. Inside his head he could hear this clearest of voices, and it was unmistakably Aggie's.

'*Jack, can you hear me*?' That was what she had asked him, in Polish.

Like the bald man who had heard from his Thelma, Jack's eyes immediately filled with tears, and his throat tightened up so much that he wouldn't have been able to say anything out loud if he had wanted to. It was Aggie, his beautiful lost Aggie, there was no mistaking it. He looked across at Tamara Thorne, and his chest was physically hurting with grief and resentment, but Tamara Thorne still had her eyes closed, and was still waving her arms from side to side.

Aggie – he thought – *Agnieszka, is that really you*?

There was a long moment of silence, but then he heard Aggie's voice again, still quite clear, but much smaller this time, as if she were speaking to him from very far away.

'Jack, *słyszysz mnie*?'

He had no tissue so he had to smear the tears away from his eyes with the back of his hand. *Yes, Aggie, I can hear you. Where are you? Speak to me, Aggie!*

Another long silence, and then Aggie said, '*Są dwa kilometry na północ . . . a potem jeszcze trzysta metrów na zachód . . . od wsi Truskaw.*'

What? He could hardly hear her, let alone understand what she was saying to him. She was trying to tell him that somebody was two kilometers to the north of Truskaw then three hundred meters to the west.

He recognized the name Truskaw immediately. Truskaw was the village in the Kampinos Forest to which Grzegorz Walach and Maria's great-uncle Andrzej had been trying to escape during the war, but where they had finally been overwhelmed with terror.

'*Są pogrzebani tam, gdzie ścieżka rozdziela się na trzy,*' Aggie continued. She sounded as if she were reading from a script, or a diary, like Maria. '*Pod skałami w kształcie głowy wiedźmy.*'

Jack understood that. 'They are buried where the path divides into three . . . under the rocks that look like a witch's head.'

Who is? he asked her, but this time the silence went on and on and she didn't say anything more.

'Aggie!' he managed to choke out, and everybody seated around him turned and stared. Even Tamara Thorne opened her eyes and looked at him.

'I'm sorry,' he said. He stood up awkwardly and knocked over his folding chair.

'You *heard* somebody, Jack?' asked Tamara Thorne.

'I'm sorry,' he repeated. 'I shouldn't have come here. I'm sorry I disturbed you. I – ah – I have to get back to my customers.'

He picked up his chair and then he made his way back between the bookshelves. Bindy came hurrying after him and caught up with him just as he reached the door.

'Jack! Are you all right, Jack? Oh, God – you look so *pale.*'

'I'm fine, Bindy. I knew I shouldn't have come. The last few days . . . well, that Owasippe business probably disturbed me more than I realized.'

'No, it's me who should be sorry,' said Bindy. 'I should have seen that this wasn't a good time for you.'

'Never mind,' Jack told her. 'Give my apologies to Tamara. Tell her I may even get around to reading her book.'

As he stepped out of the door, Bindy said, 'Jack?'

'What is it?'

'Nothing. I just wanted to make sure that you were OK. I do care about you, you know.'

He kissed her on the forehead. She was slightly sweaty and her skin tasted of maca root moisturizer. 'Thanks, Bindy. Take care of yourself.'

Where the Bones Are

When he returned to the restaurant, he found that Sparky was in the kitchen, wearing a white apron that almost reached the floor and a white chef's cap. He was using his hands to mix ground pork and ground beef with onions and crushed Saltine crackers in a large brown bowl.

'I teach him to make *schnitzla*,' said Mikhail, proudly. 'More useful than wait on table.'

'That's great, Mikhail,' Jack told him. But when Mikhail had gone back to his range to fry up some more onions, Jack said to Sparky, with an intensity that was almost ferocious, '*How did you know?*'

'How did I know what, Dad?'

'How did you know that medium woman had a message for me?'

'I told you, Dad. It was all in your star chart. "Somebody has a message for you, and it's a woman."'

'Yes, you were right. A woman *did* have a message for me. I heard her speaking to me, right inside my head. But do you have any idea who it was?'

Sparky looked up at him, his hands still deep in the bowl of ground pork.

'No,' he said, in a little ghost of a voice.

'It was your mom. At least I think it was. You know that I don't believe in any of that life-after-death baloney. But it sounded exactly like her.'

Two tears suddenly rolled down Sparky's cheeks. 'It was *Mom*? You really heard her?'

Jack came around the table and put his arms around Sparky's shoulders. 'I don't know how it was done, Sparks. Maybe I was tricked. Some of these mediums, they have ways to fool you into thinking that they're putting you in touch with dead people, but it's nothing but a scam. Like, they'll find out little personal details about you before the séance starts, so you'll really believe that it's your dead Aunt Jemima talking to you.'

Sparky took his hands out of the bowl and carefully scraped the *schnitzla* mix from his fingers, using a spoon. Then he went to the sink and washed them.

'Hey – you don't finish yet, Sparky!' called out Mikhail. 'Now you have to squish into patty!'

'I'm sorry, Mikhail,' said Jack. 'You'll have to finish them off yourself. Sparky and me, we have a couple of important things to talk about.'

'OK,' said Mikhail. 'But you come back, Sparky, for more lesson in cook! You have touch like good chef!'

Jack and Sparky went upstairs to their apartment. Jack went to the fridge and took out a beer for himself and a Dr Pepper for Sparky. They went into the living room and Sparky sat down on the end of the couch, looking up at Jack both expectantly and anxiously.

'This is so hard, Sparks,' said Jack. 'At first I wasn't going to tell you, but then I thought, I have to. After all, it was *you* who said that I was going to be given a message, and you were right, and so you deserve to know what it was and who gave it to me.'

'Do you believe that Mom's still here, someplace?' asked Sparky. He looked around the room, almost if he thought she might be standing in the corner.

'What?' said Jack. 'In heaven or something? I don't know. It would be nice to believe it, wouldn't it? But I don't think I can.'

'If she's not in heaven, how did she speak to you?'

'I have absolutely no idea. But the message she gave me was that somebody was buried in the Kampinos Forest, not too far from a village called Truskaw. Well, she said "they", so I'm assuming that she was talking about more than one.'

'Did she tell you who they were?'

'No, she didn't, but considering that this was a message from beyond, she was pretty specific about *where* they were. Two kilometers north of Truskaw and three hundred meters to the west, that's what she said. Apparently they're buried where the path splits up into three, under some rocks that look like the head of a witch.'

'She said all that? What . . . what did she sound like?'

'Really calm, like she always used to, when she was alive. Not upset in any way at all, but not much expression, if you know what I mean. It was almost like she was reading it. She started off sounding really clear, but then her voice got fainter and fainter.'

'Did she say anything about Malcolm?'

'No, she didn't. Well – she might have done, but if she did I couldn't hear it.'

Sparky looked thoughtful. 'She must have had a reason for telling you about these buried people.'

'I agree, Sparks. Like I said, she didn't tell me who they were, but if I had to hazard a guess, I'd say that they could well be your great-great-grandfather Grzegorz, and his friend Andrzej – you know, Mrs Koczerska's great-uncle. I never even *heard* of Truskaw before last week. It seems like too much of a coincidence that this is the second time in five days that somebody has mentioned it to me.'

'What are you going to do?' asked Sparky.

'Well, you said, didn't you, that some woman far away was going to confirm that this message was true? I'm going to call Maria Koczerska and see if her friend at Warsaw University can shed any light on it.'

'She can,' said Sparky, emphatically. 'She *will*.'

'You also said that I'm going to fall in love with her.'

'That's what your stars say.'

'Don't I have any choice in the matter?'

Sparky looked away. Jack was trying to be light-hearted about it, but he could tell that Sparky didn't want to talk about it any more.

'Do you have any homework?' Jack asked him.

'Not tonight. Well – some, but it's only reading a chapter of *Moby Dick*, and I can do that when I go to bed.'

'OK – why don't you go back down to the kitchen and help Mikhail to finish off those *schnitzlas*? If I can manage to get through to Mrs Koczerska, I'll come down and tell you.'

When he called Maria Koczerska, she told him that she was just about to go out for an evening of Polish dancing. He thought that there was no point in being anything but totally honest with her, so he told her all about the séance and what he had heard Aggie saying to him inside of his head.

Strangely, Maria didn't sound at all surprised.

'All right, Jack,' she told him, when he had finished. 'Tonight I will email my friend Krystyna at the Institute of History and see what *she* has to say about this.'

Jack said, 'I just hope she's not too skeptical about it, just because I got the message through a psychic. I know what these academic women are like. They always want empirical proof of everything – even what day of the week it is.'

'I think you will find, Jack, that Krystyna has a very open mind. Anyhow, I promise you that I will contact her and let you know what she says as soon as I can.'

'Just off the top of your head, Maria, do *you* think Aggie could have been talking about Grzegorz and Andrzej?'

'Who knows, until we look for them?' said Maria. 'But like so many thousands of others, Grzegorz and Andrzej must be there somewhere in that forest. All of Kampinos is a cemetery, and almost every tree marks somebody's last resting place.'

Jack was washing his teeth that evening, ready for bed, when he had a return call from Maria.

'I have spoken to Krystyna,' she said. 'This weekend she will go to the forest and try to find the place you spoke about. If she does, she may make some preliminary excavation there.'

'What did she say when you told her where the information came from?'

'To be honest with you, Jack, I didn't tell her that it had come from a medium. I said instead that after she had sent me my great-uncle Andrzej's diary, I had managed to locate some old Polish immigrants in Chicago who had been eye-witnesses to the mass executions at Palmiry. I said that the details about the burial site had come from them.'

'You lied to her, in other words? I thought you said that this Krystyna was very open-minded.'

'Yes, of course, and she is. But there was no point in putting her open-mindedness to such a test. Not until she finds these rocks like a witch's head, if they exist, and then digs down to

find if there is anything there. If there are no rocks there, or
nobody buried underneath them, we can simply blame senile
old men with faulty memories.'

The following Tuesday morning, Sally came into the restaurant
and sat herself up at the bar. Jack came up to her and said,
'What's it to be, ma'am?'

'A Dead-End Special with a side order of Frustration, please.
Undersheriff Porter just emailed me from Muskegon and we've
had to agree that all of those scouts committed suicide of their
own free will, without any apparent threat or coercion.'

'Oh.'

'Yes. Oh. We've questioned everybody involved with the
Thirty-ninth Scout Group and we could find no cult activity of
any kind, religious or otherwise, no online suicide pacts, no
systematic bullying, nor any evidence whatsoever of sexual abuse.

'The Muskegon Sheriff's Department searched a twenty-
square-mile area of the forest surrounding the Owasippe Scout
Reservation with dogs, metal detectors and infra-red heat-seeking
equipment mounted on helicopters. Nothing was found that could
have had any material relevance to the scouts' suicides, nor to
the deaths of Sandra Greene and Weldon Farmer, from Michigan
Wildlife Conservancy, which does appear to have been a mutu-
ally agreed suicide.

'Several of the scouts' relatives and friends received letters
and postcards from them, but none of them mentioned being
frightened, like Malcolm. Undersheriff Porter is of the opinion
that we shall never know why any of them committed suicide.
Like, ever.'

'So what does that mean? Case closed?'

'No . . . but unless I receive any further evidence from
Muskegon, or some scout comes forward and tells me that they
all agreed to commit suicide so that they could go to a better
life on another planet, there's no place else for me to take it.'

Jack wondered if he ought to tell Sally about Tamara Thorne's
séance, and the message he had received from Aggie, but he
decided against it. It wouldn't help her to solve the mystery of
what had happened at Owasippe, and it could make things much
more complicated. Nearly three quarters of a century had elapsed

between Grzegorz Walach and his friend Andrzej killing themselves in the Kampinos Forest and the scouts killing themselves at Owasippe, and even if Sparky was convinced that there was a connection between them, how could they prove it, and even if they could – how would it help?

'You want a real drink?' he asked Sally.

'Love to,' she said, 'but no. I have to go interview a husband and wife whose daughter has been found dead with a plastic bag stuffed in her mouth. Muslims. It seems like their daughter was fond of short skirts and dating American boys and they wanted her to go to Pakistan and go through with some arranged marriage.'

'Tragedy stops for nobody, does it?' said Jack.

'You said it, buster.'

Jack had just finished phoning through his orders for fresh vegetables when his phone rang. It was Maria Koczerska.

'I have heard from my friend Krystyna in Warsaw. On Saturday she and her friend from the historical institute went to the Kampinos Forest, to the location that you told me.'

She paused, and said, 'Please – hold on for a second, Jack. My cleaner is just leaving and I have to pay her.'

She put down the phone. Jack waited for over a minute, and then he heard her pick it up again.

'And?' he said. 'What did they find? Please – don't tell me they didn't find anything at all.'

'They measured exactly two kilometers north from Truskaw and then three hundred meters to the west and they found the rocks. Krystyna said they were not sure at first that this was the right place because the rocks look like a witch only from a certain angle. She has sent me a photograph of them and I can email it to you, too.'

'What about excavation? Did they do any digging?'

'Yes, they did. Not very deep, only a few centimeters, but almost at once they found a human shoulder bone. That is when they stopped, because they have to obtain special authority to exhume human remains from the forest. It is a national park now, after all.'

'So she's going to do that?'

'Yes,' said Maria, 'she filled out an application today and she has sent it to the park authorities. She is also seeking assistance from the historical institute to help finance the exhumation. It has to be done very carefully, with everything being properly photographed and recorded.'

'Well, that's pretty amazing, isn't it?' said Jack. 'My late wife tells me that there's somebody buried in a forest in Poland, and where they're buried, and they're actually there, for real. I can hardly believe it.'

'I told Krystyna this,' said Maria.

'You told her I went to a séance?'

'Yes. Well, I had to. She wanted to talk to my Polish immigrants about what they had seen when these people were buried, and who they thought they were, and who did it – so of course I had to admit that my immigrants were all invented. Apart from that, Jack, it is so extraordinary. I thought it was very important for her to know how you came by such information.'

'So – when you told her the truth – what did she say?'

'She said she would like to speak with you on the phone.'

'Yes – well, of course. I'd be glad to, although I don't know what else I can tell her. My late wife spoke to me inside of my head and told me this stuff. I don't know how, or why.'

'Maybe you need to try to get in touch with your wife again.'

Jack said, 'No, Maria. No way. She's gone. She's dead. I don't want to have to go through all of that grief a second time.'

'I understand. But I will give you Krystyna's number in Warsaw, her number at the university and also at home, and you can call her whenever you are able to.'

'Thanks, Maria.'

'There is one more thing, Jack. I just wanted to tell you how much this all disturbs me. On the one hand I am deeply curious to know what happened, and Krystyna is, too, but at the same time I wonder if it is wiser not to know. I have a feeling that if we find out, we will regret it. Andrzej and Grzegorz killed themselves for a reason, and maybe it is safer for us if we never discover what that reason was.'

Apparition

Although there was a lull in the restaurant around seven forty-five p.m. before the eight o'clock customers came crowding in, Jack didn't call Krystyna that evening. In Warsaw it would have been two forty-five the following morning, and he was sure that she wouldn't take too kindly to being phoned at that time.

By the time he had closed the door on his last customers at one-thirty a.m. he was too tired to think about phoning anybody. He went upstairs to his apartment, took a short hot shower, and climbed into bed to watch *Highway Patrol* on This-TV. After fifteen minutes, unable to keep his eyes open any longer, he switched off the bedside light and went to sleep.

He dreamed that it was dark. He dreamed that it was silent. Then he heard people talking. He couldn't hear distinctly what they were saying, but it sounded like a woman and a boy. Their conversation continued for what seemed like twenty minutes or even longer, although there were several lengthy pauses in between their sentences, like the conversation of two people who are both preoccupied with doing something else, like reading or sewing or playing a video game.

After a while, Jack opened his eyes, or dreamed that he was opening his eyes. His bedroom was totally dark, like his dream, or maybe this was part of his dream, because he could still hear the voices, the woman and the boy, having their desultory, long-drawn-out conversation. They sounded as if they were in the living room.

He lay there for a while, straining his ears, trying to make out what they were saying, but his bedroom door was closed, and all he could hear was the cadence of their voices, and not their words.

He sat up. *Am I dreaming this, or am I awake?* But then he looked at the digital clock on his nightstand and saw that it was 2:47 am and he knew that he was awake. If he was awake,

though, who was that talking in the living room at this time
of the morning?

He climbed out of bed, crossed the bedroom floor and opened
the door. The living-room door was two doors off to the right,
on the opposite side of the corridor, and there was a light shining
underneath it. Hanging on the wall in between was a large
framed black-and-white etching of angels, gathered around Mary
and the infant Jesus. The angel Gabriel was staring directly at
Jack as if he wanted to know what he was doing there. *At night*,
he seemed to be saying, *this is* our *domain*.

Jack made his way stealthily down the corridor and stopped
outside the living-room door. For the first minute or so, there
was silence, as if the woman and the boy knew that he was
there, and had deliberately stopped talking, waiting for him to
betray himself by making a noise, or sneezing, or losing his
patience and opening up the door.

He took hold of the door handle and he was about to open
the door when he heard the boy say, 'I told them they would
lose. I even told them what the score would be – three–five. Of
course when they lost and it was three–five, they blamed me.
They said I was a jinx.'

'That was so mean of them,' said the woman. 'Supposing
you had told them they were going to win, and they *had* won?
They wouldn't have blamed you *then*, would they?'

Jack held on to the door handle but he didn't open it. If he had
heard only the boy's voice, he would have gone in, because it was
Sparky's voice, and Sparky did have a tendency to walk and talk
in his sleep. But it was the woman's voice that made him hesitate.
It was the woman's voice that gave him a freezing, prickling
feeling. It was the same voice that he had heard inside his head
at Tamara Thorne's séance. Aggie. His dead wife, Agnieszka.

Again, there was silence. Then the woman said, 'It's going
to happen again, unless you can do something to stop it.'

Another long pause.

'I know. But what can *I* do? Nobody's going to believe me,
are they? And I don't even know what it is myself.'

'You have to find out. That's the point.'

More silence. The clock in the hallway suddenly struck three
and Jack's heart almost stopped.

'Dad's going to talk to some woman in Poland,' said Sparky.

'Oh. You mean the one he's going to fall in love with?'

Silence.

'I shouldn't have told you that.'

'Why not? I still love him, but I can't expect him to live alone for the rest of his life.'

At that point, Jack opened the door. The first thing he saw was Sparky sitting cross-legged on the couch, with his eyes closed. He was wearing his pale-green pajamas and his hair was sticking up on the crown of his head, as if he had just climbed out of bed. The only light in the living room came from a standard lamp with a parchment shade which stood right behind him.

Jack looked across at the far end of the room, and froze. Sitting in a wing chair by the window, in a long white nightdress, her face pale, was Aggie. Her blonde hair was shining in bright filaments in the lamplight, but her eyes were only shadowy smudges. Her thin-wristed hands were clasped in her lap and her feet were bare. She looked almost exactly as she had looked on the day that he had last seen her, on the day she had died. He could even see the blue veins in her ankles.

Jack opened and closed his mouth, but he couldn't speak. He knew that Aggie couldn't be real, and that she must be some kind of mirage. She didn't even *look* real – or at least she didn't look solid. He could see right through her, to the back of the wing chair she was sitting in, with its tapestry cushion.

Five long seconds passed, and then he took an unsteady step toward her, and then another. Because her eyes were so shadowy, it was difficult for him to tell if she could see him or not. She didn't move as he came closer – didn't raise her hands or try to stand up or change her expression.

'Aggie,' he said, hoarsely; but as soon as he spoke her name she vanished, leaving nothing but the empty chair and the crumpled cushion.

Jack closed his eyes for a moment and then opened them again, in case she had reappeared, but she had totally gone.

You were dreaming, Jack, he told himself. *You were hallucinating. What you saw was nothing but wishful thinking. You're overtired, that's the trouble, and still grieving. Not only that – all of this weirdness with the scouts committing suicide at Owasippe and the stories about Grzegorz Walach killing himself in the Kampinos Forest, it's really thrown you off balance.*

All the same, he was sure that he had heard Sparky talking to her, and he was equally sure that he had heard her talking back to him.

He turned around. Sparky was still sitting cross-legged on the couch, his eyes still closed. Jack went over and sat down next to him.

'Sparks?' he said. 'Sparky?'

Sparky still didn't respond, so Jack took hold of his forearm and gently shook him. 'Sparky? Wake up! It's Dad!'

Sparky abruptly opened his eyes and looked around the living room.

'Mom?' he said, in a voice that was thick with sleep.

'Hey, dude, it's me. You've been somnambulating again.'

Sparky stared at him in bewilderment.

'Where's Mom? She was here. I saw her. She was right there, sitting in that chair.'

'Your mom's gone, Sparky, you know that. She's never coming back. You were dreaming, that's all.'

'But I . . .' Sparky began, but then he realized that Jack must be right, and that he must have been asleep all the time.

'OK,' he said, and stood up, and furiously scratched his head.

'Get yourself back to bed,' said Jack. 'It's school tomorrow and we can't have you nodding off in the middle of algebra.'

Sparky looked up at him and Jack could see such pain in his eyes.

'She was here, Dad. I'm sure she was here. I was talking to her, and she was talking back to me. I can even remember what she said. She said, "You have to stop it, or else it's going to happen again."'

'What do you think she meant by that?'

'She meant the scouts committing suicide. She meant the white thing that we saw in the woods. I mean, that's what we were talking about.'

Jack put his arm around Sparky's shoulders and guided him back to his bedroom. 'I think this whole thing has been too darn traumatic for both of us, don't you? Let's both get some sleep and try to make a fresh start tomorrow. Maybe we could go boating on the lake this weekend. That would blow some of the cobwebs away.'

As he climbed into bed, Sparky said, 'Dad?'

'What is it?'

'Mom said one more thing. She said, "Tell your father I still love him."'

Jack was about to say, 'I know,' but instead he simply said, 'Sleep well, Sparks,' and closed the bedroom door.

Cry for Help

He went back to bed but he found it impossible to get back to sleep. He could hear garbage trucks in the street outside and police sirens and somebody playing dance music. Not only that, he was arguing with himself. Did I really see Aggie? Did I really hear her voice? He knew that it was impossible, but then he also knew that, under stress, the human mind can imagine all kinds of strange things. His old college friend Joe had suffered from alcoholic hallucinosis when he had given up drinking, and he had been convinced that he could hear Chinese policemen gambling in the corridor outside his hospital room.

Jack was still awake as it began to grow light outside, and he was beginning to think about getting out of bed and perking himself a strong cup of coffee and maybe making a start on his accounts. He threw back the bedspread and swung his legs out of bed and it was then that his phone warbled.

He looked at the time – 5:37 a.m. Who the hell was calling him at 5:37 a.m? He picked up the phone and squinted at the caller ID screen. *Out of area.*

Usually he didn't answer calls unless he knew who was ringing him. But this time he lifted the receiver to his ear and said, 'Nostalgia.'

A woman's voice with a Polish accent said, 'Is this Mr Wallace?'

'Who wants to know?'

'I am sorry to disturb you, Mr Wallace. I know that with you the time is very early. This is Krystyna Zawadka from Institute of History at Warsaw University. Maria Koczerska's friend.'

'Oh – oh, yes. I was planning on calling *you* later today.'

'Mr Wallace, I am calling you from Truskaw, in Kampinos Forest.'

She hesitated. Her voice had sounded very strained and shaky, and it wasn't just the distance between them – the line was as clear as if she had been calling him from across the street.

'Are you OK?' Jack asked her.

'No, not OK. My colleague Robert and I, we came out to the forest this morning to visit again the place that you told Maria about – the place by the rocks like the head of a witch. We have not yet received permission to excavate the bones there, but we wanted to take photographs and draw preliminary maps.'

She hesitated again. Jack could hear that she was breathing in quick, suppressed gasps, as if she had been running.

'So what's happened?' he asked her.

'I don't know. Something happened and nothing happened. But we had been there for only fifteen minutes, taking photographs, when we both began to feel as if we were being watched. It made us both very anxious, and we kept looking around to see if we could see anybody spying on us, but we could see nobody.

'We took more photographs, and Robert began to make measurements with his theodolite to draw his map, but all the time we became more and more frightened, although neither of us could understand why.'

'But you still didn't see anybody?'

'No . . . although we could hear branches breaking and a rustling sound behind the trees. Oh God, I began to feel so scared, my heart was beating so hard and I kept turning around and around to make sure that nothing terrible was coming up behind me.'

'Nothing terrible like . . . *what*?'

'I don't know, Mr Wallace. That was what made it all the more frightening. I didn't know what I was frightened of, and yet I was so terrified I thought I might literally drop dead on the spot. Robert must have felt the same, because he kept turning around, too, and making noises like *huh*! *huh*! *huh*!

'What was so strange was that neither of us tried to run away. I felt there was no point in trying to run away. Whatever it was that was frightening me so much would never let me escape. The thought came into my mind that the only way to stop myself feeling so scared would be to kill myself – to take my knife and cut my own throat.'

Jack said nothing, but he couldn't help thinking that a very similar feeling may have overwhelmed Malcolm and the rest of the scouts, and those two wildlife researchers he had found in the pool.

Krystyna was panting more quickly and sounding more and more distressed, but then she took a deep breath and managed to recover herself. 'Robert – it was Robert who saved me, I think. He let out a great shout, and dropped his theodolite on to the rocks, which he would never do, because it costs so much, maybe twelve thousand *zlotys*. Then he ran off into the woods, still shouting.

'For some reason I felt then that I could get away, and so I ran in the opposite direction, back along the path to Truskaw. I am here now, calling you from the BP gas station. I thought of calling the forest rangers, but what could I say to them? That Robert and I became so frightened of nothing at all that we both ran away? But now I do not know what to do next. I should go to look for Robert, I suppose, but I am very scared to go back there.'

Jack said, 'I'm sorry, Krystyna, I'm not too sure what I can do to help you.'

'It was you who heard the message from your late wife, telling you where to find these buried bones. Perhaps you think that I am being stupid, but surely there must be some psychic connection between you and this place in the forest.'

'I don't really believe in psychic connections, Krystyna, to tell you the truth,' said Jack. At the same time, however, he was thinking how clearly he had heard Aggie's voice inside his head, and how he had heard Sparky talking to her in the living room, and how he had actually seen her sitting there, if only for a few moments, before she had melted away.

'But how could you know exactly where this place was?' Krystyna asked him. 'How could you describe it down to the very last meter?'

'Don't ask me,' said Jack. 'I simply told Maria what my late wife told me, during that séance. I don't know how *she* could have known, either.'

'There must be *some* connection, Mr Wallace, even if it isn't psychic. We don't yet know who the bones that are buried here belong to. But if they *are* the bones of Maria's great-uncle

Andrzej and your great-grandfather, the feeling of absolute terror that Andrzej wrote about in his diary is exactly the same as Robert and I experienced.'

Krystyna paused again, and then she said, 'There is one distinct possibility – inherited memory, or what we call past life experience.'

'Inherited memory? You mean remembering something that happened to your great-grandfather, even though you weren't even born yet?'

'Exactly. I myself have made several studies for the Institute of History of people who have seem to have inherited memories from their ancestors, sometimes going back hundreds of years. It is a well-recorded phenomenon. After all, if you can inherit the physical appearance of your forebears, their eyes, their nose, their hair color, who is to say that you cannot inherit what is inside their brain, as well?'

'Krystyna – even if that's possible – I still don't really see how I can help you.'

'Please . . . I beg you to come here, and to visit the place for yourself. Maybe then we can learn why we felt such terror there. If we can understand what causes it, then I am sure that we can find out how we can overcome it. They felt it in the forest during the war . . . we can still feel it now. But what can it be?'

'Krystyna, I run a Polish restaurant here in Chicago – an extremely *busy* Polish restaurant. I can't just up and leave it.'

'Don't you have anyone who could take care of it for you, just for a few days? The university will pay for all of your travel and all of your accommodation and other expenses.'

'I don't know. I feel like I'm getting myself involved in something that has nothing to do with me at all.'

Krystyna said, 'The last thing I would want to do is put any emotional pressure on you, Mr Wallace, but if you thought you heard the voice of your late wife telling you about this location, don't you think that there was some reason for this?'

Jack was silent for a while, although his mind was churning over like a washing machine. 'I'll have to think about it,' he said, at last. 'I would have to bring my son as well. He has Asperger's and he needs special care.'

'I understand. But I can arrange for the university to pay for your son, too.'

'Let me think about it and get back to you, OK? I promise I'll call you later today. Meanwhile – what are you going to do about finding your friend?'

'I'm not sure, Mr Wallace. The only thing I can do is go back to where we left our Land Rover and see if he has managed to return there, too. If he hasn't, I will have to talk to the forest rangers. But Robert is not a fool. He is a qualified surveyor. I am sure he will find his way back somehow. Right now he is probably more worried about me than I am about him.'

'I'll talk to you later, Krystyna,' said Jack. 'And by the way, please call me Jack. Only the tax inspectors call me "Mr Wallace".'

'Jack – yes,' she said, very softly, as if she were being reminded of somebody whose name she had known a long time ago. And then she hung up.

The Face of Fear

When Sparky appeared in the kitchen, Jack was already beating eggs to make them an omelet for breakfast. Sparky looked puffy-eyed, as if he too had slept badly.

He sat down at the table and dry-washed his face with his hands. 'So what time are we leaving?' he asked.

Jack was about to pour the beaten eggs into the skillet, but he hesitated. 'Ex-squeeze me? What do you mean, "what time are we leaving?"'

'It says in your star chart that we're going away this afternoon. We are going away, aren't we?'

'Jesus, that's some star chart you've drawn up there. It doesn't tell you what time I'm going for a crap, does it?'

'I guess it might do. But we *are* going away, aren't we?'

'I know how you know. You overheard me on the phone this morning, didn't you?'

Sparky emphatically shook his head. 'It says in your star chart that we're going away for at least three days. Beyond the eastern horizon, that's what it says. It doesn't say exactly where. It's somewhere out of the line of sight of your present array of planets, beyond the curvature of the Earth.'

'I see.' Jack started gently cooking the eggs, folding them back as they began to set so that he could tilt more runny egg mixture around the skillet. When they were almost ready, he tipped grated mozzarella cheese and slices of smoked ham on top of them.

'OK,' he said. 'I had a call from Maria's friend from Warsaw, Krystyna. She and a friend of hers went to that place in the forest by the witch's-head rocks to take some pictures. The trouble is, they got so scared that they both ran away, in opposite directions.'

'They got scared? What of?'

'Nothing! Nothing that they could see, anyhow. Just scared.

I guess they must have felt the same way that we did, at Owasippe. In fact Krystyna said she was so scared that she thought the only thing she could do was to cut her own throat, the same way Malcolm did.'

'Oh, no. That's terrible. What about her friend?'

'She still doesn't know what happened to him. He ran off shouting and that was the last she saw of him. She promised to call me once she had found him, but I haven't heard anything from her yet. She wants me to fly to Warsaw to check this place out, and see why it frightened them so much – although, seriously, what the hell do I know? I'm a restaurateur, not a ghost-buster.'

He cut the omelet into two and slid each half on to separate plates. Then he poured himself a mug of black Java coffee and sat down.

'You still haven't answered my question,' said Sparky, unblinkingly.

'What – when are we leaving? Sometime later today I guess, if I decide to go. There's a direct flight with Polish Airlines around five and another one around nine. It's a nine-hour haul, so we wouldn't get there till ten tomorrow morning.'

'Are you going to call the school and tell them I'm taking some time off?'

'Hey, whoa, hold your horses! I haven't even made up my mind if we're going yet.'

'You *will*, Dad. You have to. Mercury is rising and Mercury is the planet of travel and communication. It's also the planet of the nervous system, so we'll be finding out more about fear, and other feelings.'

'So that's it? Some *planet* says we have to go?'

Sparky shook his head. 'We were always going to go, whatever. That's our destiny. The stars and the planets don't make us do things. All they do is tell us in advance what we're going to do before we do them.'

Jack cut a forkful of omelet and thoughtfully chewed it. 'I'm not sure I like the idea of destiny. I'd prefer to believe that we can change our lives, if we want to.'

'We can,' said Sparky. 'The only thing is that – even when we change them – we end up doing what we were destined to do anyway.'

'So there's no escape?'

'No, Dad. There's no escape.'

Krystyna called Jack at 12.17 that afternoon to tell him that Robert had still failed to reappear. She had returned to their Land Rover, which they had parked in a clearing about 150 meters away from the witch's-head rocks, but she had found that it was still locked and Robert had the keys.

'I was lucky and two forest rangers came driving past. I told them that Robert had disappeared, and not come back, so they gave me a ride back to their ranger station.'

'You didn't tell them why he ran off?'

'What could I say to them? How could I say that we were so frightened that we thought of killing ourselves? They would have thought that I was mad.'

'So what are they going to do if he doesn't show? Send out a search party?'

'They will look for him tomorrow, if there is still no sign of him. But it is late now, and there is no chance of finding him in the dark. The forest is over four hundred square kilometers, and it is not only trees – it is swamps and sand-dunes and rivers, too. Very primeval.'

Jack said, 'I'll be with you by tomorrow morning. I'm still not exactly sure what I can do to help, but my son seems to think that we don't have any choice. He says it's our destiny.'

'Your son sounds very wise. How old is he?'

'Twelve, going on thirteen. But I'm not sure if I'd call him wise. More like mystical.'

'Maybe this is what is happening here, Mr Wallace. I'm sorry – I mustn't forget to call you Jack. Maybe this *is* mystical, rather than real.'

'I'll call you back when I've booked our flights, OK? We can discuss expenses when I get to Warsaw.'

Jack hung up, and then sat back in his office chair, hoping that he had made the right decision. But Mercury was in the ascendant, and Sparky was insistent, and he knew that he had no alternative. Apart from that, in a strange way, he *wanted* to go.

*   *   *

Two women were waiting for them as they came out of the shiny modern baggage hall at Warsaw Chopin Airport. One woman was thin and quite tall, with short hair the color of gingerbread, and a pale but handsome face, with wide-apart green eyes. She was wearing a light gray suit and cream-colored blouse, with a ginger-colored cameo pinned to her collar. She had a very determined expression on her face, the slightest of frowns, as if she were finding it hard to focus, and under her arm she was carrying a tan leather-look attaché case.

The other woman only came up to her shoulder. She had messy chopped-about blonde hair, and heavy black-rimmed spectacles that only just managed to perch on the end of her short, snubby nose. She was wearing a black-and-scarlet gypsy-style dress and red wedge-shaped sandals. She was holding up a home-made cardboard sign that had MR JACK WALACE scrawled across it in felt-tip.

'OK,' Jack said to Sparky out of the corner of his mouth, as they trundled their suitcases toward them across the marble flooring. 'Which one is Krystyna?'

'Search me.'

'Come on, you're the astrologer. I'm supposed to fall in love with one of these women. Which one is it?'

Sparky hissed, as they came closer, 'I don't *know*, Dad; I don't have your star chart with me right now!'

They walked up to the women and smiled. 'Hi,' said Jack. 'I'm Jack Wallace and this is Alexis, but he usually goes by the name of Sparky.'

The tall woman with the gingerbread hair held out her hand. 'So pleased that you could come, both of you. Welcome to Warsaw! I am Lidia Kuś, one of the junior researchers at the Institute of History, and this is Doctor Krystyna Zawadka.'

Well, I sure got that wrong, thought Jack, as the short bespectacled woman gave him a toothy smile and held out her hand, too. *I thought Krystyna was the tall one. And I'm afraid that Sparky's slipped up here, astrologically speaking. I can't see myself falling in love with* either *of these young ladies, even if they can boast more degrees between them than a meat thermometer.*

'Good to meet you,' said Jack, shaking her hand. 'I just hope we can be of some assistance, although to tell you the God's honest truth I'm still not sure how we can.'

They walked together out of the airport terminal. The morning was glaringly bright, and as they crossed the parking lot a strong warm wind was whipping from the west, which made the pennants on top of the airport building flap like applause.

'Did your friend show up?' Jack asked Krystyna.

'Robert? No. This is one of the first things I want to do now that you are here, is go to the Kampinos Forest and look for him. We will settle you in your hotel, have an early lunch, and then go, if that's all right with you. It's about thirty kilometers, that's all. It will take us less than an hour to get there.'

'Haven't you reported him missing yet?'

'Robert is a grown man,' said Krystyna. 'He has not been missing for long enough for me to call the police.'

She led them across to a silver Toyota hybrid with the dark blue letters *Uniwersytet Warszawski* printed on the doors. She unlocked the car with her remote control, and then she added, 'I have of course told the forest rangers and they are keeping their eyes open for him – but as I said to you on the phone, Jack, the Kampinos Forest is immense. Whole battalions of the Home Army hid there during the war and the Germans could never find them.'

Once everybody had climbed into the car, she sat in the driver's seat and started the engine. 'You are not frightened of woman drivers, Jack?'

'It depends how they drive.'

'I will drive especially carefully for you. My foot is a brush!'

They drove out of the airport and headed along the straight divided highway toward the city center. As she drove, Krystyna said, 'Actually, I am very worried about Robert. Why has he not tried to get in touch with me? Why did he suddenly run away like that? I couldn't see anything chasing him. There are several lynx in the forest, but a lynx will usually only attack you if you corner it or if you appear to be threatening its young. Running away – that is not a great idea. Sometimes the lynx will become excited and come after you. But Robert knew that.'

She reached a red stop light and turned to look at Jack. He had to admit that even though her blonde hair was choppily cut, it was attractive in a boyish way, and she smelled of some soft peachy perfume.

'However, I don't think that Robert was being chased by a lynx,' she added. She spoke with the same serious emphasis as Sparky.

'So what do you think it was?' Jack asked her. 'A Forest Ghost? A *nish-gite*?'

'I don't know. That is why I have asked you here, so that we can find out.'

'But what if it is a *nish-gite*? What do we do then?'

Krystyna crossed herself, but didn't answer him. The lights changed to green and she released the parking brake and set off again.

They stopped outside the shining green tower block of the forty-four-story InterContinental Hotel on Ulica Emilii Plater, in the very center of Warsaw. Krystyna led them across the lobby to the reception desk and said, 'Jack – we have booked a suite for you here, for as long as you need to stay. All your expenses will be met by the university, so you don't have to worry. There is a fitness center right at the very top of the hotel, if you are interested – also swimming pool!'

Sparky looked around the high, gleaming lobby, wide-eyed. He didn't say anything but Jack could see how impressed he was. The best hotel they had ever stayed in before was the Holiday Inn at Pewaukee, Wisconsin, when they had visited his cousins.

Krystyna took their registration cards from the receptionist, and as she did so she took off her heavy-rimmed spectacles. Jack almost laughed. It was like one of those *True Romance* comics where the boss goes up to his secretary and says 'Why, Miss Jones, without your glasses . . . you're beautiful!'

Krystyna without her spectacles was very pretty, with high Polish cheekbones and wide gray eyes. She had a little upturned nose, which had been overwhelmed by those thick black spectacle-frames, and pouting pink lips that looked as if she was permanently on the verge of blowing a kiss.

Jack was particularly taken with the little cinnamon dusting of freckles across her cheeks and the bridge of her nose.

She handed across the registration cards for Jack to sign and date. As she did so, she narrowed her eyes and said, 'Jack? Everything is OK? You do not have too much jet lag?'

'No, no, Krystyna. I'm fine. Let's just sign ourselves in here and then we can find ourselves something to eat. I don't know about you, Sparks, but I'm as hungry as a horse.'

Sparky nodded, still hypnotized by his surroundings.

They went up to their hotel room on the 27th floor. They had a large bedroom with twin beds and a living room with a desk and a couch and two armchairs, all decorated in neutral colors, and coldly air-conditioned. Sparky went straight to the window and looked out. Across the street from their hotel stood an immense gray building with a spire on top, over two hundred meters tall, built in the wedding-cake style of the Soviet era.

'That is the Palace of Culture and Science,' said Krystyna. 'Supposedly it was a gift from Joseph Stalin to the Polish people, but it was the Soviet way of dominating our city center. My father says that he would demolish it – himself, on his own, if necessary, with a pickax, but I always say to him that history is history. We should learn lessons from it, not pretend that it didn't happen.'

'Some building,' said Jack. 'Looks more like the palace of Ming the Merciless.'

'Excuse me?'

'Ming the Merciless in *Flash Gordon*. No? Never mind . . . forget it.'

Still looking out of the window, Sparky mumbled, 'We mustn't get lost.'

'Oh, I don't think you will get lost in the city center,' smiled Krystyna. 'In any case, you can always ask somebody to direct you.'

'*No* . . . in the forest, I mean. We mustn't get lost in the forest.'

'You mustn't worry, Sparky. We will all stay together and we are taking Borys with us who knows the Kampinos Nature Reserve better than anybody.'

Sparky turned around, still looking anxious. 'I need to draw another chart. I tried to draw one on the plane but it didn't make any sense. It kept on saying that nothing was going to happen to us.'

'Well, that must be a good prediction,' said Krystyna. 'If nothing is going to happen to us, we will all stay safe, yes?'

'*No*. You don't understand. Nothing is going to happen to us. That's what it said. Nothing good. Nothing bad. *Nothing*.'

'You mean like The Nothing in *The Never-Ending Story*?' asked Jack. Sparky had watched that movie again and again until Jack could almost repeat the lines by heart. 'The Nothing that tries to swallow up the whole world?'

'*No* – because that was just a story. This is *real* nothing.'

Krystyna glanced at Jack and said, 'Are you quite sure that you couldn't use some rest, Jack? It was a long way from Chicago. You must both be feeling very tired.'

'I'm not tired,' Sparky insisted. 'I just have to work out what's going to happen to us in the forest.'

'OK, Sparks,' Jack told him. 'Why don't you stay up here in the room and rest and have something to eat on room service? I'll go downstairs to the restaurant with Krystyna and Lidia.'

Sparky nodded, and went over to his purple carry-on bag to find his paper and his pencils. Jack picked up the room-service menu and said, 'What do you want to eat, sport? They have cream-cheese *pierogi*, if you fancy them.'

Sparky was busy laying out his drawing materials on the desk. 'Waffles, please,' he said. 'Waffles and maple syrup and bacon.'

'You must find it very hard, Jack, running a restaurant and also being a single father to Sparky,' said Krystyna, as they sat over brunch in the DownTown Café on the second floor.

'Let's put it this way, it isn't easy,' Jack told her. 'He misses his mom so much, even though he doesn't talk about her very often. It doesn't help that he has Asperger's, and finds it so difficult to get along with other people. He'll look at your face, but he can't read your expression, so he's never quite sure if you're joking or serious or what.'

'He seems very dedicated to his astrology.'

'It's his obsession. The strange thing is, though, that his predictions pretty often turn out to be right – or nearly right, anyhow. If Sparky hadn't insisted on it, I never would have gone to that séance and I never would have heard Aggie's voice telling me where those bones were buried.'

Krystyna poured brown sugar into her coffee and stirred it. 'I can't imagine what we're going to find in the forest – well, that's if we find anything at all. I can still feel that terror. It was like falling into deep, cold quicksand. It was worse than that. When you are sinking in quicksand you wave your arms and you kick your legs and you struggle desperately to survive. But in the forest I felt as if it would be better if I simply gave in, and killed myself. At least I would no longer be so terrified.'

'Believe me – I know exactly what you're saying,' Jack told her. 'That sounds so much like the feeling that Sparky and I had at the Owasippe scout camp. But I'm sure we *heard* something, too, and felt it. It was like a wind blowing.'

He paused, and then he said, 'I don't know. I still don't see how *nothing* can make us feel so frightened. Maybe it's something to do with the cougars and the lynxes after all. Maybe when they're threatened they've developed some kind of smell that really scares us. Skunks and muskrats do it, don't they?'

At that moment, a short stocky man in a brown canvas jacket came up to them. Although he couldn't have been more than forty years old, he was bald-headed, with a broad, amiable face that looked as if it had been knocked around a bit during his lifetime. He had a V-shaped scar on his chin and no front teeth at the top.

'Ah, Borys!' Krystyna greeted him. 'Jack, this is Borys who is going to be our guide. Borys is a forester. He helped us so much when we were preparing a history of the fighting in the Kampinos Forest at the beginning of the war, when the Germans invaded. I think he knows every single tree by name.'

'*Znam ten las lepiej niż tyłek mojej żony.*' Borys grinned. 'I know the forest like the backside of my wife.'

'Have you told Borys what happened when you and Robert went into the woods?' Jack asked Krystyna. 'He knows why you went there, and what you were doing?'

Krystyna nodded. 'I've told him everything. He knows all about your great-grandfather, and Maria's great-uncle, and the diary. He knows about your séance, and the message.'

'Has he ever come across anything like this before? Anybody else getting frightened the way that you two did?'

'He has heard of the Forest Ghosts, or the *nish-gite*.'

Jack saw Borys pull a pretend-scary face.

'Ever see one yourself, Borys?' he asked him.

Borys shook his head. In Polish, he said, 'Sometimes you can hear something rustling in the bushes. Sometimes, behind the birch trees, you can see something moving. Something white. But that could be anything – just an elk, maybe, with the sun shining on its fur, running away. Or just the sun itself. Who knows?'

'Ever felt frightened, the same way that Krystyna and Robert did?'

'I don't believe in ghosts. People who believe in ghosts make them come to life.'

'But have you ever felt uneasy, in the woods? Like, there's somebody watching you?'

Borys shrugged and lifted his rough-hewn hands. His skin was so cracked and leathery it looked almost as if he were wearing gloves made of tree bark. 'Of course! Everybody does. It's a well-known feeling. It's self-preservation, I suppose, like birds immediately flying away when you come close, even though you are no threat to them at all, because you have absolutely no chance of catching them.'

'So what do we do, when we get to the forest?'

'We search, systematically. I will bring my dog. We look to see if Robert has left any kind of trail behind him as he ran away, which he must have done. There's no way you can run through the undergrowth without breaking branches and scuffing up the ground and leaving a scent. But also we look for anything unusual that could explain why Robert and Krystyna got the wind up so badly!

'When we get there, I will tell you more. It will be easier to explain once you can see the terrain for yourself.'

'OK, Borys, *dziękuję* – thank you.'

'We should go,' said Krystyna, checking her over-large Tissot Chronograph. 'We want to search as much as possible before it gets dark.'

'I'll go get Sparky,' said Jack. He left the restaurant and walked across to the elevators. As he did so, he glimpsed something flicker across the mirror at the end of the corridor, something white. He quickly turned around to see what it was, but it had vanished, whatever it was. Probably nothing more threatening than one of the kitchen staff wearing a white apron, or a chambermaid bundling up a sheet. He told himself to stop being so jumpy. He was tired, that was all, and distracted.

He let himself into the hotel room. Sparky's room-service tray was resting on the coffee table by the couch, and all his star maps were spread across the desk, but there was no sign of Sparky.

'Sparks!' Jack said, walking across to the bedroom door, which was open. 'We're leaving for the forest now! Are you ready?'

'Dad?' said Sparks. For some reason he sounded alarmed. 'Dad – come listen to this!'

Jack found Sparky standing at the end of his bed, staring at the telephone receiver, which was lying on his pillow.

'What's up, Sparks?'

'*Listen!* I was going to make a call to my friend Kenny at school and tell him I was in Poland, but when I picked up the phone I heard this voice!'

Jack picked up the phone and put it to his ear. 'I don't hear anything. It was probably the hotel switchboard, asking you what you wanted.'

'No, it wasn't! Listen!'

Jack listened hard. At first he heard nothing at all, not even static. But then he heard the faintest of voices say what sounded like '– *save us* –!'

It was so tiny and so strained that it was almost inaudible, like a tiny person in a fairy-story trapped under a bell-jar. All the same, Jack could tell that it was a woman.

He kept on listening, with Sparky staring at him anxiously, and then he heard it again, more distinctly this time: '– *save us, you have to – save us . . .*'

'It's a woman,' said Jack. 'I thought she was speaking Polish at first, but she's not.'

'It's *Mom*,' said Sparky. 'I know it is. It's Mom.'

'Oh, come now, Sparks. It can't be. I know it sounds a little like her, but it can't be.'

'*You* heard her, didn't you, when you went to Bindy's bookstore?'

'I know I did, but that was inside of my head. I only imagined that I did. This is some real live woman. We can both hear her.'

'– *you have to save us, please* . . .'

Jack said, into the receiver, 'Who is this? Excuse me, ma'am – I think you probably have a wrong number here. This is the InterContinental Hotel, room two-seven-twelve.'

'– *buried – we're buried* . . .'

'You're buried? Where are you buried?'

'– *both of us – buried* . . .'

'Yes, I hear you. You're buried. But where?'

'– *where the path divides three ways – underneath the rocks* . . .'

Oh Jesus, thought Jack, *it* is *her. It is Aggie. And she's telling me the same thing that she told me during the séance.*

He sat down abruptly on the side of the bed. 'What is it?' Sparky asked him.

He held up the receiver so that Sparky could hear it, too. The voice came and went, sometimes quite clear and other times so faint that it was barely audible.

'– *you have to save us – please – we can't – not for ever* . . .'

Suddenly, the phone jangled loudly, which made Jack start, and frightened Sparky so much that he actually shouted out loud.

'Yes?' said Jack.

'Jack? Are you OK? This is Krystyna.'

'Oh, sure. Krystyna. Hi.'

'Listen, Jack, I don't mean to chase you but we should seriously think about leaving for Kampinos now. We want to give ourselves as much time as possible to look for Robert.'

'Of course, yes. We'll be right with you.'

He put down the phone and looked at Sparky. 'They want to leave for the forest right now. Are you sure you want to do this? To tell you the God's honest truth I don't even know how we got ourselves involved in this. Maybe we should just forget about it and take the next plane home.'

'But that was *Mom*. You heard her. She wants us to save those people.'

Jack didn't need to remind Sparky that his mother was dead, and that those people who were buried under the rocks had been dead even longer. But neither could he deny that the voice on the phone had been Aggie's, or somebody who had sounded uncannily like her.

'I just want to make sure that you're up for it, Sparks, that's all. I don't know whether this is going to be dangerous, but it could be scary.'

'I've drawn up my *own* star chart, as well as yours,' Sparky told him, although he kept glancing at the phone as if he expected to hear his mother's voice again. 'I don't think the chances us of being killed or seriously injured are very much greater than normal.'

'That's not very reassuring.'

'I know. But if we are going, we ought to go.'

They both looked at the telephone receiver lying on the bedcover. It remained silent. Whatever connection they had made before, in this world or the next, it was broken, at least for now.

Into the Trees

They drove out of Warsaw in two cars. Jack and Sparky were driven by Krystyna, in her Toyota, while Borys and Lidia followed behind in a mud-spattered Suzuki SUV with bull bars fitted on the front. Borys had brought his black-and-tan Rottweiler, which sat in the back seat with his tongue hanging out like a bright-red necktie.

This morning's sun had been covered by high, thin clouds, so the afternoon looked hazy and out of focus.

Krystyna had changed into a light yellow cotton bush jacket and white jeans, and brown hiking shoes. As she drove she kept up an almost non-stop monolog, telling Jack and Sparky everything she knew about the way that the Germans had taken so many thousands of Polish intelligentsia out to the forest and shot them, burying them in mass graves and planting trees on top of the graves in the hope that nobody would ever discover what they had done.

Although more than two thousand bodies had been exhumed after the war, only four hundred of them had ever been identified.

'I expect *God* knows who they are,' said Sparky, solemnly, from the back seat.

Krystyna glanced at him in her rear-view mirror, and gave him a little smile. 'Yes, Sparky,' she said. 'I am sure that He does.'

Beyond the outskirts of Warsaw, the highway north-westward toward the forest was straight and flat, for kilometer after kilometer, with scrubby landscape on either side, and occasional houses with orange-tiled roofs and gas stations advertising *Autoserwis*. Even as they approached the turnoff for Palmiry, which would take them into the forest toward Truskaw, the forest itself appeared very low on the horizon, more like a dark green ocean when the tide was out than a forest.

The narrow road to Palmiry was rough and pot-holed, and

their car jolted and swayed from side to side. Behind them, Borys and Lidia's Suzuki almost disappeared in the dust they were stirring up.

'One day you must pay a special visit here to Palmiry Cemetery,' said Krystyna. 'For now, though, we can stop for just a moment and you can see for yourself what it means. I have brought you this way because I think it is important for you to have a feeling of what they suffered, men like your great-grandfather and Maria's great-uncle.'

She parked by the side of the road and Borys parked close behind her. The five of them climbed out of their vehicles and walked through the trees. It was immensely silent here, although between the trees Jack could see the glitter of scores of cars in the parking lot.

They came to a huge clearing in the forest, surrounded by pines that seemed to be impossibly tall, their tops swaying in a breeze that couldn't be felt down here on the ground. Here stood row after row of white stone crosses, between long concrete paths. At the very far end of the cemetery, among the trees, stood three crosses like the crosses that had been erected at Calvary.

On each grave there was a red-and-yellow glass candle holder. Some of them had fallen over and broken, but an elderly man was slowly walking up and down between the crosses, picking up the pieces.

Some of the visitors were moving up and down the pathways. Some were kneeling in front of the graves and praying. It was so silent, though, that Jack felt as if he were watching a movie with the sound turned off.

Krystyna crossed herself, and closed her eyes for a moment. 'Sometimes I think I can hear them,' she said. 'They are like a crowd of people who fill up a town square during the day, all that hustle and bustle, but now there is no more hustle and bustle, and they have all gone. They have left nothing but empti- ness behind them.'

They drove as far as they could down a track between the trees. Nearer Warsaw, the Kampinos Forest was swampy, almost like the Everglades, but out here, to the west, the pines grew on

high white sand dunes, which gave the strange impression of
a forest growing in a desert.

The track grew narrower and narrower, until the branches
were scraping and squeaking against the sides of their vehicles.
At last, however, they saw Krystyna's pale-blue Land Rover in
a small shady clearing up ahead, and they circled around and
parked.

'Your friend hasn't been back here, then?' said Jack, climbing
out of the car and looking around. The forest was warm and
smelled pungent with pine.

'No. Oh, God. I hope nothing terrible has happened to him.'

'If Robert is here to be found, Krystyna, we will find him,'
Borys asserted. He unfolded a map of the Kampinos Forest and
spread it out across the hood of his Suzuki, pointing with his
stubby index finger to a red X that he had drawn on the map.
'Here – this is the place by the rocks where the bones are buried.
It is just a few meters through the trees, that way. When Krystyna
ran away, she went further south, to this village you see here,
Truskaw. Robert on the other hand ran in almost exactly the
opposite direction, to the north-west. In that direction it is all
forest, kilometer after kilometer – pine forest and sand dunes.
It is impossible to run through this kind of terrain without
leaving a trace.

'What we will do is start where the bones are buried, and
then spread out and walk north-westward, but always within
sight of each other. Look for footprints, of course, but also look
for anything else strange. It doesn't matter how insignificant.'

Lidia said, 'What if we start to feel panicky, Krystyna, like
you did?'

'If that happens you must call out, and immediately we will
all join up together again,' said Krystyna. 'I know that Robert
and I both panicked, but yesterday evening I talked to a friend
at the university who is a doctor. She says that nobody really
knows what causes panic attacks, but you can almost always
control them by regulating your breathing. Some people do this
by breathing into paper bags.'

'Which I'll bet we conveniently forgot to bring with us,' said
Jack.

'We shouldn't need them. If *we* panic, my doctor friend said that all we need to do is join together and breathe steadily and reassure each other that there is nothing in this forest which can cause us harm.'

'Well, let's pray there isn't.'

Borys laid his hand on Sparky's shoulder and said, '*Boisz się, chłopcze?* Are you scared, young man?'

Sparky shook his head. In a flat, toneless voice, he said, 'You can only be scared if you don't know what's going to happen to you.'

'But you do?'

'Yes.'

Jack looked at Sparky then and thought for a split-second how much he looked like his late mother. The sun was shining down through the pines in shafts, so that the forest appeared like the inside of a church.

Borys went to the back of his Suzuki, opened the tailgate and let his Rottweiler jump down. The dog immediately circled round and round him, excitedly wagging his tail. 'This is Diablik,' said Borys. 'He is very stupid – *durny* – but he is a great tracker. He can smell a cat through concrete.'

Sparky edged back until he was standing close to Jack. Sparky had always been frightened of dogs, even little yappy ones. Jack said, 'It's OK, Sparks. He's perfectly harmless,' although he had to admit that he, too, found Diablik a little intimidating. There was something about the way Diablik kept licking his wet black lips and wuffling and baring his teeth, as if he couldn't wait to take a bite out of somebody's face.

Before he closed the tailgate, Borys lifted out a large under-and-over shotgun. 'Extra insurance,' he said, in Polish. 'Just in case there *is* something there!'

'Well, you just be very careful with that, Borys,' Krystyna warned him. 'We don't want any accidents.'

They left their vehicles and walked through the trees until they came to one of the many cycle paths that criss-crossed the nature reserve.

About a hundred meters further along, the path divided into three, one branch heading almost due south, one due west, and one north-westward. Where it divided, the path was overshadowed by a lumpy outcropping of dark gray boulders, hunched up like a woman crouched over a cauldron. As they came nearer, Jack could see the resemblance to a witch even more distinctly. She had a pointed hat, a long sharp nose and a protuberant chin, and eyebrows made of shaggy dry roots.

Just past the witch-like rocks, the north-westward path had been cordoned off with blue-and-white tape with the words *Kampinoski Park Narodowy – Niewchodzic.*

'This is where we found the bones,' said Krystyna, lifting up the tape and ducking underneath it. Borys held it up so that Lidia and Jack and Sparky could follow her.

The excavation was covered by a plastic sheet which was fastened down by tent-pegs. Krystyna pulled out the pegs and folded the sheet aside so that they could see where she and Robert had been digging. They didn't appear to have gone down very deep, only about fifteen centimeters. Protruding from the sandy soil, however, Jack could see what looked like the end of an upper arm bone.

'We dug further down than this, and uncovered a few bones that are definitely human,' said Krystyna. 'However, we covered them over again since we didn't want to get into trouble with the park authorities.

She folded back the plastic sheet and walked across to the rocks. 'Robert dropped his theodolite right *here*, and then he shouted something, I don't know what it was. He climbed up this slope very quickly and then went running off between those two tall pine trees up there, still shouting. I didn't see which way he went after that, because I was running away myself, in the opposite direction. Look, you can still see the impression of my boots in the path.'

Jack listened, and looked around. Although there was so little wind today, the forest sounded as if it were softly speaking to itself – as if the trees were discussing the arrival of these new interlopers. *Who are they, and what do they want? These are not hikers or cyclists or joggers. These are people who want to know more about our secrets.*

Borys approached the sandy slope where Robert had started to run away.

'Here,' he said, 'you can see his footprints clearly. Look how deep they are! He was climbing up here like a mountain goat!'

He slung his shotgun across his back, and then he said, 'Come on, then, let's see if we can follow his trail. Krystyna – you brought Robert's scarf, yes?'

Krystyna took a dark-brown knitted scarf out of her purse and handed it to Borys, who held it in front of Diablik's snout. Diablik breathed in deeply, three or four times, like somebody smoking a joint, and then immediately started to snuffle around the ground. It took him only a few seconds to pick up Robert's scent, and then he barked, loudly, and started to drag Borys up the slope.

'Steady, Diablik! Steady!' said Borys. 'You have four legs! I only have two!'

Once they had reached the top of the slope, the five of them spread out, so that they were just within sight of each other through the trees, with Borys in the center. Diablik was straining at his leash so hard that he was breathing in a strangulated whine, and his paws were scrabbling on the sand. He led them between the two tall pines, and then further into the forest. Now the only sounds were the shuffling of their footsteps, Diablik's panting, and – every now and then – the harsh scraping cry of nutcrackers.

'The scent is still strong!' Borys called out after a while. 'I can see also where Robert was running! Broken branches and footprints! He was still running fast!'

The deeper into the forest they penetrated, the thicker the bushes became. At times Jack had to wade thigh-deep through spiky shrubbery, and as he did so he kept his eye out for Sparky, to make sure that he was managing to keep up. But this afternoon Sparky seemed like a boy on a mission – as if he needed to prove that the predictions he had made with his star charts were really going to come true. Jack had noticed that when he talked to him, he was only half-listening, and his mind appeared to be someplace else. Now Sparky was forging ahead through the forest with a tall walking stick that he had made for himself out of a fallen branch, not looking right or left – not even glancing around from time to time to see where Jack was. Maybe he was thinking of Malcolm, and wondering if he could really find something here in the Kampinos Forest that would solve the mystery of Malcolm's suicide. Maybe he was thinking of his mother, and why her voice had led them out here, to this wilderness.

After more than forty minutes, Jack was becoming tired and thirsty, as well as having been snagged and lacerated by brambles and bitten by midges. He was about to shout to Borys that maybe it was time for them to stop for a while and have a break, when he heard a quick, plunging rustle in the bushes only a few meters to his right, as if a large animal was pushing its way through them.

He stopped, and listened. For nearly thirty seconds he heard nothing at all, except for those wretched nutcrackers screeching at each other. *Arrrrrkkk!* Pause. *Arrrrkkk!* Pause. *Arrrrkkk!* Then, suddenly, there was more rustling in the bushes, and this time the bushes actually shook.

'Borys!' he shouted. 'Borys!'

Borys pulled Diablik to a choking standstill. 'What is it? What is wrong?'

'There's something in the bushes here! It sounds like an animal!'

'OK, I will come take a look.'

'Sparks!' called Jack. 'Wait up a moment! Krystyna! Lidia! Wait up!'

Borys came over and peered into the bushes. He also unreeled more of Diablik's leash so that Diablik could take a sniff around.

'If there is any animal there, Diablik will find it.'

'It sounded pretty big,' said Jack. 'For a moment there, all of those bushes were going totally crazy.'

Now Krystyna came over to join them, with Lidia following closely behind.

'Have you found anything?' she asked.

Jack said, 'I thought I heard some kind of animal in the bushes, but I guess it must have gone by now, whatever it was.'

'No,' said Borys. Just to make sure, he poked into the bushes with his shotgun. 'No, there is nothing here now.'

He wound in Diablik's leash, and then he said, 'Maybe this is a good time anyhow for us to stop and take a rest. Like I say, your friend's trail is still very clear. I am sure that we will find out where he went.'

They sat down on the ground in a small sunlit clearing and

Krystyna passed around bottles of water and Grześki chocolate wafer bars. Sparky still looked preoccupied and so after a while Jack said, 'Penny for 'em, Sparks.'

'What? Oh, nothing.'

'Is there something you've seen in one of your star charts?'

A tiny red spider was crawling across Sparky's bare knee. Sparky held his finger poised over it as if he were about to squash it, but then he pursed his lips and gently blew it away.

'My star charts aren't always one hundred per cent accurate,' he said, solemnly.

'Well, yes, I understand that,' said Jack. 'Astrology is not what you call an exact science, is it?'

'I have to rely on stars and planets, Dad – that's the trouble. The nearest star is Alpha Centauri which is four-point-three-six light years away, and the nearest planet is Venus which is twenty-five-point-five million miles away, so it's not surprising if I sometimes get things wrong.'

'Have you made some prediction that you *want* to be wrong?'

Sparky looked at Jack with an expression that said *you know me too well, don't you*? In spite of the fact that he found it so hard to read other people's expressions, he was never able to hide his own feelings. Not from Jack, anyhow.

'He's dead,' he said. 'That's what my star chart told me.'

'You mean Robert, this guy we're looking for?'

Sparky nodded. 'I don't know how, or where, but I think he must be dead. The signs are all there.'

Jack said, 'OK. But let's keep this to ourselves for the moment, shall we? I don't want to upset Krystyna and then find out that he's *not* dead, after all.'

There was a long pause, and then, 'You like Krystyna, don't you, Dad?'

'Yes, Sparks, I do. But don't jump the gun. I haven't fallen in love with her. Not yet – even if I ever do. When I fell in love with your mom, I felt like I'd been hit by a truck. That hasn't happened yet.'

'I don't *mind*, you know, if you do fall in love with her.'

Affectionately, Jack scruffed up Sparky's hair. 'Come on, we'd better get going. It's a quarter of four already. But you won't say a word, will you, about Robert? Not until we find him. *If* we find him.'

He stood up. As he did so, there was another rustling sound in the bushes about thirty meters off to his left. All of them heard it this time – Krystyna and Lidia and Borys, too. Diablik pricked up his ears and let out a short, sharp bark.

A nutcracker cried out *Arrrrkkkkk!* and *Arrrkkkk!* After that, there was a moment's utter silence, not even the breeze stirring the tops of the trees. Then suddenly there was an explosive noise of branches breaking and leaves shaking, and the bushes shook violently from side to side as something ran through them. It must have been at least as large as a warthog – maybe even bigger.

'Go get it, boy!' said Borys, and reached down to unfasten Diablik's leash. But Sparky yelled out, '*No!*'

'What's the matter, *chłopcze*?' Borys asked him. 'Diablik is a match for anything – even a lynx!'

'*That isn't a lynx!*' Sparky screamed at him.

'OK, OK! It isn't a lynx! So what is it?'

'I don't know, but please – you mustn't let Diablik go!'

Borys turned to Krystyna and shrugged. Krystyna said, 'Keep him on the leash, Borys. Whatever it is, we don't want him running off after it, do we? Let's find Robert first.'

The bushes rustled again, a little further away, and even further to the left. All of them looked at each other apprehensively.

'Lynx, I will bet you money,' said Borys. 'Lynx or an elk. They're both very shy.'

The five of them spread out again, although not as widely as they had to begin with. Up above the trees the sky was still blue, but the sun was gradually beginning to sink, and the shafts of light that shone through the forest were now slanting diagonally. The air was becoming cooler, too, and different birds were starting to sing – warblers and thrushes.

Jack began to sense a strange atmosphere in the forest. Now that night was approaching, he felt that all of the undiscovered bodies buried beneath the forest floor were beginning to stir. Although so many bodies had been exhumed after the war, it was still believed that there were hundreds more whose graves had never been found. He could almost imagine a hand reaching up from out of the sandy soil and grabbing his ankle, in a desperate appeal for its owner to be dug up.

Diablik plowed on, his head down, sniffing and snorting as he followed Robert's trail. The trees began to thin out, and eventually they reached an open clearing, about three hundred meters wide, with white sand dunes and wild grass. Krystyna came across to Jack and checked her enormous wristwatch. 'Sixteen-twenty. We've covered almost six kilometers now. Borys says that Robert's footprints in the sand are quite deep, so he was still running by the time he got here. But Robert wasn't very fit, you know. He never played any sports and he liked his beer. I don't know how long he could have kept it up.'

'I guess it depends what was after him. Or what he *imagined* was after him.'

'Your son is very quiet. Is he all right?'

'Sparky? Yes, he's OK. He's always been kind of introspective.'

'Why do you call him Sparky? Is there a reason?'

'Oh, that started when he was about two years old. We took him out to stay with his cousins in the country, outside of a town called Dekalb. At night, of course, you can look up and the whole sky is filled with stars, not like the city, where it's all light-pollution. He thought they were sparks, like sparks from a barbecue. "Sparks! Sparks!" I don't know if that's what started him off being so interested in astrology.'

They were still talking when they heard more rustling from the bushes up ahead of them, where the pines grew thicker again. This was a loud, frantic rustling, which sounded as if somebody had seized hold of the bushes in both hands and was violently shaking them.

'I don't believe *that* can be an animal,' said Krystyna. 'What kind of animal could do that?'

'I think you're probably right,' Jack told her. 'Borys! You want to bring Diablik? Let's find out what the hell that is!'

'Don't let him off the leash, though!' Krystyna cautioned him. 'We don't want to lose him!'

Jack and Borys started to clamber and slide over the steeply sloping dunes, heading toward the bushes at the fringe of the forest. When Sparky saw where they were going, he shouted out, 'Dad! *No*, Dad! Dad – there's nothing there!'

Jack turned around and waved to him. 'It's OK, Sparks! We'll be fine!'

If there's nothing there, he thought, *then there's nothing for us to worry about. But if there* is *something there, and it's aggressive, then Borys has his shotgun.*

Forest Fever

As they approached the bushes, however, the shaking abruptly stopped, and the forest was silent again. Even the songbirds had stopped twittering. It was growing gloomier, too. Not only was the sun sinking, it had disappeared behind a dark bank of cumulus cloud which was rising up from the south-west with almost unnatural rapidity, like a speeded-up movie.

Jack and Borys turned to each other, wondering if they ought to continue, but Diablik kept on whining and straining at his leash and he was obviously pining to go after whatever it was that had been causing all of that commotion in the undergrowth.

'What do you think?' said Jack.

Borys shrugged. 'Like your son says, it's probably nothing. But . . . OK. . . . let's take a quick look, anyhow, just to make sure.'

They followed Diablik through the tangle of bushes and into the trees. It was still silent here, and shadowy, too, and the forest was growing chilly. Jack stopped for a moment, and looked around, and Borys looked around, too, hefting up his shotgun.

'I don't see anything,' said Jack. 'If there *was* anything here, it's either gone, or it's hiding. I vote we go back and pick up Robert's trail again before it gets too goddamned dark.'

As he turned around to go back, however, he thought he glimpsed a white shape, running between the trees. He turned around again, and peered into the forest, frowning, but it had vanished.

Borys said, 'What? You saw something?'

'I don't know. It could have been an elk. But it was white. It reminded me of something we saw in the forest in Michigan.'

Borys stayed still for a few seconds, his head lifted, listening intently. After a while, he said, 'No. If it had been an elk, or any other animal, I would have been able to hear it.'

'What about a human?'

'Well, humans are much more cunning than animals,' said Borys. 'They know to stop still and stay silent. But ask yourself what is a human doing in a forest like this, running and hiding and shaking bushes?'

He tugged at Diablik's leash, and whistled between his teeth, and snapped, '*Tutaj piesku!* Here, boy! *No chodź, nieposłuszny kundlu!* Come here, you disobedient mutt!'

Jack looked over his shoulder one more time, and as he turned he thought he glimpsed that fleeting white shape a second time, out of the corner of his eye, although it was so quick that he couldn't be sure. But Borys was right. It had to be an animal. What would anybody in their right mind be doing, playing hide-and-go-seek in the depths of a forest, at this time of day?

Borys gave Diablik another deep sniff at Robert's scarf. Diablik snuffled around in ever-widening circles, and then picked up Robert's scent again. Immediately he began tugging Borys across the sand dunes, and the rest of them followed. They kept the trees on their left, although they could see more thick forest up ahead of them – even taller, and even darker. They stayed even closer together now, looking into the trees from time to time, although none of them really knew what they were looking for, or what was making them feel so uneasy.

'Did you *see* something, Dad?' asked Sparky, as they came closer to the tree line ahead of them.

'I'm not sure. But you know what we saw in the woods at Owasippe? That white thing, whatever it was?'

Sparky said, 'I thought so. That's what it said in the stars.'

'What did it say in the stars?'

'You can't get away from it. That's what it said. You can't get away from it. It's everywhere.'

'What is?'

Sparky didn't answer. Diablik had reached the trees now, and Borys had stopped him and made him sit. He sat there panting, with his long red tongue hanging out.

'We have a choice now,' said Borys, in Polish. 'It is dark in the forest and already we will need our flashlights. We can continue for maybe another half-hour, or else we can mark this spot and come back tomorrow. There is a path only about seven hundred meters in that direction, and a half-hour's walk will take us back to the place where we left our vehicles.'

Jack understood most of what Borys was saying, but Krystyna quickly translated for him.

'In that case, I vote we take a rain check,' he said. 'Sparks and me, we're both pretty bushed. And if we don't hear from Robert by tomorrow morning, we'll be able to call the police to help us look for him.'

Krystyna said, 'I agree. I'm very tired, too. I can't think why Robert ran so far, but if anything was chasing him, it doesn't look as if it caught up with him, does it? I can't get a signal on my cell out here. He's probably back in Warsaw wondering where *I* am.'

The five of them headed eastward, along the edge of the forest. The heavy gray clouds had now covered the sky almost completely, and Borys switched on his flashlight so that he could occasionally shine it into the trees.

'You don't really think that Robert is back in Warsaw, do you?' Jack asked her.

Krystyna shook her head. 'No. But I can't imagine what else might have happened to him. I don't *want* to imagine what else might have happened to him.'

They had walked no more than two hundred meters further when Diablik let out a single sharp bark and dashed off into the forest, only stopping when he came to the end of his leash.

Borys yanked at his leash and called him, but Diablik barked again, and then again, and danced around and around until he was all tangled up, and hopping on three legs.

'You know what you are?' Borys shouted at him. 'You are the stupidest dog I have ever known!'

He stalked after Diablik and freed him from his twisted-up leash. 'Now, come on!' he shouted, but instead Diablik scampered off into the trees again, tugging Borys after him. About fifty meters away, he stopped, and picked something up in his teeth. He came trotting back with it, wagging his tail.

Jack heard Borys say, 'What's that you've got there, Diablik? Here – give it to me! Give it to me, you mutt! What is it?'

Diablik seemed to be reluctant to let it go, and snarled when

Borys tried to wrench it out of his jaws, but after a brief
tussle Borys managed to pull it free. Almost immediately,
though, he hurled it down on to the ground. '*Jesus Christ!*' he
shouted. '*Jesus! Holy Mother of God! Jesus!*'

'Borys?' said Krystyna. 'What is it?' She started to walk
toward him, but Jack caught the sleeve of her jacket and said,
'No, Krystyna – wait up. Let me check it out first.'

She turned back to him with an unspoken question on her
face, but he shook his head to warn her that Diablik might have
found something that she didn't want to see.

'All right, yes,' she said, and let Jack go. As Jack
approached him, Borys was still grimacing in revulsion, and
furiously rubbing his hand on his pants. He jerked his head
toward the thing that he had thrown to the ground. 'Jesus
Christ,' he repeated. 'Do you see that?'

At first Jack couldn't make out what it was, but then he
hunkered down close to it and turned it over with a twig. Diablik
was watching him intently all the time, panting harshly, as if
he was eager to have it back once Jack had finished with it.

It was a severed human foot, with a bright blue nylon sock
rolled halfway down it. Whoever had removed it, they had cut
all the way through the cartilage where the leg bones were
connected to the ankle bone, exposing stringy white tendons
like broken elastic bands and raw red flesh. It was no wonder
Diablik was so keen to get his teeth into it.

Krystyna came up behind them. 'What is it?' she said, boldly.

'A *foot*,' said Borys. 'A man's foot, by the look of it.'

Krystyna came closer so that she could see it for herself. She
stared at it for a long time, with her hand pressed over her
mouth in horror. 'Oh God,' she said at last. 'Oh God, I'm sure
that's Robert's. Robert always wore blue socks like that.'

'Now I think it *is* time to call the cops,' said Jack. He took
out his cell and slid it open but there was still no signal. 'We'd
better get back to our vehicles, and find the nearest ranger
station. You know where that is, don't you, Borys?'

'Of course, yes. Close to Palmiry.'

'You think we should take the foot with us or leave it here?'

'No, no, we should take it with us,' said Borys. 'I will leave
a marker so we know where we found it. Diablik would have

happily eaten it if we had given him the chance. We don't want some other animal to walk off with it. There might be other body parts around here somewhere so we don't want to forget where it was.'

Diablik sniffed the air, and then barked again, and tried to pull Borys even further into the forest.

'Where are you going now?' Borys demanded, but Diablik kept on pulling, and barking, and in the end Borys said, 'Maybe he's picked up the scent of something else.'

Borys released the brake on Diablik's leash and Diablik immediately bounded away. He didn't even reach the leash's eight-meter limit before he found something else, and picked it up in his teeth, and started to worry it, shaking it from side to side as if it were still alive.

Borys went up to him and again had to wrestle with him to pull it free. Once he had done so, he dropped it immediately on to the ground and called back, 'The other foot! Shit! It has a blue sock, too – just the same!'

Jack looked back at Sparky, waiting with Lidia by the edge of the forest. 'I think it's time I got Sparky out of here,' he told Krystyna. 'He had bad enough nightmares when he saw a dog being run over.'

'OK, you're right,' said Krystyna. 'But if these are Robert's feet – my God, where is Robert?'

Borys said to Jack, 'Here, Jack, hold this, please,' and handed him his shotgun. Jack was surprised how heavy it was. He sloped it over his shoulder while Borys knelt down, unbuckled his large canvas satchel, and took out a crumpled plastic supermarket bag. His nose wrinkled up in disgust, Borys picked up the severed foot and dropped it in. Then he stood up and walked back to the first foot that Diablik had found and dropped that in, too. He twisted the bag in a knot and stowed it in his satchel.

'All right,' he said. 'Now we can go.'

As soon as they started walking back the way they had come, however, Diablik started barking again, and tried to pull Borys back toward the interior of the forest.

'Heel!' Borys shouted at him. 'If there is anything more to find, you stupid dog, let the police find it!'

He dragged Diablik back to the edge of the forest where

Sparky and Lidia were waiting, even though Diablik continued to bark repeatedly and tug at his leash.

'Come on, Sparks,' said Jack, putting his arm around his shoulder. 'I think we've had enough for one day, don't you?'

But Sparky looked back toward the forest and said, 'Diablik wants us to go that way.'

'I know. But Diablik's already found something pretty nasty and I don't think it's up to us to see what else might be lying around.'

'What did he find?'

Jack looked over at Krystyna but Krystyna simply shrugged. Sparky was bound to find out sooner or later, so why not tell him now? After all, Jack had never lied to him or hidden anything from him, especially since Aggie had gone. After 'Your mother has just died', what could he possibly say to him that was worse?

'Feet,' he said. 'Somebody's feet. With their socks still on. But no somebody to go with them. Just their feet.'

Sparky nodded. 'I thought it might be something like that. The stars showed somebody who couldn't run any more. Mercury turned retrograde in Leo.'

'I see. What exactly does that mean?'

Sparky drew circles in the air with his finger, first one way and then the other. 'Mercury is the planet of forward movement. You know, like progress. But when Mercury turns retrograde everything gets snarled up. Traffic, airline schedules, everything. There's something else about Mercury, too. Mercury is a psychopompos.'

'A what?'

'A psychopompos. It means a spirit guide. That's a being who helps people to cross from the real world into the afterlife.'

'I'm not too sure I like the sound of that. That sounds a bit too much like dying.'

Sparky looked at Jack without blinking. Jack was beginning to feel seriously bad about having brought him here – to Poland, to this creepy, godforsaken forest – but at the same time he recognized that neither of them had really had a choice.

Unlike other young people, Sparky could never take anything

for granted. He needed to understand the workings of the world, both physically and spiritually, and he was never happy until he did. He would never rest until he knew why Malcolm had killed himself. Coming here to the Kampinos Nature Reserve had at least given him a chance of finding out.

'OK, Sparks . . . so what are you suggesting?' Jack asked him.

'I think we should let Diablik show us what it is that he can smell.'

Again, Jack glanced at Krystyna.

'What if it's a body?' he said. 'Or parts of a body?'

'It probably is,' said Sparky, flatly.

'Don't you think it's going to give you nightmares?'

'Malcolm gives me nightmares already. He keeps coming to see me in the night.'

'Malcolm? You didn't tell me that.'

'He keeps trying to talk to me, but he can't because his throat's cut and all he can do is bubble.'

Borys said, 'We have to make up our minds, Jack. Soon it will be much darker.'

'We need to go and look for him,' Sparky insisted. 'He may be still alive.'

'Is this wise?' asked Lidia. 'Whoever cut off this poor man's feet, he could still be here. He might attack us, too.'

'There's nobody here,' said Sparky. 'There's nothing.'

'And what makes you so sure of that?' Lidia retorted. 'You are just a boy. This is the first time you have ever been to this forest.'

'Look,' said Jack, 'let's give it another twenty minutes. If we haven't found anything by then, we'll call it a day.'

Diablik was so overexcited by now that he was tangling himself up in his leash again, and although Borys kept snapping at him to keep quiet, he wouldn't stop barking.

'All right,' Krystyna agreed. 'Twenty minutes but no more.'

The five of them walked back into the forest, with Diablik leading the way and Borys grunting with effort to restrain him. It was much darker now. Borys switched on his flashlight and gave it to Jack, while Krystyna took out a small halogen flashlight of her own. The forest smelled dry and musty and aromatic, and every now and then they heard the spectral *woo! woo! woo!* of long-eared owls, followed by the cries of their young, which sounded like kitchen cupboard doors with rusty hinges.

'I don't know what I'm doing here,' complained Lidia, as she stumbled over a patch of scrub. But Diablik suddenly stopped pulling at his leash, and made a whining noise in the back of his throat, and Borys said, 'Wait. Wait just a minute. I think I can see somebody up ahead of us. Just there, Jack, can you see?'

Jack pointed the flashlight directly in front of them. Borys was right. A man was standing between the trees about thirty meters away, facing toward them. He was balding, with a sandy-looking moustache, and he was wearing a faded blue denim jacket, a tan checkered shirt and jeans. Jack's flashlight made his eyes glitter, but he didn't call out to them, or wave, or show any sign that he had seen them.

'*Robert!*' cried Krystyna. 'It's Robert!'

She hurried toward him, with the beam of her flashlight criss-crossing between the trees. 'Robert – what are you *doing* here? What's happened?'

Borys and Jack followed her, but Jack noticed that Diablik now seemed to have lost all his wild enthusiasm for the chase. He was growling softly, and dragging his paws in the sand, so that Borys had to pull him along behind him in a series of jerks.

As they came closer, Jack realized that something was badly wrong with Robert. He was standing at an odd tilt, with his knees bent, and the way that both of his arms were hanging down made him look like he was pretending to be a zombie. He was opening and closing his mouth, and Jack was sure that he saw him blink, but he wasn't looking in their direction.

'Sparks,' said Jack, taking hold of Sparky's sleeve. 'I want you to stay right here, OK. Don't go any further.'

'He's not dead, though, is he?'

'No, he isn't. But I still want you to stay here.'

'Dad, I'm not a kid. I'm *twelve.*'

'I know, Sparks. But just let me check out what's happened here, OK?'

'I will stay with him,' said Lidia. 'If Diablik does not want to go near, then neither do I.'

Sparky reluctantly stayed where he was, while Jack caught up with Borys and Krystyna. Diablik was pulling so hard in the opposite direction that Borys had to let his leash all the way out, and even then he kept on scrabbling to get as far away from Robert as he possibly could.

When he came closer, Jack saw that although he was standing upright, Robert had no feet, only the peg-like ends of bloody white leg bones. The hems of his jeans had been rolled up, and were soaked dark crimson. His hands were bloody, too.

'Robert,' said Krystyna gently, touching his unshaven cheek. 'Robert, it's Krysta! Can you hear me? Who did this to you, Robert?'

Robert's eyes rolled around and tried to focus on her. A long string of bloody dribble slid from his mouth on to his jacket.

'Listen to me, Robert! It's Krysta! What happened? Who did this to you?'

'*Ja*,' he croaked. '*Sam to sobie zrobiłem.*'

'You did it to *yourself*?' said Krystyna. 'How? Why did you do it?'

'More to the point,' said Jack, 'how come he's still standing up?'

Borys circled around behind Robert. He took one look, crossed himself, and then beckoned to Jack to join him. Jack came around and shone the flashlight on Robert's back. Between Robert's legs he saw the trunk of a young pine tree, with flaking orange bark. It had broken at an acute angle slantwise, to form a sharp point, and that point was penetrating the crotch of Robert's jeans.

Jack said, 'Jesus. What are we going to do?'

Borys shook his head and said, 'I don't know. I just don't know. How far do you think it goes up inside him? It must go up far enough to keep him standing up, so I don't know if you and I would have the strength to lift him off it. Even if we did, he may bleed to death.'

Krystyna looked at them over Robert's shoulder and said, 'What is it?'

'He's impaled on a tree trunk,' said Jack. 'We're not sure what we ought to do next.'

'Impaled? What do you mean?'

'It's stuck right up between his legs. That's what's keeping him upright.'

'Oh, God,' said Krystyna. Then she leaned forward to Robert again and said 'Robert?' very gently. 'Can you hear me, Robert? We're going to get some help for you.'

Robert grunted, and nodded.

Krystyna said, 'I don't think we dare to move him. Borys – why don't you go for help? You know your way out of the forest better than any of us. We can stay here with Robert. If you leave Diablik with us, and your gun, we should be all right. But if he did this to himself, there shouldn't be any danger.'

Robert grunted again, and said something that sounded like, '*Pan.*'

'*Pan*? *Pan* Who?' asked Krystyna. Pan was Polish for 'mister.' But Robert's head abruptly slumped forward and he didn't answer.

Borys gave Diablik's leash to Krystyna. Both Sparky and Lidia kept their distance, although they had heard Jack say that Robert was impaled and they were both staring at him in helpless horror.

Just as Jack was about to take Borys's shotgun, he heard a rustling sound, off to their left. He shone the flashlight into the trees, and saw a white shape flicker for a split-second, and then vanish.

Borys turned around and frowned in that direction, too, lifting his shotgun and easing off the safety catch. 'I heard something,' he said.

'That white thing again, whatever it is.'

They waited, and listened, and then the rustling was repeated, but much nearer this time, and off to their right.

'Dad,' said Sparky. 'Dad, I'm *scared*, Dad!'

Now the rustling grew louder, and a wind began to whistle through the forest, with an eerie down-the-chimney sound. Sand and dried pine needles started to snake around their feet, and pine cones rattled softly across the forest floor. Jack thought he heard something crackling, close behind him, but when he quickly looked around, there was nothing there. In spite of that, his heart beat painfully hard in his ribcage, and he could almost hear the blood pumping in his ears. He suddenly realized that he was frightened – not just apprehensive, or anxious, but critically frightened for his life.

Krystyna and Lidia must be feeling the same sense of panic, because Krystyna dropped her flashlight and clutched her hands to her head as if she were being deafened, and Lidia ran a few steps in one direction and then ran back again, panting. Even Borys was hopping around and around in confusion, as if he were performing a Native American rain dance, his eyes staring wildly.

Jack glimpsed the white figure running behind the trees again, and this time he felt as if he had been drenched by a bucket of ice-cold water. He snatched Sparky's hand and shouted to the rest of them, '*Run! We have to get out of here! Run!*'

Krystyna stared at him as if she couldn't understand what he was trying to tell her. 'Here – take my hand!' he said. He tried to push his flashlight into the side pocket of his jacket, but he fumbled and it fell to the ground and immediately went out. He was panicking too much to worry about picking it up. He seized Krystyna's hand and the three of them began to run together back the way they had come, tripping and stumbling as they weaved their way through the forest.

Krystyna kept trying to turn her head. 'Lidia! Borys!' she panted. 'Are they behind us?' But Jack was filled with such dread that all he could think about Borys or Lidia was that if they were caught first, it would give him and Sparky and Krystyna more chance of escaping.

They kept running, even though they were gasping for breath and Jack felt as if his knees were going to give way. In the darkness they kept colliding with tree trunks, so that they were scratched and bruised, and it was all they could do to keep hold of each other's hands.

It was only a few minutes before they saw the pale gray sand dunes behind the trees. They realized that they had nearly reached the edge of the forest, but their feeling of panic only grew more intense. With every step she took, Krystyna was letting out little screams of fear, and Sparky was moaning in that weird ululating way he sometimes did when he was having a nightmare.

Jack thought: *It's after us, whatever it is. It's after us, and it's going to overtake us when we cross the sand dunes, and it's going to rip us apart and we're going to die. Our skeletons are going to be scattered and our insides unraveled like firehoses and our eyes will be staring at the sky and seeing nothing.*

He kept running, awkwardly tugging Krystyna along with one hand and Sparky with the other, but he couldn't help thinking: *This is hopeless; we're never going to get away. The best thing we can do is kill ourselves. Then, at least, that terrible white thing won't catch us.*

He could feel the weight of his clasp-knife inside his jacket pocket, knocking against his hip. He could cut Sparky's throat, and then Krystyna's, and then his own. At least they would be spared the agony of being dismembered while they were still alive.

'Krystyna!' he panted. 'Krystyna, wait up!'

'No, Jack!' she gasped. 'It will kill us! We will all die!'

Jack stopped running, and tried to stop Krystyna and Sparky, too. He managed to pull Krystyna to a halt, but Sparky twisted his hand out of his and went on running into the darkness.

'Sparks! Come back! *Sparks*, come back here!'

But all he heard was Sparky's footsteps, and his low, siren-like moaning. After a few seconds, even those were gone, and there was nothing but the whistling of the wind from out of the forest, and the trees swishing, and the snapping of twigs.

'*Sparks*! *Sparky*! *Alexis*!' Jack shouted. '*Come back here, Sparks, right now!*'

'We must keep on running, Jack,' Krystyna pleaded with him, tugging at his hand. 'If we keep on running, we will catch up with Sparky. *Please!*'

'Krystyna, it's no use. You know it's no use. We're never going to get away.' He paused, and then he shouted one more time, 'Sparks! Come back here!'

The wind was rising and the pine trees all around them were beginning to creak like coffins.

'So, what can we do?' said Krystyna. Although she was still breathless, she sounded less hysterical and more resigned.

'I was thinking that we could end it ourselves, right here and now. At least it wouldn't hurt. But now Sparks has run off . . .'

Still holding his hand, but much more tightly now, Krystyna

looked up at him, her blonde hair blowing across her face. 'It's the finish, Jack, isn't it? It's so strange. When I first saw you, at the airport, I had the feeling that you and I would die together.'

The wind was blustering so loudly that Jack could hardly hear her, but from the look in her eyes and the movement of her lips he thought he could understand what she was saying. Their panic was now so overwhelming that they had both become unexpectedly composed. Jack thought of the stories he had read about the Home Army fighters in Warsaw, during the war, who had calmly shot themselves rather than allow the Nazis to take them prisoner. Better death than torture. Better to end it all quickly than suffer the pain of being torn apart alive.

Just as that thought entered his head, they heard a loud shot, not far away, somewhere in the forest. Then, almost immediately afterward, another shot. This was followed by a long pause, and then a third shot.

'That must have been Borys!' said Krystyna. 'Maybe he has managed to shoot it, whatever it is.'

'Borys!' she called out. 'Borys, was that you?' But the wind was too strong for anybody to have heard her. 'Borys! Lidia! We're over here!'

Jack said, 'Let's just get out of here.' The shots had somehow broken the spell of his panic, and he was beginning to think more rationally now. 'We need to find where Sparks has gone first.'

'But Borys and Lidia—'

'Come on; Borys knows his way around this forest. Like his wife's backside, that's what he said. They'll be OK.'

They continued to jog side by side through the trees, glancing behind them from time to time, but the wind was dying down, and Jack no longer had that cold tingling feeling in his back that they were being pursued. As they cleared the tree line and came out on to the sand dunes, he was already breathing much more calmly. Up above them the clouds were gradually rolling away, and a bone-white gibbous moon was shining, which gave the forest the appearance of a brightly lit stage set.

'What was it, Jack?' asked Krystyna, brushing back her hair. 'What was it that frightened us so much? It was only a wind, after all. A *wind*, nothing else! I didn't *see* anything, did you?'

'Maybe,' Jack told her. 'I'm not too sure.' What could he tell her – that for a split-second he had glimpsed a white shape running behind the trees, but he had absolutely no idea what it was?

'All I know is I never want to feel as panicky as that again – like, *ever*. Now, I'd better try to find Sparky, before he wanders too far off.'

He walked back toward the tree line, cupped his hands around his mouth and shouted out, 'Sparky! Sparks! Can you hear me?'

He called again and again, walking along the tree line as he did so. But all he heard in response was long-eared owls hooting, as if they were ghosts, mocking him. After a while he said, 'I'll have to go back into the forest and look for him.'

'What about Robert? We can't just leave him there.'

'I know, and I don't intend to. But the poor guy's dying if he isn't dead already, and I can't help him. We have to contact the emergency services somehow.'

'I'll go,' said Krystyna. 'You keep on looking for your son. Maybe you can also find out where Borys and Lidia have gone to. They must have run the wrong way and gotten themselves lost.'

Jack said, 'You know that *I'd* go for help, don't you, if it wasn't for Sparky?'

'Of course,' said Krystyna. She looked past him, into the forest, and said, 'Do you think that it's gone now – whatever it was that was chasing us? I don't want anything to happen to *you*.'

'I have no idea. It could be that Sparky was right about it, and there's nothing there at all. Maybe it was just us, getting the heebie-jeebies for no reason. But for just a minute back there, I swear to you, I could have killed all of us, myself included, rather than have it catch up with us.'

Krystyna touched his sleeve, as if she were reassuring herself that they were both still alive. 'For just a minute, Jack, believe me, I would have let you.' She looked away for a moment, and then she looked back at him. 'I would have begged you.'

Unhappy Ending

After Krystyna had left him to call for help, Jack cautiously re-entered the forest. The moon was still shining brightly, but within minutes it would glide down behind the jagged treetops and disappear, and it was already too gloomy for him to penetrate more than two hundred meters without losing his bearings. The last thing he wanted to do was get lost himself.

Before he started calling out for Sparky, he stood perfectly still and listened, just to make sure that he couldn't hear any rustling or any footsteps or any unnatural breeze blowing. Now, however, even the owls were silent, and the only sound was the creaking of the trees and the furtive burrowing of pine voles.

'Sparky!' he shouted out. 'Sparky! Where are you, Sparks? It's Dad here!'

He gave a piercing two-fingered whistle and then shouted out again. 'Sparks! It's Dad here! Where are you, son?'

He whistled twice more, and then listened. Nothing, except for some pine cones dropping.

Next he called out for Borys and Lidia, and whistled for Diablik, too. Again, nothing. He might just as well have been alone.

He was still shouting and whistling when he heard twigs crackling, somewhere to his left. At first it was too shadowy for him to see who it was, but eventually a pale figure appeared out of the darkness, walking directly toward him. He was about to shout out, 'Hold it right there! I have a gun!' but then he realized that it was Sparky.

'Sparks!' he said, and hurried toward him. He wrapped his arms around him and gave him a hug. Unusually, Sparky didn't respond, but kept his arms dangling by his sides and made no attempt to kiss him.

'Hey, buddy, are you OK? For a moment there, we seriously thought we'd lost you!'

'I wasn't lost. Where's Krystyna?'

'She's gone to get help. We still don't know what's happened to Borys and Lidia. I just wish I hadn't dropped my goddamned flashlight.'

'They're dead. I knew they were going to die.'

'They're *dead*? How can you know that?'

'Didn't you hear those shots? They're both dead, and Diablik, too. Borys shot them, and then himself.'

'You didn't see him do it, though?'

'No.' Sparky seemed strangely disinterested, and not at all frightened any longer.

Jack said, 'Come on, Sparks . . . Borys could have just let off a few shots to scare off whatever was chasing after us.'

'No, he didn't. I saw it in the stars. They were very specific. They said that one thing could lead to another.'

'What does that mean?'

'If we found Robert, the *duch* would find us.'

'The ghost?'

'Yes . . . and if that happened, the stars said that two of us would die. That's why I wanted us to keep on running. I didn't want *us* to die – not you and me, or you and Krystyna.'

'Jesus, Sparks, why didn't you tell me this before we went looking for Robert? I mean, you practically encouraged us to go look for him, didn't you? We were just going to take his feet with us and go for help. We weren't going to go into the forest at all.'

'I needed to see if it was true.'

'The ghost?'

'Yes. I have to know why Malcolm killed himself.'

'But if you're right about Borys and Lidia, Sparks – that means that two people have died and you're responsible. Indirectly responsible, anyhow. That's just terrible.'

'I'm not responsible, Dad. It was there, in the stars. Two people were going to die, although the stars didn't say which ones they were. It was always going to happen, no matter what I did.'

'Oh, really?' Sparky was making Jack feel both anxious and angry. He always found it difficult to control his temper when Sparky started talking in this measured, emotionless way. He always sounded so rational, but as far as Jack was concerned there was nothing rational about astrology whatsoever. 'So what did the stars have to say about this so-called *duch*?'

Sparky's eyes darted from side to side, almost as if he were reading his words from an autocue. 'It's like I said before, Dad. It's nothing, but it's everywhere. We should go now.'

'I don't get it, Sparks. Well, I do and I don't. I thought I saw this white thing back there, running around behind the trees. It was just like we saw in the woods at Owasippe. Is *that* the ghost?'

'We should go now.'

'Sparks – I just asked you a question. That white thing I saw – is *that* the ghost?'

'I told you. There's nothing. We should go now.'

Jack didn't want to push Sparky much harder. He was obviously disturbed and distracted and when he became really upset it would sometimes take him weeks to get over it. All the same, he said, 'Sparks – listen to me, we're going no place. We're going to stay here until Krystyna gets back with the forest rangers and the paramedics. There's no way we can leave Robert stuck on that tree stump like that – and, if you're right about Borys and Lidia, we can't leave them, either. Supposing one of them is only wounded?'

'But we don't know where they are,' said Sparky. Jack wished that he would stop speaking in that deadly monotone. 'How can we help them if we don't know where they are?'

'That's not the point. You don't just go off and leave somebody when they might need you.'

Sparky didn't say anything to that, but turned away and walked over to a sloping granite rock that protruded from the sand. He sat down with his back to Jack, his arms folded, making it quite clear that he was only staying here on sufferance. Jack was tempted to tell him to stop sulking, but he knew from experience that would only make things more difficult. Back at home, he might have given him a hard time for acting so moody, but he couldn't really do that here, in the Kampinos Forest, with the moon already touching the trees.

* * *

They waited for nearly two hours before they saw headlights and blue emergency lights flashing through the trees and heard the labored whinnying of all-terrain vehicles.

During all of that time, Jack had continued to shout out '*Borys!*' and '*Lidia!*' over and over, and whistle for Diablik, but Sparky had continued to sit on his rock with his arms folded, saying nothing, although he did get up once to go behind a tree and relieve himself.

Jostling slowly across the sand dunes came two police Pathfinders, a Jeep from the Kampinos National Park and a Mercedes G-Class from the ambulance service, with Krystyna's Toyota trailing at least two hundred meters behind them. They circled around and parked, their blue lights still rippling. Six police officers and two paramedics climbed out, as well as Krystyna. She came hurrying over to Jack, followed by two officers in uniform and one in a black leather jacket and jeans, with his hands in his pockets.

'You found Sparky!' she said, and she went across to Sparky and laid her hand on his shoulder. 'Sparky?' She smiled. 'Are you OK?'

Sparky said nothing and irritably shrugged her away. Krystyna frowned at Jack but Jack simply shook his head to indicate that she should leave him alone for now.

'Any sign of Borys, or Lidia?' she asked.

Jack shook his head again. 'Nothing. And I've been calling them ever since you left.'

The police officer in the black leather jacket came up to Jack and held out his hand. He was several kilos overweight, with a stomach that bulged over his belt, and with his short gray hair and bulbous nose he reminded Jack very strongly of Meat Loaf, the rock singer. Jack could smell alcohol on his breath.

'Komisarz Piotr Pocztarek, sir, from the Masovian Command. Panna Zawadka here has been explaining to me what you were doing in the forest.'

'*Professor* Zawadka,' Krystyna corrected him.

'My apologies,' he said, with barely disguised sarcasm. '*Professor* Zawadka. She says that you were searching for her missing colleague. I am still not clear, though, why you all ran out of the forest – what alarmed you so much?'

'I told you,' said Krystyna. 'We don't really know. We could hear something coming after us, but we couldn't see it, so it could have been anything. A man, or a wild animal. We had just seen my colleague impaled on a tree, with his feet cut off. You can't blame us for being afraid.'

The uniformed police officers and three forest rangers had now all switched on heavy-duty flashlights, and the rangers were explaining to the officers the best way to search the forest, in parallel zig-zags between the trees. 'That way, there is much less chance of you missing anything.'

'What about your friend from the university, and the forester who was with you?' asked Komisarz Pocztarek.

Jack looked over at Sparky, who still had his back turned. 'We don't know. We heard shots, but we think they might have simply gotten themselves lost.'

'OK, *dobra*,' said Komisarz Pocztarek. 'I think the best thing that you can do is take us to Professor Zawadka's colleague, as quick as you can. I've called up a helicopter from Capital Command which should be here in twenty minutes or so.' He turned around and beckoned to the two paramedics. One of them was carrying a lightweight aluminum stretcher and an oxygen cylinder, while the other was carrying a metal box of emergency equipment.

'You don't mind if Professor Zawadka takes my son back to Warsaw, do you?' asked Jack. 'We only flew in from the States this morning and he's pretty much exhausted.'

'I don't see why not,' said Komisarz Pocztarek. 'I will want to talk to Professor Zawadka some more, and maybe to your son, too, but it can probably wait until tomorrow morning.'

As soon as he heard that, Sparky stood up, ready to go.

Jack said, 'I'll see you later, Sparks. Make sure you order yourself some supper on room service, a cheeseburger or a sandwich or something. I shouldn't be too late, with any luck.'

Sparky didn't answer but walked off toward Krystyna's car. Krystyna said, 'Forgive him, Jack. He must be very tired, and traumatized, too. This has been a terrible shock for all of us.'

Once Krystyna had driven Sparky away, Jack followed the police officers and the paramedics into the forest. The trees deadened their voices and their flashlights made the trees look flat and two-dimensional, as if they were cut out of cardboard.

'You understand Polish?' Komisarz Pocztarek asked Jack.

'Pretty much, yes.'

'The good professor wasn't just being hysterical, was she? You, too, felt that something was coming after you?'

'I felt it, for sure. Absolutely. I couldn't get out of the forest fast enough.'

'But? You don't sound convinced that it was real, or if you all just lost your nerve.'

'Wait until you see this poor guy stuck on a tree stump, and then tell me what you think.'

But it was Borys and Lidia and Diablik that they came across first. One of the *policjanci* up ahead of them shouted back, 'Here, *panowie*! There's two of them, dead! And a dog!'

Jack and Komisarz Pocztarek hurried to catch up with them. The police officers and the forest rangers were standing around, brightly illuminating a triangular space between three pine trees. There was so much blood on the ground and up the tree trunks that it looked as if somebody had been drunkenly splashing around a five-liter can of bright red paint.

Lidia was lying face-down with her arms neatly by her sides and her legs together. Jack could have thought that she was planking if the whole of the back of her head hadn't been blown off. Her remaining hair stuck out wildly like the petals of a large scarlet dahlia, with a beige mush of pellet-peppered brains for its center.

Next to her lay Diablik, on his side, with his red tongue hanging out. He had been shot in the stomach, which had almost taken his back legs off. Jack imagined that he had probably been jumping up when Borys had shot him.

Then there was Borys himself, lying on his back with his double-barreled shotgun held in both hands, its muzzle pressed underneath what had once been his chin. He had blasted his face off completely, except for two eyeballs still attached to their optic nerves, one each side of his head, and both staring in opposite directions.

Komisarz Pocztarek crossed himself. 'This was Borys Grabowski, yes?'

'Borys, yes,' said Jack. 'I didn't know his surname.' His stomach was beginning to twist into tight, painful knots, and his mouth was flooding with bile. At the same time, however, he found that he was unable to take his eyes off the grisly carnage that was lying on the forest floor in front of him. He had never realized how deep the sinus cavities were, behind the human face. They looked like a dark array of unexplored caves.

'Did he give you any sense that he was capable of committing an act like this?' asked Komisarz Pocztarek. 'Was he bad-tempered? Belligerent?'

Jack shook his head. 'No, not at all. He was friendly, and helpful. He had a great sense of humor, too.'

'This is not so humorous, though, is it?' said Komisarz Pocztarek. He sniffed and wiped his nose with the back of his hand. 'Sorry. I'm allergic to pine trees.'

Jack took several deep breaths and pressed his hand against his stomach to try and stop it from churning over so loudly. Then he said, 'I'd better show you where Robert is. I doubt if he's still alive. In fact I think he may have died while we were still there. You see that canvas bag? His feet are in there.'

Komisarz Pocztarek went over to Borys's canvas sack. He took a ballpen out of his pocket and used it to lift up the flap, and peer inside.

'Holy shit. Professor Zawadka told us about his feet. I didn't know whether to believe her.'

He came back, took hold of Jack's elbow and steered him away, until the bodies were out of sight behind the trees. 'Are you OK?' he asked him. 'You're not going to puke?'

'I'm thinking about it. At least my lunch is.'

'I know how you feel. I was having dinner with my family at the Restaurant Dziupla in Truskaw when they called me. I was halfway through my hunter's stew. I can definitely feel it sitting there, like your lunch, trying to make up its mind if it wants to stay where it is.'

He sniffed again, and then he turned back and called out to one of the officers to get in touch with the Masovian Command forensic team again, to see when they expected to arrive here.

'Make sure they're bringing a sniffer dog! But for now you can start a spiral search all the way around here, at least five hundred meters. You're looking for anything – footprints, weapons, discarded clothing, bloodstains. Anything.

'Now,' he said to Jack. 'Let's go.'

Flanked on either side by three of the six police officers, two forest rangers and both paramedics, they made their way through the forest as fast as they could. The beams from their flashlights criss-crossed through the trees and their equipment belts jangled. After a few minutes they came to the clearing where Robert was still standing. His head was hanging down, his chin on his chest, but this time a large black carrion crow was sitting between his shoulder blades, pecking at the back of his neck. As soon as it saw them coming, the crow croaked and noisily flapped its wings and flew away.

They approached Robert cautiously, shining their flashlights on the ground all around him to make sure that they didn't tread on anything that might be evidence.

While the police officers and the forest rangers searched the clearing, the two paramedics put down their stretcher and their metal box and gently lifted Robert's head up. His face looked ghastly, like a Halloween mask made out of pale gray rubber. His mouth was hanging open and his eyes were milky.

'Deceased,' said Komisarz Pocztarek. 'Don't think there's very much doubt about that. That's one hell of a way to die. Your feet cut off and then sodomized by a fucking tree. Mother of God. I've seen some sick things in my time, believe me, but this just about beats them all.'

He borrowed a flashlight from one of the uniformed officers and walked slowly around Robert's upright body, examining it closely, especially where the splintered tree trunk had been forced up between his legs.

'He was still alive when we first found him,' said Jack. 'The only thing he said was "I did it myself".'

'Yes, Professor Zawadka told me that. But I find that hard to believe, don't you? If he did do it himself he must have been very drunk, or delirious. I've had a couple of cases where people have deliberately cut their own legs and arms off – their penises, too – but that's a recognized psychotic condition, body integrity identity disorder, and after they've done it they usually call for help.'

He shone the flashlight into Robert's face. 'Let's just say this: they don't usually go to find a tree stump to sit on.'

He was still staring at Robert when one of the uniformed officers came up to him and said, 'I think you ought to see this, sir.'

They followed him to the edge of the clearing, and he hunkered down and pointed to the ground. Almost hidden under a fibrous thatch of twigs and dry pine needles lay the brown leather handle of a large camping knife, smothered in bloody fingerprints. Only the handle, though – the blade had broken off completely.

'Well, that could be the weapon that was used to cut off his feet,' said Komisarz Pocztarek. 'The fingerprints will tell us if he really did it himself. I think it's far more likely that somebody did it for him – that same somebody who chased you away.'

'Robert did say one more thing,' Jack told him. 'He said "*Pan*". I'm sure that's what it was, anyhow. He said it quite clearly.'

'"Sir"? "Mister"? Why would he have said that? That was all? He didn't give you a name?'

'Sorry,' said Jack. 'He didn't say anything else after that. Borys and me, we thought about trying to lift him off that tree stump, but we decided that we probably weren't strong enough, and even if we did it would do him more harm than good. One of my restaurant customers was mugged once, and stabbed in the chest when he wouldn't hand over his wallet. He made the mistake of taking the knife out, and he bled to death in five minutes flat.'

Komisarz Pocztarek looked around the clearing. High above their heads, the carrion crow let out another scraping cry, impatient to continue its interrupted meal.

'You can go and join your son now, sir,' he told Jack. 'It looked to me like he needed his father. I will have one of these officers drive you back to the city and I will contact you tomorrow, if that's OK.'

Jack said, 'Thank you, I appreciate it. I'm just about beat.'

Komisarz Pocztarek beckoned to one of the uniformed officers, and spoke to him quickly and quietly. The officer said to Jack, in English, 'Come with me, please, sir,' and began to lead him back through the forest.

Jack had only walked about fifty meters, though, before his stomach violently contracted. He leaned against a tree and vomited bile and half-digested bacon and sausages, and then retched, and retched again.

The *policjant* patiently waited for him, whistling *Hej Sokoly* between his teeth.

InterContinental Hotel, Ulica Emilii Plater 49, Warsaw

When Jack quietly opened the door to his hotel suite, he saw that the desk lamp in the living room was lit and that the TV was still on, although the sound was muted. He crossed the living room toward the bedroom, but as he did so he saw that there was a blue blanket spread out on the couch, and that a mop of blonde hair was sticking out from under it.

He gently drew down the top of the blanket and saw that Krystyna was lying there, fast asleep.

'Krystyna?' he whispered. 'Krystyna?'

She opened her eyes and blinked at the back of the couch, obviously uncertain where she was. Then she turned her head around and stared at him.

'*Jack*,' she said, in a thick, sleepy voice.

'What are you doing here? Why didn't you go home?'

She pushed the blanket aside and sat up, tugging her fingers through her hair. 'Oh, God. I'm so glad you woke me up. I was having such a scaring dream.'

Jack went to the bedroom door, slid it back, and looked inside. Sparky was sprawled across the bed like a human starfish, his mouth open, breathing deeply.

'Was he OK?' asked Jack. 'He was in such a weird mood when he came out of the forest.'

'That's why I stayed,' said Krystyna. 'All the way back he was nervous and jumping and talking to himself. I kept asking him what was wrong but he didn't seem to understand what I was saying to him. I didn't want to leave him in case he had a fit or something like that, or did himself some injury, like Robert.'

She paused, and then she said, 'Robert was dead, I expect, when you reached him?'

'Yes. I don't think he stood any chance of survival, anyhow.'

'What did that detective say?'

'He was very doubtful that Robert could have done that to himself. I mean, how can you cut your own feet off, for a start?'

'There was that rock-climber who got stuck and cut his own arm off.'

'Well, sure. But Robert wasn't stuck, was he? And cutting his feet off would have made it much harder for him to get away, not easier.'

'I don't know,' said Krystyna. 'I don't understand any of this, and I'm much too tired and upset to think about it any more.'

Jack checked his watch and saw that it was five after eleven. 'We'd better get you home, Professor. Do you live far from here?'

'Old Sadyba. It's only fifteen minutes away by taxi.'

'I'll call reception and tell them to have one waiting for you.'

Krystyna tugged on her boots and laced them up. 'We should meet again tomorrow,' she said. 'I expect that detective will want to talk to us again, in any case. I'll come back here around twelve-thirty. That will give me plenty of time to get some sleep.' She nodded toward the bedroom. 'I just hope that Sparky is better in the morning. I think he was shocked and frightened more than anything else.'

'You're probably right. But thank you for being so thoughtful and staying with him. I really appreciate it.'

He stepped forward and kissed her on the right cheek, then the left, then the right again. For a moment he was holding her, and he felt the urge to kiss her on the lips, too, but he knew that this three-kiss goodbye was nothing more than everyday Polish politeness. In the old days, a Polish gentleman would have lifted her hand and kissed the back of her wrist.

'I'll see myself down to the lobby,' she said, as he took her to the door. 'You stay here and keep an eye on Sparky.'

'*Dobranoc*, Professor. Sleep well . . . and thank you.'

Krystyna walked off toward the elevators, but when she reached the corner she turned her head and looked at him over her shoulder. Jack wasn't at all sure what to read in her expression, but by the way she hesitated he wondered if she didn't really want to go.

He was woken up while it was still dark by a whispering, secretive voice. He opened his eyes and lay there for a moment, listening. He couldn't make out any words, but the whispering sounded very conspiratorial, like somebody planning a malicious practical joke, or a theft, or describing some forbidden activity that they had seen or done. *Whisper-whisper-whisper hee-hee-hee.*

He lifted his head up. The bedroom was still dark, except for the bedside clock, but a soft white light was flickering intermittently from underneath the bathroom door. Jack reached over to the far side of the bed and said, 'Sparks? Are you awake?' But there was no Sparky there, only the twisted sheets, which were damp with perspiration.

'Sparks!' he called out. 'Everything OK in there?'

But the whispering continued, and the soft white lights continued to flicker, and Sparky didn't answer.

Jack climbed out of bed and walked over to the bathroom door, but he hesitated before he opened it. He was torn between fatherly concern and the possibility that Sparky might be doing something that he didn't want Jack to see, like masturbating with the aid of pornographic videos on his iPhone. He thought of the number of times he had heard his father's footsteps coming along the corridor and he had hastily pushed his copy of *Penthouse* under the bed.

He stood there, undecided, for nearly a minute. But the whispering went on, and the light seemed to flash even more brightly – too brightly for an iPhone. It was more like an old-fashioned black-and-white TV, or a fluorescent light strip that was just about to give up the ghost.

'Sparks?' he said, leaning his head against the door. 'Sparks – what are you doing in there? Are you OK?'

There was still no answer, so he tried knocking. 'Sparks – what the hell's going on in there?'

'Don't come in!' Sparky called back. But his voice was very strange, almost like two or even three voices all shouting at once, all in different octaves.

The whispering abruptly stopped, although the lights

continued to flicker. Jack waited a little while longer, and then he said, 'Sparks – can you hear me?'

'Don't come in!' Sparks repeated, in a much higher voice this time, almost a scream.

'Sparks, I need to know what the hell you're doing in there. What's all this whispering? And you got some kind of light flashing – what's that?'

'*Don't come in! Don't come in! Don't come in!*'

Jack pulled down the door handle and tried to open the door, but Sparky had bolted it. Jack knocked again, with his fist this time, and much louder.

'Open this goddamned door, Sparks! I mean it! It's the middle of the night and I want to know what you're up to in there! What's this whispering, for Christ's sake? What's with all these lights?'

'Dad, *please*—'

'Please, nothing! Either you open this goddamned door right now or else I'm going to kick it in! I mean it!'

'No, Dad! *No!*'

But Jack stepped back two paces, and then kicked the bathroom door as hard as he could. The screws that were holding the bolt in place were torn out of the doorframe, and it took only one more kick for the door to judder wide open. Jack stepped into the bathroom and there was Sparky with his back to him, standing naked in front of the washbasin. His face was reflected in the mirror, but his eyes were closed.

'Do you mind telling me just what in the hell you're doing?' Jack demanded. 'It's three-thirty in the goddamned morning and we've both had the worst day that anybody could possibly imagine, but here you are whispering and flashing the lights on and off. What's wrong, Sparks? Are you sick or something?'

'Dad, please leave me alone.' Sparky was so tense that his buttocks were clenched and his shoulder-blades were protruding as sharp as two axes. He still didn't open his eyes. His voice, too, still sounded as if two or three people were speaking at once, or as if it had been recorded and then re-recorded – fractions of a second out of synch.

'Come back to bed, Sparks,' Jack told him.

Sparky stayed where he was. Jack came right up to him and

laid a hand on his shoulder. Sparky flinched, almost as if Jack
had given him a mild electric shock. His skin felt very cold and
clammy, even though he must have been very hot in bed to have
sweated so much.

Jack said, 'Sparks – you have to come back to bed, son. If
you're still feeling like this in the morning, we can call for a
doctor.' He paused, and then he said, 'Where's your mom's
pendant? I thought you wore it all the time.'

Sparky opened his eyes. For a fraction of a second Jack
thought that Sparky had rolled them up inside of his head,
because they were blind and white, without any irises. But then
he blinked, and they looked normal again. He still didn't seem
to be his normal self, though. He could often be introspective
and difficult to talk to, but ever since he had emerged from the
forest he had given Jack the impression that he had discovered
some secret he was determined to keep to himself. In a word,
he not only looked introspective but *sly*.

'My pendant?' he said. 'I must have lost it.'

'You're kidding me. Where?'

'Someplace in the forest, I guess.'

'You sound like you don't even care.'

'Of course I care. But if it's lost, it's lost. I'm never going
to find it again, am I?'

Jack didn't know what to say to that. It had been his impression that his mother's pendant had been one of Sparky's most
precious possessions.

'So what was all that whispering?' he asked, as they went
back into the bedroom. Sparky picked up his blue-and-orange
Chicago Bears pajamas from the floor beside the bed and tugged
them on. Jack couldn't help noticing that his penis was erect.
Maybe his first guess had been right, and Sparky had been
masturbating, but somehow he didn't think so. Something else
had aroused him, although he couldn't imagine what.

They climbed back into bed and Jack switched off the light.

'You do know, don't you, that you can tell me anything, and
everything?' he said. 'I'm your dad, for God's sake. You surely
don't think it's going to go any further.'

Sparky twisted the bedcover around himself and turned over,
with his back to Jack. 'I don't have anything to tell you.'

'Not even what that whispering was about?'

'It wasn't whispering.'

'It sure sounded like it.'

'It was tree talk.'

'*Tree* talk? What the hell is tree talk?'

'You wouldn't understand.'

'Well, you could try me. I'm not that dumb.'

'I'm too tired, Dad. I'm going to go to sleep.'

'Come on, Sparks. You can't just say it was tree talk and then not tell me what it is.'

'I wish I'd never mentioned it.'

'Jesus. *I* wish you hadn't, either.'

Sparky didn't respond to that. Jack waited for over a minute but Sparky said nothing more, and a few minutes later he began to breathe deeply and evenly, with a little catch at the end of each breath, and Jack knew that he had gone back to sleep.

Krystyna joined them for a late breakfast the next morning at the same table in the DownTown Café where they had sat only yesterday with Borys.

Outside it was a warm breezy day and Krystyna had arrived wearing a pale pink cardigan with embroidered flowers on it, and jeans. Her hair had been blown by the wind but Jack thought that only made her look fresher and more attractive.

'Komisarz Pocztarek will be coming here at one,' said Jack. 'I told him that you would be here as well, so he can interview us all together.'

'It was on the TV news this morning,' said Krystyna. 'It's in the papers, too. "Massacre in Kampinos Forest". I tried to call Borys's wife, Kasia, last night, and again about an hour ago, but I there was no answer.'

She looked across the table at Sparky, who was listlessly pushing a slice of smoked sausage around his plate with his fork.

'How are you today, Sparky?' she asked him. 'Feeling any better?'

Sparky shook his head but didn't even raise his eyes to look at her.

'Well, it was very traumatic for you,' said Krystyna, laying her hand on his arm and smiling at him. 'But I'm sure that you'll get over it, given some time.'

Sparky pulled his arm away and said nothing. Jack said to him, 'If you don't want to eat that, why don't you go back upstairs and watch TV?'

Still without saying anything, Sparky pushed back his chair, stood up and said, 'I'm going out for a walk, if that's OK with you.'

'Of course it is. Try to get back here around one, though. That's when Komisarz Pocztarek is coming to talk to us again.'

Krystyna said, 'Why don't you go across to the *Patyk* – the Palace of Culture? I believe they have a James Bond exhibition at the moment, with all the props from the movies, and his car.'

Sparky looked at her as if she had said something completely unintelligible. 'I might,' he said, and then he left them.

'Hard work, bringing up young people,' said Krystyna, when he had gone.

'Tell me about it. His Asperger's makes it even harder. And of course he's old enough now to realize how different he is from the other kids at school. He has regular therapy sessions, and I've tried everything. Even herbal remedies, like St John's Wort. But, you know – it's not a condition you can really cure.'

'It's sad. He's such a good-looking boy. Like his father.'

'I think he looks more like his mother,' said Jack. 'But his mother was always very open, very sociable. Sparky keeps things bottled up. I'm worried about how that experience in the forest might have affected him.'

'Yes. He was behaving very strangely on the way back to the city last night.'

'He got out of bed in the middle of the night and locked himself in the bathroom, and started whispering, and switching the lights on and off. Even when he went back to sleep he was very restless. I asked him what he was whispering and he said it wasn't whispering, it was "tree talk", whatever that means.'

Krystyna put down her coffee-cup. 'Tree talk – is that what he called it?'

'That's right. He wouldn't tell me what he meant. He said I wouldn't understand and he wished he'd never mentioned it.'

'But tree talk, in Greek mythology, that's the conversation that trees have when somebody intrudes into their forest. If you learn the language of the trees, apparently, you can hear them whispering and understand what they are saying to each other. Usually, it's a warning. Haven't you ever been into a forest on a day when there is no wind at all, but suddenly you hear this swishing of leaves? That is supposed to be the trees, telling each other that you are trespassing.'

'You don't seriously think that trees can talk to each other?'

'I don't know. It's possible. They have found out that house-plants react to sound, like music, or human conversation, so that they are aware when somebody comes into the room. They can also make a clicking sound, with their roots, to warn each other that somebody is there.'

'Now that is seriously creepy.'

'Professor Guzik was telling me about it once,' said Krystyna. 'He teaches ancient culture at the university. He said that the Greeks believed the trees would alert each other whenever a human entered the forest, and that they would pass the message on to Pan, who of course was the god of the woods.'

'*Pan*.' Jack frowned. 'That was what Robert said, isn't it?'

Krystyna stared at him, but then she said, 'No. He couldn't have meant Pan. It's ridiculous.'

'It's more than ridiculous. It's insane. But it's what he said, isn't it? And with his very last breath, practically. *Pan*. Maybe he wasn't saying "mister" at all.'

'No. This isn't possible. It's all just mythology. It's no more real than, say, Medusa and the Gorgons. Or Pegasus the flying horse. Or – I don't know – Cerberus the three-headed dog, who guarded the gate to hell.'

'I still think there might be something in this tree talk,' said Jack. 'When Sparky and I went into the woods at the scout camp in Michigan, we both heard this rustling sound. Pretty much the same thing happened here, in the Kampinos Forest. Both times, this strong wind started blowing, and both times we started to panic.'

'Perhaps you should meet Professor Guzik,' said Krystyna. 'He's a great expert on mythology, and what was probably real and what wasn't. I remember him telling me that

Polyphemus – the giant with one eye in the middle of his forehead – he probably existed. He was a shepherd on a Greek island who would catch stranded fishermen and kill them and eat their brains.'

Jack looked down at the pale yellow scrambled eggs on his plate. 'Thanks, Krystyna. You sure know how to kill a man's appetite.'

Komisarz Pocztarek was over thirty minutes late. He came up to Jack's suite on the twenty-seventh floor, accompanied by a young female detective with a large mole on her upper lip and a dark gray suit that was two sizes too tight for her.

Sparky had returned from his walk, although he wouldn't tell Jack or Krystyna where he had been. He sat at the desk in the corner of the living room, staring out of the window and tapping out an irritating rhythm with a pencil.

Komisarz Pocztarek looked as if he hadn't slept. He was wearing the same black leather jacket and the same shirt as yesterday, with his red necktie loosened. He smelled of cigarette smoke and Jack noticed that the fingers of his right hand were tinged amber with nicotine.

He sat down and flipped open his notebook. 'First of all, I have to tell you that it appears as if Robert Wiśniewski did actually cut off his own feet. We found the blade of his camping knife and it was covered in his own blood, and the fingerprints on the handle were his. It also looks certain that he impaled himself on that tree stump. It was probably broken off beforehand, but before he severed his feet it appears that he used his knife to whittle the top of it so that it was even sharper, and would penetrate his body more easily. We found no traces that anybody else was involved.'

'What about Borys and Lidia?' asked Krystyna.

'All the circumstantial evidence suggests that Borys Grabowski shot Lidia and then his dog and then reloaded his shotgun and shot himself. Murder-suicide, or possibly a suicide pact. We have no idea what the motive could have been, apart from what you have already told us about you all panicking. But unless some new evidence turns up, we are not actively looking for anybody else.'

'So, does that mean that my son and I can go back to the States?' Jack asked him.

'Of course, although I will need to know how to get in touch with you, if it is necessary. And today I would appreciate it if each of you could give me again your account of what happened when you went looking for Mr Wiśniewski in the forest.'

'Sure. The sooner we get this over with, the better.'

Komisarz Pocztarek interviewed each of them separately, while the other two waited downstairs in the bar. His questions were detailed and laborious. Where were you standing in relation to the others when you first began to feel panicky? Why do you think you became so frightened? When did you hear the shotgun blasts? How long do you think it was between each blast? How long was it before your son reappeared from the forest? Did he say anything to you? If so, what?

Jack told him about the white figure that he had seen behind the trees. What did he think it was? Komisarz Pocztarek asked. A person, or an animal? Could he describe it in detail? How many times did he see it, and how long did each appearance last? Could it have been a trick of the light – some kind of optical illusion?

'You don't think I really saw anything?' asked Jack.

'Of course I do. But our sniffer dog found no trace that anybody else had been in that part of the forest except for you five. So I am inclined to think that if it wasn't an optical illusion, it was an animal of some kind. And no matter how well-trained it might be, there is no animal that I know of which can cut a man's feet off and stick him on a tree stump, and then kill two people and a dog with a shotgun.'

Jack felt like telling him not to be facetious, but then he thought: *Let's just get this over with. All I want to do now is go back to Chicago and back to my restaurant. I want to get Sparky away from here, too.*

It was Krystyna's turn to be interviewed next. She was only twenty minutes or so, but when she came out she looked tired and strained, and her eyes were swollen, as if she had been crying.

'Sparky, it's your turn,' she said. Sparky stood up and

marched out of the bar without a word, while Krystyna sat down in the chair that he had just vacated and ordered herself a vodka-tonic.

'Are you OK?' Jack asked her.

'Not really. Robert was such a good friend to me, always, and Lidia, too – and Borys. I think when Komisarz Pocztarek started to ask me questions about them it really hit me for the first time that they were all gone, and that I will never see them again, ever.'

Jack reached over and squeezed her hand. 'I'm sorry, Krystyna. This has been some kind of nightmare, hasn't it?'

'Yes! But the trouble is that we still haven't woken up from it, have we? We still don't know why we panicked so much and why they killed themselves like that. It could have been *us,* too! We came so close to doing it ourselves!'

'Maybe we'll never know. I'm just going to make sure that from now on I stay well clear of *any* woods, believe me.'

The waiter brought Krystyna's cocktail and she stirred the ice noisily before she drank it. 'God – I needed that,' she said, relaxing back in her chair. But then she looked across at Jack and said, 'Komisarz Pocztarek told me that you saw something in the forest when we found Robert – something white. He asked me if I had seen it, too, but of course I hadn't. You didn't tell me that.'

'I just didn't want to scare you any more than you were scared already,' Jack told her. 'I only saw it for a second, and I have absolutely no idea what it was. Borys thought that it could have been an elk.'

'What did it look like?'

'I don't know. It was always behind the trees. White, and very quick. It could have been an animal, I guess. It looked more like somebody dressed up in a sheet, pretending to be a ghost.'

'My God. That *is* scaring. But you really can't think what it was?'

Jack shook his head. He could see it, in his mind's eye, but its shape and its flickering movement still made no sense.

After another fifteen minutes, Sparky reappeared, with Komisarz Pocztarek and his partner close behind him.

'How was it?' Jack asked Sparky, but all Sparky did was shrug and say, 'OK, I guess. Can I have another Coke, please?'

'Sure. Just go to the bar and tell them to put it on twenty-seven-twelve.'

When he had gone, Komisarz Pocztarek came and sat down next to Jack. 'I talked to your son,' he said, with cigarette breath. 'You told me about his psychological condition and of course I took this into account.'

'But? I sense a "but" coming.'

'Well, yes. There is nothing to suggest that he was in any way involved with the killings of these three people, but he gives me the strongest feeling that he knows something about it which he did not wish to tell me.'

'Any idea what?'

Komisarz Pocztarek looked at Jack steadily. 'I have been in this business for a very long time, sir, and I know when some-body is trying to hide something from me. I also think that you agree with me – and that you, too, believe that your son is not telling us everything that happened to him in the forest.'

He turned around to make sure that Sparky wasn't yet returning from the bar. 'I am not trying to suggest that he is lying. I am not saying that. But I am ninety-nine percent sure that he is not telling us the whole story.'

'I don't know what he could possibly know that I don't know,' said Jack. 'He was with me the whole time . . . well, except for those ten minutes or so when we got separated.'

'Yes?'

Komisarz Pocztarek could obviously sense that Jack was thinking hard. *Should I tell him how much Sparky's mood had changed, when he reappeared out of the forest? What had caused him suddenly to start being so sulky and stand-offish? Had it been nothing more than shock and exhaustion, or had he seen or done something that he didn't want anybody to know about?*

'I think he found the whole experience very traumatic,' said Jack. 'It seems like he's hiding something but that's only because he doesn't want to think about it. I feel pretty much the same way myself.'

'Well, OK,' said Komisarz Pocztarek. 'But if he should tell

you any more about what happened in the forest, I would like
to be the first to know.'

They both stood up, and shook hands. He had left the bar
by the time Sparky returned with his glass of Coke.

'What did he say to you?' asked Sparky.

'He thinks that you're hiding something.'

'Hiding something? Like, what?'

'How should I know, if you're hiding it? But if you must
know, I agree with him. *I* think you're hiding something, too.'

Sparky slumped down in his chair and sucked at his straw.
Jack waited for him to respond to him, but he didn't. Jack
glanced across at Krystyna but all Krystyna could do was make
a face that meant: *'Kids, what can you do?'*

'You're not flying back to the States tonight, are you?' she
asked him.

'No . . . and in any case, there are no more direct flights out
today. I'm hoping to get a decent night's rest tonight, God
willing. We'll have to make an early start tomorrow, though.
There's a Lot flight around seven-fifty in the morning.'

'Why don't you stay one more day?' Krystyna suggested.
'Can you do that, or is it impossible? I would like so much to
talk to you some more about what happened in the forest. In
fact, I think I need to. It was so disturbing. Also, I could arrange
for us to meet Professor Guzik.'

'I don't know,' said Jack. 'I've left my manager in charge of
my restaurant and this is one of the busiest times of the year.'

'Please,' Krystyna pleaded with him. He looked at her and
he thought that her eyes were exactly the same gray as Lake
Michigan on a rainy afternoon.

'OK, I'll try,' Jack told her. 'I'll have to make a few phone
calls, but I'll try. You don't mind staying one more day, do you,
Sparks?'

Sparky took his straw out of his mouth and said, suspiciously,
'Who's Professor Guzik when he's at home?'

He called Tomasz at six twenty-five that evening. In Chicago
it was eleven twenty-five in the morning, just before Nostalgia
opened for lunch.

'Tomasz, how are things going?'

'Fine, Boss, fine! No problems! When you come back?'

'I was hoping to stay one more day, if that's OK with you.'

'Sure, fine. Stay so long as you like. Everything going good. I have usual argument with Bobak's about sausage delivery, short again on *kiełbasa*, but otherwise everything good.'

'Great. I'll see you Saturday, then.'

'Before you go, you have visitor this morning. I was going to text you.'

'A visitor? Who was it?'

'Very tall skinny woman. Gray hair like twisty bread. She leave her number for you. Wait up, and I will find it.'

'No, don't worry, Tomasz. I think I know who it was. Tamara Thorne.'

'That is correct. Tamara What-you-say. Yes. She say she need to speak with you.'

'Did she say what about?'

'All she say was, she have important message for you.'

'She didn't say who the message was from?'

'No. Just important message.'

'OK, Tomasz. Thanks.'

Jack hung up. Sparky was sitting on the couch in front of the TV, playing *Aliens: Colonial Marines*. The last time Jack had been given a message through Tamara Thorne, it had come from Aggie – or, at least, it was supposed to have come from Aggie – and it had led him and Sparky here, to Poland, and into the Kampinos Forest. He didn't like the sound of this at all. He supposed that he could have asked Tomasz to give him Tamara Thorne's number, and called her, but he would rather delay hearing what her message was until he got back to Chicago. Usually, he only felt comfortable if he was in charge of things, but here in Warsaw he felt that he had lost his oars and was being carried along by the current.

'Early night, tonight, buddy,' he told Sparky.

Sparky didn't answer, but kept on shooting his smartgun at aliens.

'And none of that whispering tonight, if you don't mind. I badly need my sleep.'

Sparky frowned at him irritably, as if he had no right to ask him that, and then went back to his game.

White Vision

Jack slept, and dreamed about Aggie. It was a windy afternoon in early fall, and they were walking through the woods, with red and yellow leaves whirling all around them. At the moment the woods were sunny, but in the distance the sky was almost black and threatened an electric storm. Aggie was wearing a long white dress of billowing chiffon with a bow at the back, and she was walking very fast so that Jack was having difficulty keeping up with her.

Aggie! But she wouldn't turn around, and kept on walking faster and faster. *Aggie! Agnieszka!*

The wind was rising and the leaves were rustling louder and louder. He shouted again and again at Aggie to slow down so that he could catch up with her, but she didn't seem to be able to hear him. *Aggie! Agnieszka!* But she walked so fast that within a very short time she had disappeared, and all he could see was a blizzard of leaves.

He slowed down, and then stopped. He couldn't imagine why she had walked away from like that. He knew that they hadn't argued. Why had she left him?

The leaves continued to rustle, like interfering busybodies, *rustle, rustle, rustle.* But then he realized that it wasn't the rustling of leaves that he could hear, but somebody whispering. Whoever it was, they were speaking too quickly and too softly for Jack to be able to make out what they were saying, although they sounded very urgent, and very secretive.

He opened his eyes. The bedroom was dark, but white light was dancing underneath the bathroom door, and he could see at once that Sparky was no longer lying next to him. He was in the goddamned bathroom again, god damn it, whispering and playing with the lights.

Jack heaved himself wearily out of bed and went up to the bathroom door. He listened for a while, but he still couldn't understand what Sparky was saying. Like last night, his voice sounded very strange, as if two or three or even more of him were all whispering in chorus.

Jack wondered if he ought to knock and confront him again, or if he ought to leave him to whisper until he grew tired of it and came back to bed of his own accord. It had always worried him that Sparky's difficulties in communicating with other people might lead him one day to explode with frustration and hurt somebody – or himself. Because of that, he always took care when Sparky had done something wrong to explain why he was disappointed with him, and not simply yell at him, although he often felt like it.

This time, he didn't knock. He didn't have to. He had replaced the bolt on the bathroom door where he had kicked it open last night, but only by pushing the screws loosely back into their holes, so that the chambermaid wouldn't notice the damage.

He was about to go back to bed when the whispering suddenly began to grow louder, and even more urgent, and it began to sound malicious, too, with guttural noises that came from the back of the throat. Jack thought: *No, I can't put up with any more of this. If I let Sparky go on whispering, who knows how long he's going to go on for. It could be hours, and I might not get any sleep at all.*

He pushed open the door, and as he did so the screws dropped out of the bolt-keeper and it fell to the floor with a clatter. '*Sparks!*' he cried, but instantly the bathroom was flooded with dazzling white light, as if an A-bomb had detonated in total silence, and Jack had to hold his hand up in front of his eyes to stop himself from being blinded.

For a fraction of a second, he thought he saw a white figure standing in front of the basin, like some grotesque angel, although it was so bright that it was impossible to see it clearly. It seemed to have a face, which was turned toward him, with eye sockets that were nothing but shadows, and a dragged-down mouth, but that may have been nothing but an optical illusion. Jack was already seeing one after-image after another, amoebic green shapes that swam in front of his eyes, and which blotted out the figure altogether.

He was seized with such fear that he wet his pajamas. Warm piss, all the way down to his ankles. He lurched back, jarring his left shoulder on the door frame. Then he staggered back into the bedroom, rolled across the bed and headed for the sliding door that led through to the living room. In a series of frantic jerks, he managed to tug the door open, but he was panicking too much to think of sliding it shut behind him. All he could think of was getting away.

He stumbled to the windows. It was still dark outside, but twenty-seven floors below him the city was glittering with lights. Opposite, the Palace of Culture and Science was floodlit in green, like a huge rocket ship designed by a maker of wedding cakes, all ready on the launch pad. It made the night look even more surrealistic, and Jack felt completely dislocated from reality, as if he had woken up in a different world altogether, a science-fiction world of unrelenting terror, from which it was impossible for him to escape.

He tried to find a catch to open one of the windows, but they were all sealed. He would have jumped out, if he could. He thumped the glass with both of his fists, but it was toughened, and it didn't even crack. Panting, he looked back toward the bedroom door and saw that the white light was flickering even more brightly, although it was more spasmodic than it had been before. The white figure was coming after him. God alone knew what it had done to Sparky.

He grasped the arms of the heavy black leather chair behind the desk, and lifted it up. He nearly lost his balance, but he managed to swing the chair around and hurl it at the windows, grunting with effort as he did so. It simply bounced off the glass with a loud bang and tumbled on to the floor.

Desperate, he looked around. He could go for the door that led out to the corridor, and then take the stairs or an elevator down to the lobby, if the white thing wasn't following too close behind. But then he realized with a feeling that was right on the edge of madness that he didn't want to. He had completely lost the instinct to save himself. It was the same utter hopelessness that had engulfed him in the woods at Owasippe, and in the Kampinos Forest. If anything it was even more overwhelming than that. He was terrified that the white thing was going to catch up with him, because he was sure that it would rip him apart while he was still alive, twisting his arms and legs right out of their sockets. At the same time he knew that trying to escape was futile. Even if it didn't catch him tonight, it would catch him one day.

In a terrible flash of insight, he understood now why Robert had cut off his own feet. *He had done it to prevent himself from running away.* Robert had understood that suicide was the only possible way out. If he killed himself, he would never be gripped by that panic again, ever. He would find peace, even if he didn't find absolution.

Jack quickly went across to the coffee table in the middle of the living room, where there was a complimentary plate of fruit – apples and oranges and plums and pears. He picked up the fruit knife. It wasn't very sharp, but it had a serrated edge. If he locked himself in the living-room toilet, he should be able to saw through his wrists, and then his throat, and open up enough arteries to bleed to death before the white figure could get to him.

He had already opened the toilet door and switched on the light when Sparky appeared in the bedroom doorway, naked again.

'*Dad?*' he said. His voice was soft and hoarse, as if he had a head cold.

Jack hesitated, and then took a step back. 'What is it? Where's that thing gone?'

'There's nothing here, Dad. Only me.'

'For Christ's sake, Sparks. I *saw* it. I saw it with my own eyes.'

Even as he said those words, though, he realized that his panic was already subsiding. There was a very long moment when neither of them said anything, but just stood and stared at each other. Gradually Jack began to get his breath back, and his heart stopped pounding. He looked down at the fruit knife he was holding and the idea of rasping his way through his wrists with it suddenly seemed ludicrous.

He switched off the toilet light and closed the door. Sparky was standing there, hugging himself and shivering. Even though Jack had tried to turn the temperature up, the air-conditioning was still unpleasantly chilly, and he was suddenly aware how wet and clinging his pajama pants were.

He walked past Sparky without saying a word and cautiously put his head around the bedroom door. There was no white thing in sight, and the only light was coming from the strip-light over the bathroom basin. He crossed over to the closet, hesitated for a moment, and then flung both doors open. No white thing in there, either.

'I told you, Dad,' said Sparky. 'There's nothing there.'

'I saw it, Sparks! I saw it clear as day! It was like . . . I don't know what the hell it was like. It was so goddamned bright I could hardly even look at it.'

'There was only me in the bathroom, Dad.'

'The lights were flashing on and off. And you were whispering, just like you did last night.'

'No, Dad.'

'Don't tell me "no", Sparks. I heard you, and I saw that thing with my own eyes. Why do you think I ran out of the room?'

'Maybe you were hallucinating,' Sparky suggested. 'I read in *Psychology Today* that stress can do that to you sometimes.'

Jack was about to snap back at him, but from experience he knew that it was pointless. Sparky would go on repeating the same thing, over and over. 'Maybe you were hallucinating. I read in *Psychology Today* that stress can do that to you sometimes.' What the hell was a twelve-year-old doing, reading *Psychology Today*?

'So why aren't you wearing your pajamas?' he demanded.

'I was hot.'

'You were *hot*? This goddamn air-conditioning is set to "igloo".'

'In bed I was hot. I took off my pajamas and then I went for a leak.'

Jack went back into the bathroom and took a look around. There was no evidence that anything unusual had happened here, although the mirror over the basin was faintly fogged over, and he was sure he could detect some faintly herbal odor, as if somebody had been burning sprigs of thyme. He sniffed, and closed his eyes for a moment to help him concentrate. If anything, the bathroom smelled like the forest, but it was probably just the hotel soap.

'OK, buddy,' he told Sparky. 'Put your pajamas on and get

back into bed. I'm just going to take a quick shower. We can talk about this in the morning.'

'There was nothing there, Dad,' Sparky repeated.

'All right, buddy, whatever you say. There was nothing there.'

After a short, hot shower Jack put on a T-shirt and a clean pair of shorts. He had just lifted up the covers to get into bed when the doorbell chimed in the living room.

When he went to answer it, he found two broad-shouldered security men in olive-green uniforms standing outside in the corridor. One looked exactly like Lech Wałęsa, with a gray moustache like a yard broom.

'Sorry to trouble you, sir, but we have had complaint.'

'Complaint? What kind of complaint?'

'In the room below, they say that you are throwing furniture. Crashing, banging. All kinds of noise.'

Jack shook his head. 'Throwing furniture? Are you kidding? Not unless we've been doing it in our sleep.'

One of the security men craned his neck sideways so that he could look past Jack into the living room. 'So – nothing?'

'That's right. Nothing.'

For the rest of the night, Jack found it impossible to close his eyes. If Sparky hadn't been sleeping so soundly, he would have gone down to reception and asked them to change their rooms. But when he thought about it rationally, it was hard to believe that the white figure from the forest had followed them here, to the twenty-seventh floor of a brand-new hotel in the center of Warsaw. If the white figure was nothing more than a figment of his own imagination, it would make no difference, would it, whatever rooms they slept in?

He was convinced that he had heard that chorus of whispering, and he was sure that he had seen that blinding white figure in the bathroom, if only for a split-second. But it was more than likely that Sparky was right, and that he had either been dreaming or hallucinating. He had heard of people having recurrent nightmares after they had been through deeply traumatic experiences, and what he had seen in the Kampinos Forest had been enough to push the sanest person over the edge.

By creating that frightening white figure, his brain might simply have been trying to give his panic some shape that he could understand, in the same way that children believed there were bogeymen underneath their beds, or witches hiding in closets.

Next morning it was gloomy and it was raining hard. When Jack opened the drapes, he saw that Warsaw was veiled in gray. He stood there for a while, watching the traffic and the pedestrians hurrying along Emilii Plater with multicolored umbrellas. Sparky was still asleep, his head buried under the bedcovers.

While Jack was dressing, the phone warbled. He picked it up and it was Krystyna.

'Jack? How are you this morning?'

'I've been better. What time am I going to see you today?'

'Around twelve would be good. I have called Professor Guzik and he is going to meet us at the Batida Café near the University.'

'What have you told him?'

'Not much, except that you are interested in tree talk, and that you think you may have actually heard some trees communicate.'

'Great. He probably thinks that I'm a head case already.'

Sparky was still asleep at eleven-thirty, when it was time for Jack to think of leaving. Jack gently shook his shoulder and asked him if he wanted to come with him.

'No. I don't feel good. I'll just stay here and play some games.'

'Make sure you order yourself something to eat, OK?'

'I'm not hungry. I don't feel good.'

'Well, make sure you stay here. I shouldn't be too long. Call me if you need to.'

Sparky buried himself under the covers and said, 'I'm OK. I don't feel good, that's all.'

Jack left him, hanging a *Do Not Disturb* tag on the outside door-handle. He wasn't at all sure that he was doing the right thing. Maybe it would have been wiser to take the first flight back to Chicago, and try to forget about white things that haunted the woods. But he knew that Sparky would never let it go, and he also had a feeling that if he didn't discover what they were, and why they had panicked him to the point of killing himself, they would follow him doggedly for the rest of his days.

He pushed his way in through the doors of the Batida Café and immediately saw Krystyna sitting at a table on the left-hand side. She was talking to a mousy-haired young man in a crumpled green linen suit. There was a strong sweet smell of coffee and cakes in the café, and the wide glass display counter was crowded with doughnuts and pastries, white and pink and chocolate and covered in sprinkles.

Jack walked up to the table and said, 'Krystyna. Hi.'

The mousy-haired young man had been eating a caramel-frosted doughnut. He immediately jumped up, wiping the frosting off his fingers with a paper napkin.

'Aleksander Guzik,' he announced, and held out his hand. 'Krystyna has already told me much about you. I gather that you are the great-grandson of Grzegorz Walach, the great violinist. Amazing! It is an honor to meet you, sir.'

Professor Guzik had a round, well-fed face and huge round spectacles with amber plastic frames. He wore a wispy moustache, the same mousy color as his hair, which he had obviously grown to make himself appear more mature, although it actually made him look more like a third-year student than a full professor.

'Coffee, Jack?' asked Krystyna. 'Maybe a cake, or a sandwich? Did you eat breakfast yet?' She had pinned up her hair with barrettes today, which gave her a more sophisticated air, and she was wearing a smart gray jacket with a pink crystal butterfly pinned to her lapel.

'Coffee will do me, thanks,' Jack told her. 'Double espresso, no cream.' He pulled up a chair next to Professor Guzik and said, 'I guess Krystyna has already told you what happened in the forest.'

'It was all over the TV news, so I could hardly avoid knowing about it,' said Professor Guzik. He spoke very precise English, although it was a little sing-song, as if he were reciting poetry. 'I was so shocked when I saw that Krystyna was involved. What a terrible tragedy! I knew Robert very well. He and I went once on a vacation together, to Greece, to visit the locations of some famous mythological events.'

He paused, and then he said, 'Your son is not joining us?'

'No . . . he's trying to catch up on his sleep.'

'But it was your son who mentioned tree talk, yes?'

'That's right, he did. To tell you the truth I didn't really understand what the hell he was saying.'

'Oh . . . there is considerable scientific and anecdotal evidence that trees and plants have the ability to communicate with each other, in many different ways.'

'Well, we heard the trees rustling their leaves,' said Jack. 'Sometimes it got pretty frantic, even when there was scarcely any wind. But is that actually *talking*? I mean, if a woodsman walks into the forest with a chainsaw, do the trees warn each other that they're going to get felled, or have their branches cut off?'

Professor Guzik smiled. 'Oh, yes. And some of the ways in which plants spread the alarm to each other is even more effective than just talking.'

'Krystyna mentioned something about plants giving off chemicals.'

'That's right. Recently at Washington State University there was a fascinating study in what we call biocommunication. Edward Farmer and Clarence Ryan showed that when certain plants such as sagebrush and cabbages are attacked by herbivorous insects, they give off a chemical called methyl jasmonate. This chemical immediately sends out a message to all surrounding plants to start producing defensive substances. If the insects then eat these plants, they become very sick, and so they are discouraged from eating that same type of plant ever again.

'The same chemical will trigger lodgepole pine trees into traumatic production of resin. This acts as a vaccine against destructive insects, and protects the trees from further harm.'

'OK,' Jack acknowledged. 'So plants and trees can communicate by sending off chemicals. But that's still not actually *talking*, is it? I mean, humans can't hear it, can they? Not like those trees in the forest.'

'Well, here we begin to enter the realm of mythology,' said

Professor Guzik. He picked up his coffee spoon and started to stir his latte, around and around, as if he were trying to hypnotize Jack into believing what he had to say. 'Mythology, however, often has a basis in fact, as I have proved many times in the past. I have even published a book on the subject: *The Gods Were Real*. I don't suppose you've ever read it? It was published in English, as well as Polish.'

'I own a very busy restaurant,' said Jack. 'I'm afraid I never get the time to read too much. When I do, it's mostly cook books, or the sports pages.'

'Of course. But if you give me your address I will send you a copy and maybe you will find a few moments to look at it. It contains some information about tree talk. Tree talk is almost always associated with the forest god Pan.'

Jack had a vivid mental flash of Robert, impaled on that tree stump, croaking out the word '*Pan*', and he glanced over at Krystyna. She had her eyes on him already, as if she were watching his reactions to everything that Aleksander Guzik was telling him – or maybe she was just watching him.

Professor Guzik said, 'It was the ancient Greeks who first put a name to that causeless feeling of fear which we sometimes experience when we find ourselves isolated in a forest. The Greeks believed that the trees would rustle their leaves in order to alert Pan that people had entered the forest. Pan himself would then shake the trees and the bushes in order to frighten those people away – especially those who were intent on clearing the forest by felling trees or starting forest fires.

'This feeling of fear the Greeks called "panic" – after Pan. By instilling panic, Pan does everything he can to protect the forests and the creatures that live in them.'

'But we didn't only have that feeling *here*, in Poland, in the Kampinos Forest,' said Jack. 'We had it in the Owasippe Forest in Michigan, too. How does that figure? Those two forests are at least four thousand miles apart, easy.'

'Aha!' said Professor Guzik. 'According to the Greeks, there was not simply *one* Pan, but a swarm of Pans, each of them guarding a different forest. Nonnus wrote that Dionysus had twelve sons of Pan who helped him in his war against the Indians, all of them with different names, such as Phobos and

Xanthos and Argos and Omester. But there were even more manifestations of Pan, such as Aegipan, who was all goat, rather than half-man and half-goat; and Sybaris, who was an Italian Pan. He was conceived when a shepherd boy copulated with a she-goat.'

Jack said, 'I saw something in the Owasippe Forest, and I saw it here, too. Did Krystyna tell you? It was difficult to see exactly what it was, behind the trees, but it didn't look much like a goat. To be absolutely honest, it was more like somebody running around wearing a white sheet.'

Professor Guzik finally finished stirring his latte. He took out the spoon and sucked it. 'Yes, Krystyna did tell me this. It is very, very interesting. Of course the Greeks described Pan as having a physical appearance, as they did with all of their gods, and since he was the god of the fields and the woods, and in particular the god of shepherds and goatherds, they imagined that he would look like half a man and half a goat.

'Because of this, we find it easy to dismiss the idea of Pan as nothing but a myth. But as I say in my book, many of the gods really exist, even though they look nothing like the pictures that the Greeks or the Romans used to paint of them. Pan makes his appearance again and again in history, and in many different locations and cultures.

'There was incredible panic when the Romans fought the German tribes in the Teutoburger Forest in the year nine AD, with many of the Romans committing suicide by falling on their own swords. There was panic again in several battles in the American Civil War, such as Chickamauga and the Battle of the Wilderness, which were both fought in forests. There was panic in the Kampinos Forest when the Germans invaded in 1939. There was panic in the Hürtgen Forest near Aachen at the end of World War Two. Again and again, there are instances of panic in forests – suicidal panic – and not just because of the fighting that was going on there. The armies were damaging the forests, and the gods or the spirits or whatever you like to call them were trying to protect them.

'The same kind of panic was reported in the 1960s in the rainforests of the Mato Grosso in Brazil when agricultural companies tried to clear the land to grow soybeans. Workers were panicking so much that they were throwing themselves under their bulldozers. In the end the state government had to create the Xingu National Park – ostensibly to protect the forest and the wildlife and the ethnic tribes who lived there. But in reality it was to stop any more suicides.'

'And you think this was all down to Pan? Or *Pans*, plural?'

Professor Guzik looked serious. 'Almost every living creature on this Earth has a mechanism to protect itself. Spines, or venom, or stings, or simply camouflage. Our forests are the same. They have a spirit, an essence, whatever you like to call it. It is not a man with horns and the legs of a goat, playing a set of pipes. But it is real, and you have seen it for yourself. After the battle of the Teutoburger Forest, the Romans called it *Saltus Spiritum*, the Forest Ghost. The European Jews called it the *nish-gite*. You can look it up – not just in my book, but in many books.'

Jack's espresso arrived. He didn't know if he ought to tell Professor Guzik about his experience last night, or not. Sitting in this busy café, with the clinking of coffee cups and people talking and laughing all around them, and the rain running down the windows, his vision of a blinding white figure in the bathroom seemed even more illusory.

'Jack?' Krystyna asked him. 'You were going to say something?'

'Yes. No. It doesn't matter.'

'So I have told you all that you wanted to know?' asked Professor Guzik.

'I guess so. Except how do we get rid of it?'

'I don't understand. What do you mean, "get rid of it"?'

'My great-grandfather and his closest friend both killed themselves because this Forest Ghost made them panic so much. My son's best buddy cut his own throat, and he was only thirteen years old. These are the reasons why he and I came here, to find out who was responsible, or what.'

'But, Jack – if you don't mind me calling you Jack – the Forest Ghost is Nature. You can't punish Nature for protecting itself from human depredation. We are here on this planet as guests, and it is our duty to take care of it. If you are attacked by a shark, you cannot blame the shark, especially when you consider how badly we pollute the oceans. If a lion mauls you, or a cobra bites you, or a wasp stings you, they are only defending themselves.'

'So this Forest Ghost, this *nish-gite*, or whatever it is, we just let it go?'

'I fail to see what else you can do. It's an elemental spirit. You can't catch it and put it in prison, or kill it.'

'You can exorcize spirits, can't you?'

'You would have to ask a priest about that,' said Professor Guzik. 'But even if you could, would it be morally right to do so? In the last ten years, the Amazon basin has been deforested by two-thirds more than the entire area of Poland. What other way of defending themselves do our forests have?'

Jack didn't know how to answer that. He had never been particularly interested in climate change, or recycling, or saving energy, except for making sure that the lights and the ovens in the restaurant were always switched off, to save money. But he couldn't help thinking about Malcolm and all of his brother scouts, cutting their own throats; and of great-grandfather Grzegorz and his friend Andrzej; and Robert, and Borys, and Lidia. All of them valuable human lives; all of them needlessly lost. And for what? The sake of some trees?

Whatever Professor Guzik said, sharks that killed people were then hunted down and killed too. Dogs that attacked children were destroyed. As far as Jack was concerned, humans had an equal right to protect themselves against Nature. Nature had taken his Agnieszka away from him, and if there was any way that Jack could get his revenge on cancer, he would.

He felt the same about Pan, or the Forest Ghost, or whatever it was.

'I sense that you don't agree with me,' said Professor Guzik. Behind those enormous glasses, his eyes looked like the eyes of a goldfish, staring out of its bowl.

'Well, you're very perceptive,' Jack told him. 'But let me tell you this . . .' He held up his thumb and his index finger so that they were less than an inch apart, and then he said, 'I was panicking so much in that forest that I was *that* much away from cutting Krystyna's throat, and then my own. Then I saw Borys and Lidia with their heads blown off. Whether it's Nature or not, anything that does that to you needs to be exterminated. We exterminate rats, don't we?'

Professor Guzik shrugged and puffed out his cheeks. 'I can understand your point of view, after what you have been through. If it had happened to me, I would probably feel the same. But whatever your opinion, I don't see how you can exterminate such a thing. It is a spirit, a ghost, a will-of-the-wisp. Completely insubstantial.'

It had stopped raining by the time they left the café. Jack shook hands with Professor Guzik and thanked him. Professor Guzik said that if Jack ever managed to catch and kill a Forest Ghost, he should be sure to let him know. 'I would be most interested, believe me.'

Jack and Krystyna walked a little way along Krakowskie Przedmieście. The sun came out and made the wet gray side-walks shine so brightly that they were dazzled.

'I'd better get back and check on Sparky,' said Jack.

'Will I see you again before you go?' Krystyna asked him.

'Sure. We could have dinner this evening, if you like. It would have to be at the hotel. I can't leave Sparky on his own for too long.'

'Yes, I would like that.'

Jack took hold of Krystyna's hands and kissed her on each cheek – once, twice, three times – and this time she kissed him back. They looked into each other's eyes for a very long moment, and they both knew what they were looking for.

Bad Moon Rising

When Jack returned to the hotel, he found Sparky sitting at the desk by the window, drawing a star chart. Beside him was a plate with a few French fries and some smears of catsup left on it, as well as an empty sundae glass.

Sparky's hair was sticking up with gel and he was wearing a sweatshirt with a picture of Albert Einstein poking out his tongue.

'How are you feeling, buddy?' Jack asked him. 'You managed to eat some lunch, then?'

'I'm feeling much better, thanks,' said Sparky, without looking up from his star chart. 'Pluto and Uranus are at right angles, which was probably why you thought you saw that white thing last night.'

'Oh, I see. Pluto and Uranus. Guess I should have realized.'

'Not only that – the Sun and Uranus have also formed a square. This happens very, very rarely. It's the first in a series of seven squares of power which are going to keep reappearing for the next three years. Every time that happens, things look strange, not the way they really are.'

'Oh, OK. So what did you have to eat? Cheeseburger?'

Sparky looked up. Jack couldn't put his finger on it, but he appeared different somehow, as if he were Sparky's near-identical twin instead of Sparky himself. His face was even paler than usual, and his eyes seemed almost translucent. He probably needed a good night's sleep, just like Jack did.

'Cheeseburger with chili, and a chocolate ice-cream,' he said. The way he said it, it sounded more like a religious intonation than lunch. Then, 'How did it go with Professor Guzik?'

'Very interesting, if you're prepared to believe in mythological gods and spirits. Professor Guzik believes that trees can communicate and that we were attacked in the forest by the great god Pan.'

He went to the mini-bar, took out a bottle of Tyskie Gronie beer and tore open a small packet of pretzels. He sat down on the couch and said, 'Professor Guzik thinks there are hundreds of Pans. Maybe thousands. Every forest has its own Pan, as far as I can make out.'

He recounted everything that Professor Guzik had said to them: that these multitudes of Pans had appeared all through history in forests all over the world, causing suicidal panic.

'Yes,' said Sparky, when he had finished, almost as if he had known it all already.

'Do you believe him?' asked Jack. 'I mean, I'm totally confused about it. I don't know whether to believe him or not. What if we're feeling vengeful about something that doesn't exist?'

'You saw the Forest Ghost for yourself,' said Sparky. 'That white thing, anyhow, whatever it was. So did I. Why wouldn't you believe him?'

'Because there is no such thing as ghosts, for a start.'

'You thought you saw a ghost last night, in the bathroom.'

'Yes, but I think that was just me, being hysterical. In fact I think I probably dreamed it. It was the same as hearing your mom talking, on the phone.'

'You threw the chair at the window. You didn't dream that.'

'No. No, I didn't. But you said yourself that there was nothing there.'

'There was.'

'You mean there was something?'

'No. I mean there was nothing.'

Jack watched him drawing his star chart for a while. Then he said, 'I'd better confirm tomorrow's flight home. It's at twelve-ten but we need to be at the airport by nine.'

'We *are* going back to Owasippe, aren't we?' asked Sparky, without looking up.

'Why would we?'

'We came here to find out why Malcolm and all of those other scouts committed suicide, and why your great-grandfather committed suicide, didn't we? And now we know that it was the Forest Ghost. The *nish-gite*. It was Pan.'

Jack said, 'Even if we believe that, I don't see how going back to Owasippe is going to do us any good. If this Forest

Ghost exists, and if there's any way of catching it, I'd be the first one to try. We don't want any more kids like Malcolm killing themselves, or anybody else for that matter. But even if it's real, it's a ghost. Professor Guzik believes it's real, but even he said that it doesn't have any substance. It's a *ghost*, Sparks. We can't catch it, by very definition.'

'Actually, we can,' said Sparky. 'I've been finishing this new star chart for us and the planets say that we're definitely going to, which means that we will. It says that you and me are going to go to the west to right a great wrong, so that it never ever happens again.'

'Oh, really? But does it say *how*? I mean, that would be very useful – if we knew how.'

'All it says is that we're bringing back the answer with us, from the east, even though we don't know what it is yet.'

'Come on, Sparks – what answer? Even if we believe that people panic because of a Forest Ghost, that doesn't tell us how to catch it, or stop it, or exorcize it, or whatever you do with ghosts.'

Sparky picked up the star chart and came across to the couch to show it to him. '*There*,' he said, pointing at some of the symbols and quadrants he had drawn. 'That's us returning to the west . . . that's your star sign, Aries, and that's mine, Capricorn. Now there – that's where we go to Owasippe and right the great wrong.'

'If you say so, Sparks. Looks just like lines and squiggles to me.'

'No, Dad – you see here? This is the Moon, rising at the same time as we arrive at Owasippe. But the Moon appears in the square made by the Sun and Uranus, and that turns everything upside-down and back-to-front. That's when we realize what the answer is. It's like the answer is kept in a safe, in the heavens, but the Moon is going to unlock it for us.'

Jack swallowed beer from the neck of the bottle and shook his head. 'You got me there, Sparks. I don't understand a word of this.'

'It's easy to understand. We already have the answer, but we won't know what it is until we go to Owasippe and the Moon rises.'

'So in the great scheme of all things astrological, is this a good forecast or a bad forecast or someplace in between?'

Sparky looked down at his chart and frowned. 'Usually, when the Moon rises in a square, it's bad. Like, *very* bad. Everything goes wrong. But this time, I don't really know. It could be bad or it could be good. The trouble is, I don't know which, or who for . . .'

A Promise

'This has turned out to be such a tragedy,' said Krystyna, as they sat over dinner in the Platter restaurant on the hotel's first floor. 'I feel so guilty about Robert and Borys and Lidia. And what did we achieve? Nothing.'

'What about the skeletons you found?' Jack asked her. 'Grzegorz Walach and his friend Andrzej, if that's who they are? Will you be able to go back and dig them up?'

Krystyna shrugged. 'I have no idea. Not yet. I will certainly have to wait until the police have finished their investigation. But even if I do get permission to continue, I'm not so sure that I will ever have the nerve to go back into that forest. Supposing I start to feel panicky, all over again? Supposing I want to kill myself? Supposing I *do* kill myself?'

She reached across the table and laid her hand on his. She was wearing a small silver ring with a red garnet in it, the birthstone of Capricorns.

'Forgive me, Jack. I know you had that message from your late wife, and that you would very much like to know why.'

'No, I don't blame you. I feel the same way myself. Sparky wants us to take another trip to the forest at Owasippe. He says that if we do that, we'll find out the answer to what this Pan thing really is. But . . . I don't know. I can't say I'm very happy about it.'

'You're not going, are you?'

'I might have to. The trouble with Sparky is that he's obsessive. He won't let anything go until he's had concrete proof that it's right or it's wrong. Sometimes he frets about something that he doesn't understand until it makes him physically ill.'

'Well . . . maybe he will be able to put this Forest Ghost to rest. Let's hope so.'

'I still can't make up my mind if there really *is* such a thing,' Jack told her. 'We've heard the trees rustle and felt the wind blow and I know that I've seen some white thing running around.

I didn't tell Professor Guzik this morning but I even thought I saw something like it in our hotel bathroom last night.'

'You saw it in your *bathroom*?'

'It was like a bright white figure. So bright you couldn't even look at it. I was scared shitless, pardon my language. I almost felt like cutting my wrists right then and there. I picked up this goddamned fruit knife, would you believe, this blunt little fruit knife, and I think I would have done it. But Sparky came out and said there was nothing there, and there wasn't. I went back and searched the room, under the bed, everywhere. Absolutely zilch.'

'That is so weird. Do you think you might have *dreamed* it?'

'I guess I must have done. So – whatever Professor Guzik says – I'm beginning to believe that this Pan character could be all in the mind.'

'Perhaps you are right,' said Krystyna. 'But whatever it is – whether it's a real ghost or whether it's a psychological delusion – it frightens me too much to go back. I regret it, very much, but what happened to your great-grandfather might have to remain a mystery. What happened to *us* might have to remain a mystery, also. To Robert, and to Lidia, and to Borys.'

The waiter brought their main courses – venison medallions with loganberries for Jack and pike with sour pickles for Krystyna. For the rest of the meal, they didn't talk about the Forest Ghost again. Jack told Krystyna how his parents had started up the Nostalgia Restaurant, and Krystyna told Jack about her girlhood on the Baltic coast, in Gdynia.

They said goodbye in the hotel lobby. Krystyna said, 'You will keep in touch, Jack? If you go to Owasippe with Sparky, you promise to tell me what happens?'

'I promise. And you just let me know how you're getting on, anyhow, even if you don't have any news.'

He kissed her, and she kissed him back. They held each other for a moment, and then she gave him a little smile and said, '*Dobranoc*, Jack. Have a safe journey.'

He went outside with her and waited until the doorman hailed a taxi. Then he stood on the sidewalk and watched the taxi disappear into the traffic. Suddenly, he felt alone again.

Whispers in the Air

They had been flying for more than seven hours when he heard the first whisper. They had eaten lunch and then watched a new Johnny Depp movie and now the cabin lights had been lowered and most of the passengers had settled down to sleep or to read or to work on their laptops.

Sparky was resting his head against Jack's shoulder and was fast asleep, breathing through his mouth. Jack had closed his eyes but his mind was jumbled with too many thoughts and images and contradictory feelings for him to sleep. He kept thinking about the forest, and the rustling of leaves, and the blinding white figure he had seen in the hotel bathroom, and then about Krystyna.

He put on his headset and listened to classic pop hits for a while – Bruce Springsteen and Dr Hook and Leon Russell. He had only been listening for a few minutes, however, when his headset abruptly went dead, and then started softly to crackle, like static.

He was about to call the flight attendant and ask for a new headset when an urgent voice whispered, '*Jack – słyszysz mnie?*'

Immediately, he plucked off his headset as if it had given him an electric shock. The gray-haired man sitting in the aisle seat opposite stared at him dubiously, and kept on staring at him.

It was that woman again, that woman who sounded just like Aggie. The same woman he had heard in his head at the Tamara Thorne's séance, and both he and Sparky had heard on the telephone in their hotel bedroom. Or maybe it really was Aggie, trying to talk to him from God alone knew where. Can people really get in touch with you, from beyond? Can people really talk to you, from heaven? Aggie was lying in a casket in Saint Boniface Cemetery, two years dead. How could she speak to him now?

Cautiously, he picked up the headset again and held one

speaker about an inch away from his ear. He could hear more static, and then that whisper again.

'*Jack – słyszysz mnie? Jack – you have to find them – they're buried* . . .'

He didn't know what to do. He didn't want to go on listening but then he didn't want to stop listening, either. However surrealistic it was to hear Aggie speaking to him through an airplane headset, two-thirds of the way across the Atlantic and thirty-five thousand feet in the air, it was still Aggie, and he still loved her, even if she was dead. The sound of her voice tightened up his throat so much that if anybody had asked him right then if anything was wrong, he wouldn't have been able to answer.

'*Jack – can you hear me? They're buried – they're buried where the path divides three ways.*'

I've been there, sweetheart, he thought. *I've seen them. But right now there's nothing I can do. First of all I have to take Sparky to Owasippe, as much as I don't want to. Maybe then I'll know what I'm up against, and how to go back to the witch's-head rocks without panicking.*

'*Jack – can you hear me? Słyszysz mnie, Jack?*'

She kept on whispering to him, but her voice was rapidly becoming fainter, and the static was growing thicker and louder. He heard only one more word before she was swallowed up altogether.

'*– dependant* . . .'

He pressed the headset hard against his ear, but she was gone, and almost immediately the music came back. Queen, singing 'Somebody to Love'. The gray-haired man in the aisle seat opposite was still staring at him. Jack gave him a quick, reassuring smile, even though he thought the man looked like a lizard.

Sparky stirred, and opened his eyes, and looked up at him.

'What's wrong?' he said, and sat up straight.

'Nothing's wrong. Why?'

'You look like you've been crying.'

Jack wiped his eyes with the back of his hand. 'It's this pressurized air. Always makes my eyes water.'

Sparky kept on looking at him as if he didn't believe him, but then Jack checked his watch and said, 'Don't worry. Only

three more hours to go, and we'll be landing. What do you
want to eat tonight?'

'Pizza. Or kebab. Nothing Polish. I've had enough Polish.'

Although they had left Warsaw just after midday and flown for
over ten hours, it was only a few minutes past four in the afternoon when they arrived back at Nostalgia. Tomasz was there
to greet them, and Duane helped them to carry their suitcases
inside.

'So, good trip?' he asked Jack. 'You find out what you want
to find out?'

'Not really.' He wasn't ready yet to tell anybody about their
grisly expedition into the Kampinos Forest. 'To be honest with
you, I wish we'd never gone.'

'Everything here has run just like clockworks. No problems
at all. Except next week we have public health inspection.'

'That's OK. We got that dishwasher fixed, didn't we?'

'Everything is fine. I even got Piotr to clean all grease from
ventilator.'

'Good for you, Tomasz. I'll make sure you get a bonus for
taking care of things while I was away. And I may have to go
away again this weekend, but only for a day – maybe two at
the most.'

'That is fine, Boss. Don't worry. Oh – before I forget . . .'

He went to his maitre d' stand and came back with a page
torn from one of the check pads. Tamara Thorne had scrawled
her address on it: *1961 West Schiller Street, Wicker Park*, as
well as her telephone number and her cell number. Underneath
she had written: *Call me, another message has come through
for you!!!*

'Thanks, Tomasz,' he said, and gave him an approving clap
on the back. Then he went through to the kitchen to see how
Mikhail and Piotr and Duane were prepping for this evening's
service. Piotr and Duane were furiously chopping carrots and
mushrooms and celeriac, while Mikhail was standing over the
stove stirring a large saucepan.

'Ah, Boss, you have come back just at the right moment!'
said Mikhail. 'Taste this soup, tell me what you think.'

He handed Jack a ladle brimming with a brownish,

spicy-smelling soup, with macaroni and beans and slices of frankfurter in it. Jack blew on it two or three times to cool it, and then tasted it. It was highly seasoned – peppery, garlicky and smoky – like Aggie's cooking used to be.

'You like that?' asked Mikhail. 'Uhlan bean soup. My aunt used to make it.'

'It's great. Put it on tonight, as a special. We may even include it as a regular. Jesus – one bowl of that and you wouldn't have to eat anything else for a week!'

Mikhail gave a self-satisfied grin. But then, as Jack turned to leave, he said, 'The stuffed cabbage, with the tomato?'

'Yes, what of it?'

'This week I have very many compliments. So, after all . . . maybe your Slovak recipe is not so bad. I withdraw my objection.'

Jack left the kitchen and went upstairs. Sparky was in his room, unpacking and hanging his jeans back in his closet. Jack stood by the door and watched him for a moment and thought how lonely he looked. Not only had he lost his mother; he was locked inside a mind that could only see the world literally, without any of its subtleties and slyness. He even took the stars and the planets at face value, and believed everything that they predicted.

He went through to the living room, picked up the phone and punched out Tamara Thorne's home number. It rang and rang, and eventually a crackly message said, 'This is Tamara Thorne . . . I am otherwise engaged at the moment, but if you wish me to contact your loved ones for you, or give you any other kind of spiritual service, please leave your name and number.'

Jack tried her cellphone, and this time she answered immediately, almost as if she had been waiting for him to call her.

'It's Jack Wallace. I'm back home now. You left me a message.'

'I did, yes. It's *most* extraordinary! Somebody has been trying to get in touch with you from the other side. They sounded quite desperate.'

'Really? Do you know who it is?'

'She gave me a name but I couldn't hear it clearly.'

'It was a woman? Did she say what she wanted to tell me?'

'No. But she said that she needed to speak to you as a matter of urgency.'

Jack was tired out and he could feel a headache coming on. He was beginning to think that his mind was coming apart at the seams. In the past three days he had seen three people who had killed themselves, horribly. He had seen a dazzling figure who wasn't even there, and heard whispers and voices from people who were either dead or non-existent. Now he had an urgent message from beyond.

'Jack?' said Tamara Thorne. 'Are you still there, Jack?'

'Yes. Yes, I'm still here.'

'Don't you want to hear this message? It could be critical. Spirits hardly ever try to get in touch with the living. It's almost always the other way around.'

'Well, OK, Ms Thorne. When can we meet?'

'Right now, if you like. I'm here with Bindy, at The Bookworm.'

Jack closed his eyes for a moment. All he wanted to do was take a Tylenol, share a pizza with Sparky and then go to bed and sleep for eight hours. But if Tamara Thorne was just around the corner, he supposed that he could manage to go and find out what it was that this spirit had to tell him, whoever she was. If he didn't, he would probably lie awake all night.

'Sparks,' he said. 'I'm just going out for a while. Not long. You want to order up that pizza? Any toppings you feel like, bar pineapple.'

Sparky said, 'When are we going to Owasippe? Are we going tomorrow?'

'I don't know, Sparks. Let's recover from this trip to Poland first. What do the stars say?'

'I haven't done them yet.'

'Well, don't. I think it's about time we started making our own decisions.'

'We never make our own decisions, Dad. Whatever we do, it's down to the planets.'

Jack was beginning to believe him, but he didn't say so. Right now he didn't care what Mercury and Uranus were doing, whether they were rising or falling or square-dancing with the

Sun; he was going to go see Tamara Thorne and then he was coming straight home to bed.

He left the restaurant and walked around the corner to The Bookworm. Bindy was in the storeroom, but as soon as she heard the doorbell ringing she came hurrying out, wearing a shapeless brown dress with a beige Peter Pan collar.

'Jack! That was quick! Tamara's in back, signing books for me. How was your trip?'

'Not too happy, I'm afraid.'

'Oh, dear! I'm so sorry! What happened?'

'I'll tell you some other time, Bindy. Right now I'm bushed. I just came to see Tamara because she said it was urgent.'

'I think it is,' came Tamara's voice from inside the storeroom. 'In fact, I think it's *dreadfully* urgent.'

Jack entered the storeroom. It smelled strongly of new books. Every shelf was crowded, and there were boxes of books stacked up on every side. Tamara Thorne was sitting at a small desk, with three stacks of her latest volume all around her, which she was halfway through signing. As before, her gray hair was braided into a crown, although today she was wearing a loose gray smock and a pair of baggy black linen pants, and silver sandals. Her fingernails and her toenails were all polished silver.

'How are you, Jack?' she said, lifting her hand to him so that her bangles and bracelets all slid down to her elbow. 'Did I hear you say that your trip to Poland wasn't a happy one?'

Bindy dragged over a molded plastic chair so that Jack could sit down. 'Would you like a coffee, or a cup of tea? Or I have some wine left over from the other evening, if you feel like something stronger.'

'No thanks, Bindy. I'm not staying. I just came to pick up this urgent message from beyond the grave.'

Tamara raised one immaculately plucked eyebrow. 'I hope you're not mocking me, Jack.'

'No – honestly, I'm not,' Jack told her. 'I've had a difficult few days, that's all. In fact I think I'm more inclined to believe you now than I was the first time.'

'You've seen things? You've heard things?'

Jack nodded. 'Don't ask me to explain them, because I can't.'

'You don't have to, Jack. I can feel the disturbance all around you. Your aura is in chaos. You've triggered some force of nature – some really extraordinary force. That's why this spirit has been trying to get in touch with you – to warn you, possibly, of what you've set in motion.'

'It's not *dangerous*, is it?' asked Bindy, biting her lip.

'It's beyond dangerous,' said Tamara Thorne. 'I've never felt anything quite like it. I have no idea what it actually is. It feels very *old*, but it also feels very strange. Perhaps your message will tell us more about it.'

'OK, then,' said Jack. 'How do we go about hearing it?'

Tamara Thorne shifted the stacks of books aside. 'Take hold of my hands, Jack, and close your eyes, and try to think of nothing at all. Think of emptiness. Think of a vacuum. Think of floating in space, but a space without stars.'

Jack reached across the desk and took hold of Tamara Thorne's hands. They were surprisingly warm, and for some reason he found her grasp was both relaxing and comforting. It was like holding the hands of somebody of whom he was very fond – a mother or a sister or a friend or even a lover. He was beginning to see why Tamara Thorne was so good at empathizing with people's emotional needs.

He closed his eyes and tried to think of nothing. To begin with, all he could think of was Mikhail's bean soup, because he could still taste it.

'Is your mind empty?' Tamara Thorne asked him.

'Not totally empty, no. I'm thinking of soup.'

'Forget soup. Think of silence. Think of darkness. Think of floating.'

He thought of silence. He thought of darkness. He thought of floating. His mind was almost empty when Bindy coughed and shifted herself on the carton of books she was sitting on, and broke his concentration.

'Keep trying,' said Tamara Thorne. She began to stroke the back of his hands with her thumbs, around and around, and it reminded him of Professor Guzik stirring his latte around and around. Her stroking took him back, it took him out of himself, and at the same time he felt as if she were taking care of him, and that he could safely let go.

He almost felt as if he were dwindling into nothing, the tiniest speck in a limitless universe.

'We saw what it was,' said a young woman's voice, so loudly and clearly that he thought she must have walked into the store-room. Immediately, he opened his eyes. All he could see, though, was Tamara Thorne, sitting behind the desk with her eyes closed, still holding his hands, and Bindy sitting with her legs crossed on her carton of books, frowning at her bitten fingernails.

'We were down by the gully, looking for scat,' the young woman continued. She sounded so close to him that Jack could imagine that he felt her breath against his cheek. He looked around but there was no young woman there.

'Weldon said he felt panicky. He thought that a cougar might be stalking us. We heard a rustling in the scrub and I began to feel panicky, too. We started to jog back the way we had come. Then the rustling grew louder, and it seemed to be coming closer, so we ran faster.'

Every muscle in Jack's body was locked up with tension and he felt an almost irresistible urge to jump up out of his chair. It was only the endless circling of Tamara Thorne's thumbs that kept him sitting there. That, and his need to hear what the young woman was trying to tell him.

'We hid. We hid in a hollow, amongst the bushes. But we both realized there was no escaping it. We didn't even have to speak to each other to know what it would do to us. It kept prowling through the bushes, around and around, and I have never felt such terror in my life.

'Weldon killed me. He cut my throat but I barely felt it. When I was unconscious, he cut off my head. Then he killed himself. It was a terrible thing to do, but at least we no longer felt frightened. We had ended our lives, but we were both at peace.'

The young woman stopped talking. Jack waited, and looked around, but there was silence. Nonetheless, Tamara Thorne kept her eyes closed, and continued to stroke the back of his hands with her thumbs, over and over, as if she were expecting the young woman to say something more.

Jack thought that maybe his own awareness had broken the connection. He closed his own eyes again, and tried to concentrate on nothing at all. Darkness. Emptiness. Floating in space.

Almost half a minute went past, and then the young woman started to speak again, although now she sounded as if she were standing on the opposite side of the storeroom. She spoke much more quietly, too, so that Jack found it difficult to hear what she was saying.

'My spirit left my body. I rose up, like I was floating. I never realized that your spirit actually does that. You hear people talk about it, but it really happens. I rose up, and Weldon rose up, too, and when we rose up the thing appeared. It came through the scrub and it stood and looked at our dead bodies. It was white, and it was so bright that it was like it was burning, except that there weren't any flames, only light. I don't know how to describe what it looked like. It was scary as all hell, and its mouth was turned down like it was howling. That's what I thought of, when I saw it. It was dazzling white, like an angel, but it was howling. A howling angel.'

There was another long pause, and again Jack thought that the young woman might have finished. But then she said, 'We rose up, Weldon and me, the two of us together.' She was speaking even more softly, and with infinite sadness in her voice.

'We rose up like we were nothing more than smoke. We rose higher and higher, and I could see the whole forest stretched out below us. I could even see the sun going down, and I thought "this was my last day on Earth".'

Another pause, but when she spoke again she was clearer, and louder, almost vehement. 'I looked down, and I could see that howling angel still standing there. But then I saw a ranger, coming through the trees with his dog. I heard that dog bark, and that howling angel must have heard it, too.

'Straight off, no hesitation, its light went dim, and it disappeared into the scrub so fast that I began to think that I had never seen it at all. And you know what I thought, Jack? You know what I believe?'

When she said his name, Jack couldn't help opening his eyes. He knew who she was now – the girl he had discovered in the pool at Owasippe, with her head cut off. The girl who worked as a researcher for Michigan Wildlife Conservancy, collecting cougar scat. He couldn't remember her name, but how did she know his? She had been long dead by the time he found her.

'What?' he said, out loud. 'What do you believe?'

'This is my message to you, Jack. I know what you've been doing because the dead always know. But we hardly ever get the chance to speak out. Only when we die unjustly, and a wrong has to be righted.'

'So what's the message?'

Now – hearing Jack speak – Tamara Thorne had opened her eyes, too. She stopped stroking Jack's hands, but she held them even tighter, as if she were silently trying to give him strength and moral support.

'It was frightened, Jack. It was *frightened*. It was even more frightened than we were.'

'*What?*'

'The howling angel. The thing that *you* call the Forest Ghost, the *nish-gite*. It was frightened.'

'I don't understand,' said Jack. 'What kind of a message is that?'

He waited, and waited, but the young woman didn't answer. After a while, Tamara Thorne let go of Jack's hands and said, 'She's gone.'

'Can't you get her back? I need to ask her what the hell she was talking about.'

Tamara Thorne closed her eyes again for a few moments and then she said, 'I think she's told you everything she's ever going to. She really has gone. People think that mediums like me can call on spirits to talk to us, but we have absolutely no power to do that at all. Not many psychics will admit it, but it's true. The only time that we can talk to the dead is when they want to talk to us.'

Bindy said, 'I wanted to talk to my grandma once, to ask her where she'd left the key to her clock, but I couldn't.'

Jack sat there rubbing his neck. He felt stiff and exhausted, and now he felt baffled, too. He didn't doubt now that Tamara Thorne was a genuine medium, and that he had actually heard the voice of the headless girl he had found at Owasippe. But what was the point of hearing a message from a spirit if the message made no sense?

So it had appeared to be frightened, this Forest Ghost, or Pan, or whatever it was. He expected that cougars were frightened, when people wandered into their territory, but that didn't stop them from attacking them, and killing them.

He stood up, and held out his hand. 'Thanks, Ms Thorne. That was one experience I won't forget in a hurry. Like I say, I don't exactly know what the message was, but thanks all the same.'

Tamara Thorne shook his hand and gave him a strange, secretive smile. 'It will come to you, Jack. Unlike Bindy's grandma, she's given you the key.'

What the Stars Say

As exhausted as he was, Jack slept only fitfully that night. At three-twenty in the morning he went into the kitchen for a glass of cold water, and then he went through to the living room to stand by the window and stare out at the street.

The streetlights were too bright for him to be able to see the stars, but he was very aware that they were out there. He was aware of the planets, too, on their strange and complicated journeys around the Sun. Like Sparky, he was seriously beginning to accept that the stars and the planets were invisibly orchestrating his life, and that he had no real choice in what was going to happen to him. He had always been skeptical about astrology, but after the past few days he was beginning feel that his destiny was already charted for him, and that whatever he decided, it would make no difference.

We arrogantly believe we have choices, he thought, *but what choices do we really have, in the grand scheme of things? We are stuck to the Earth by gravity, as helpless as flies stuck to flypaper. The Sun rises and the Sun sets and it controls every day of our lives, from the time we wake up to the time we go to sleep. If the Sun and the Earth control us that much, who's to say that the other stars and the other planets don't affect us, too, in all kinds of different ways?*

He looked at his ghostly reflection in the window, and he admitted to himself that he now believed in spirits, too. He had heard Aggie's voice, and he had heard the voice of the headless girl from the Owasippe Forest. A week ago, he would have shaken his head in cynical disbelief if anybody had told him that there really was life after death, and that he would ever hear Aggie again. But now he didn't doubt it. How could he? '*Jack*,' she had whispered to him. '*Can you hear me?*'

Up until this week, his life had been nothing but practicalities. Every waking hour had been taken up with food purchasing, and menus, and staff wages, and laundry, and advertising, and accounts. He had never been as hard-headed as his chain-smoking father, or as relentlessly skeptical as his mother, but he had never considered himself to be spiritual.

After what he had witnessed this week, though, he realized that he had been converted. You couldn't see people who had blown their heads off or cut their own feet off, and you didn't hear voices from people who weren't even there – not without it changing you dramatically, and forever.

It was growing light outside, and North Clark Street gradually began to appear in front of him like a developing black-and-white photograph. He went back to bed, twisted the covers around himself, and managed to doze for another three hours. When he woke up, it was seven-thirty. He could hear a blustery wind rattling the restaurant shingle which hung outside his bedroom window, but at least the sun was shining.

He heard clinking noises in the kitchen, and the fridge door shut. He eased himself out of bed and went through to the kitchen to find Sparky sitting at the table with a bowl of Cheerios and a carton of orange juice.

'Use a glass,' he said, taking one out of the cupboard. 'Other people have to drink out of that carton, namely me.'

'I had a dream we were back in Poland,' said Sparky.

'Wasn't a scary dream, was it?'

'No,' said Sparky, with his mouth full of cereal. 'I dreamed that we were walking through the forest and we met Mom, and this man, and they were holding hands, and both of them were smiling, like they were really happy.'

Jack spooned coffee into the percolator and switched it on. 'Nice dream. Who was he, this man? Did you know him?'

'No. I never saw him before.'

'OK. But next time you have that dream, make sure that the man with Mom is me.'

'It was only a dream, Dad. How can you be jealous?'

'You'll understand one day. At least I hope you will.'

Jack sat down at the table while he waited for his coffee to perk. He watched Sparky eating for a while, and then he said, 'Did you do today's star chart yet?'

Sparky shook his head. 'I don't have to. We *are* going back to Owasippe, aren't we? We have to.'

'I don't know, Sparks. Don't you think it's better if we just try to forget about all this Forest Ghost stuff?'

'I *can't*, Dad.'

'But after what happened in Poland—'

'We *have* to go back. You know we do. We have to know what happened to Malcolm and all the rest of those scouts. We have to know what happened to my great-great-grandfather. We have to find out why they all killed themselves. Why do you think we've been hearing Mom's voice? She wants us to find out. It's really, really important.'

'But what if we actually find this ghost, or whatever it is? That's if *we* don't kill ourselves first.'

'Something will happen. I know it will.'

'Something like what?'

'I don't know. I just feel it. I feel it inside of myself.'

'Aren't you scared?' Jack asked him. 'I know I am. Well, maybe not quite so much as I was. You know when I went out yesterday evening? I met a woman round at Bindy's bookstore and she thinks that *she's* seen the Forest Ghost, too.'

'Really? Who was she?'

'Oh . . . just some woman who works for the forest conservation service.' Jack didn't want to tell Sparky that she was the same woman he had found in the pool at Owasippe, with her head cut off. 'If it's any consolation, she thinks that the Forest Ghost is more frightened of *us* than we are of *it*. That's her opinion, anyhow. She says that she saw it when a ranger showed up, and all it did was run away and hide.'

Sparky was silent for a long time. Then he said, 'I think I'm more scared of *me*.'

'What does that mean, you're scared of *you*? How can you be scared of yourself?'

'I'm scared of what's inside of me. Who I am.'

Jack laid a hand on his shoulder. 'You're just a boy, Sparks. A regular normal boy. OK, your brain works a little differently from other people, but everybody's different in some way, aren't they? Apart from that, you're my son and your mother's son, and that's what you have inside of you. Us. That's all.'

'No. There's something else.'

'Something else like what?'

'I don't know. It's hiding inside of me. Every time I try to see what it is, it disappears.

'Come on, Sparks. You're letting your imagination run away with you. You're still tired, that's all. Have a rest today. We'll talk about going back to Owasippe tomorrow.'

'We *will* go, though? We have to.'

Jack didn't answer him. But when he looked at him, he still had that odd feeling that Sparky wasn't quite himself. There was something different about him, but he couldn't work out exactly what it was. He looked so pale, with dark circles under his eyes, almost as if he were a ghost.

Jack was sitting in his office, going over the last few days' accounts, when Sally came in, looking windblown.

'The Polack returns!' she said, leaning over his desk and giving him a kiss. 'How was the old country?'

'Are you on duty?' he asked her. 'If you're not, come to the bar and have a drink while I tell you. I think you'll need it.'

'I'm off today, as a matter of fact. But I'm back on tomorrow. I have to go back to Muskegon. Undersheriff Porter says he has some new evidence he wants us to look over together.'

'Well, how about that for a coincidence? Sparky and I were planning on going back there tomorrow.' *Fate*, he thought. *Now that I've started to believe in it, I can actually see it at work.*

Sally sat down on a barstool and said, 'It's a little early, but I'll have my usual, if that's OK. Why are you and Sparky going back there?'

Jack unscrewed the Jim Beam bottle. 'It's Sparky. You know how OCD he can be. He thinks if we go back there he can find out why his friend Malcolm committed suicide.'

'I don't know how. Undersheriff Porter says there's still no evidence that any third parties were involved. And since there were no survivors . . .'

Jack took the top off a bottle of Zywiec, and said, 'Let me tell you what happened in Poland, anyhow. You won't believe it. It was almost an exact parallel of what happened at Owasippe. We went into the forest and all of us panicked. And I mean like *total* panic! Three of the people who were with us committed suicide.'

'Oh my Lord! You're kidding me, aren't you?'

As calmly and as rationally as he could, he told Sally all about their ill-fated expedition into the Kampinos Forest. She sat and listened and didn't touch her drink until he had finished. Then she knocked it back in one. 'Jesus,' she said. 'What is it with these forests?'

Jack explained Professor Guzik's theory – that forests all over the world harbored a whole multitude of spirits which the Ancient Greeks had once called Pan – spirits which defended the trees against destructive intruders, and especially humans.

'And what do *you* think?' asked Sally. 'Sounds kind of far-fetched to me. Pan – is that the guy with the goat's legs, and the pipes?'

'That's the one. But what *I* saw – that white thing – it was nothing like that. Like I said before, it was more like a ghost.'

'What time are you going tomorrow?' asked Sally. 'I didn't book my flight yet. Maybe we could go together.'

Jack caught sight of the two of them in the mirror behind the bar. *Fate*, he thought again. It was almost like watching a movie of his own life, playing out in front of him.

That night, he was woken up by the sound of voices. He rolled over in bed and checked the time. It was two thirty-three, which meant that he been sleeping for less than three hours. He lay there, straining to hear what the voices were saying. Maybe it was nothing more than the people in the next-door apartment, watching television. He knew that the husband worked the graveyard shift at O'Hare airport, and they would argue or play music or take a shower at all kinds of ungodly hours during the night.

But these voices seemed to be much quieter, and much closer, as if two people were talking intently to each other in the living room, while at the same time trying to keep their voices down so that they didn't disturb him. One of them sounded like Aggie, but he didn't recognize the other one. It was reedy, and whistly, with a slight hoarseness to it, as if its owner was suffering from a cold.

He climbed out of bed, walked across the bedroom and opened the door. He was right: the voices were coming from the living room. Not only that, a silvery-white light was playing underneath the living-room door.

Treading as quietly as he could, he went along the corridor and stood outside the door, with his head tilted toward it. The angel Gabriel stared at him disapprovingly from the etching on the opposite wall. *You again, trespassing in the middle of the night, listening to conversations that are none of your concern.*

'So you're going tomorrow?' That was Aggie, or the woman who sounded like Aggie.

'Yes – tomorrow, early.' That was the reedy voice.

'Did you ever think it would come to this?'

'I think so, yes. Not so soon, maybe. But the stars have been predicting it for years.'

There was a pause, and then Aggie said something which Jack couldn't hear clearly.

'I was always hopeful that they would understand what they had,' the reedy voice replied. 'I know now that they never will. I don't think they're capable of it. Either that, or they simply don't want to.'

Another pause. Then Aggie said, 'I always knew you were special, from the moment you were born. I always knew that God had a plan for you.'

'God?'

'Well – destiny, maybe. Whatever you want to call it.'

Jack took hold of the doorhandle. Silently, he counted to three, and then he flung the door wide open. The silvery-white light vanished instantly, and when he stepped into the room all he could see was Sparky, in his pajamas, sitting on the couch with his legs tucked up underneath him, like a yogi. His eyes were closed as if he were meditating, but as soon as Jack came into the room he opened them.

'Sparks! What the *hell* do you think you're doing? Do you know what time it is?'

'I couldn't sleep,' said Sparky, and his voice was much hoarser than usual.

'What, you're catching a cold or something? You sound like it. If you are, you need to go back to bed and keep yourself warm.'

'I'm OK, Dad. I'm not sick.'

'So what was that light I saw?'

'What light?'

'I saw a light in here, like a very bright flashlight.'

Sparky didn't answer, but Jack could see that he didn't have any kind of lamp next to him, on the couch.

'Who were you talking to? It sounded like Mom again.'

Sparky shook his head. 'I wasn't talking to anybody. There's nobody here but me.'

'Don't lie to me, Sparks. I heard you. You said that the stars have been predicting something for years. Like – *what* have they been predicting for years?'

'I don't know, Dad. It wasn't me.'

'Sparks, I'm not stupid. I heard you talking to Mom just like you were talking the other night. You said that somebody didn't understand what they had, or didn't want to understand.'

'Things are different now,' said Sparky, in his flattest, least expressive tone. 'Things have changed since then. We went to Poland. Why do you think we went to Poland?'

'We went to Poland because you insisted on it, that's why. I still don't have any idea what the hell we have to show for it, except for a whole lot of bunkum about trees talking to each other and the great god Pan. Oh – and nightmares, too. We got nightmares, or at least I did. And hallucinations. And the ongoing heebie-jeebies.'

'It does all make sense, Dad. You just have to see it from a different point of view.'

'Sparks, the only point of view I can see things from right now is that it's two-thirty in the morning and we're catching a plane to Muskegon at nine forty-five, which means we have to be up by six at the latest. I'm almost tempted to cancel it, and forget this whole thing.'

'We can't. I told you. We *have* to go.'

When he said that, Sparky's voice was even hoarser, and the way he said it was no longer flat and expressionless, but demanding.

Jack thought to himself: *Something is about to happen here. Something that's going to make all the difference to Sparky's life, and maybe mine, too.* However much he didn't want to go tomorrow, he knew that Sparky was right, and they had to.

Maybe then, at last, the voices would stop.

Return to Owasippe

They caught the nine-forty-three United Express from O'Hare to Muskegon. It was only a fifty-three-minute flight and the airline didn't serve food, so Jack had asked Duane to make them some chicken-and-salad wraps to take with them.

Sally said, 'These are delicious. And here's me, trying to diet.'

Sparky hadn't touched his. He was staring out of the window at the hammered-glass surface of Lake Michigan, and the streaky cirrus clouds that were passing beneath them like shreds of torn muslin.

'*So* many people simply don't get it,' he said, without turning around.

'So many people simply don't get what, Sparky?' Sally asked him.

'So many people don't understand that here we are – living on an actual planet.'

'I guess you're right,' Sally admitted. 'I mean, it's not something that I've ever thought about. Are you going to eat that wrap or can I have it?'

'Go ahead,' said Sparky. Sally turned to Jack for his approval but Jack shrugged and said, 'Sure. Go ahead. Better than wasting it.'

They gradually started to lose altitude. Flying over the lake was almost always bumpy, and this morning was no exception. Sparky clutched the arms of his seat and pressed his face close to the window. 'Nearly there,' he said, so that his breath fogged up the Perspex.

'He seems to be real excited about it,' said Sally. 'What does he think he's going to find there?'

'The *answer*,' said Sparky, still without looking around. 'The answer to everything.'

Sally looked at Jack and raised one eyebrow. Jack shrugged

again. He couldn't work out what Sparky was talking about any more than she could.

'Where are you meeting Undersheriff Porter?' he asked her.

'At the County Sheriff's Office, first of all, in Muskegon. Then we're coming out to Owasippe. Apparently he has some circumstantial evidence he wants to show me, *in situ*.'

'Oh, OK. So we may see you later. We may fly back later this afternoon, depending how long we stay at Owasippe, but I've booked us in at the Comfort Inn, just in case. Maybe you and I could have dinner together.'

'Undersheriff Porter has already asked me, I'm afraid. He wants to take me to some place called the Hearthstone Grill. He says I'll love it – ma-and-pa food brought up to date, apparently.' She smiled, and added, 'I think he's taken a shine to me.'

'Sounds cozy. But make sure that the only thing he shows you that begins with "circum" is "stantial evidence".'

Sally laughed, and then she said, 'Do you know something? I can't remember the last time I laughed. Yes, I can. It was with you, when your waitress dropped all of that spaghetti Bolognese right in that guy's lap. We don't laugh enough, Jack, do we? I think we've forgotten how – what with all the money worries and the violence and the general crappiness of everything. Sparky's right. We're living on an actual planet, which is amazing, but we take it totally for granted.'

The plane's wheels went down, and it began to tilt and sway as it made its way down to Muskegon Airport. As the ground came closer and closer, Sparky started to gabble something under his breath. The engines were whistling too loudly for Jack to be able to catch any of the words, but even if he had been able to, he wasn't at all sure that he would have known what they meant.

After they had landed, however, and were taxiing toward the terminal, Sparky pointed both of his index fingers upright, and touched the ends of his two thumbs together, to form a figure that looked something like a W. Very softly, Jack heard him say, '*Suck see wahbey. Man, two, suck see wahbey.*'

Undersheriff Porter was waiting for Sally in the terminal building, under the high arched roof. He smiled broadly when he caught sight of her, but his smile faded when he saw Jack and Sparky.

'Sorry, Sal, but what are these guys doing here?'

'They wanted to go back and take another look at the scout reservation, that's all. Kind of a pilgrimage, I guess you could call it, to pay a tribute to all those scouts who died.'

'I see,' said Undersheriff Porter, grudgingly. 'Although, to tell you the truth, I *don't* see. You'll find that substantial areas of the Owasippe Scout Reservation are still restricted from unauthorized entry – especially the scout huts at Lake Wolverine, and the shoreline all around the lake, and that hollow where we found those two dead cougar-shit collectors.'

Sally made an exaggerated show of covering Sparky's ears with her hands.

'Oh come on, now,' said Undersheriff Porter. 'If he doesn't know the word "shit" by now he must be arrested.' He turned around to Jack and added, 'And so will *you* be, sir, if you try to enter those areas of Owasippe which we've marked off-limits. *Arrested*, I mean. Get it? Just a friendly warning.'

He and Sally left the airport in his squad car, while Jack hailed a cab. The driver was a fat, middle-aged Native American with greasy gray shoulder-length hair and mirror sunglasses. He wore a maroon shirt buttoned up to the neck and a brown deerskin vest that was shiny with age.

First of all Jack asked him to drive them to the Comfort Inn on East Sherman Drive so that he could check in at the desk and leave their bags. If they missed the last plane back to Chicago, which left at seven twenty-five in the evening, they could stay here for the night, and catch the first plane back in the morning.

When he had registered, Jack climbed back into the cab and asked the driver to take them to the scout reservation.

'You know it's closed down for the rest of the season, don't you?' asked the cab driver, incessantly chewing gum. 'It's on account of all them kids that killed themselves. You hear about that?'

'Yes, we heard about that.'

'That place, Owasippe, *brrrr*! That was always kind of spooky. My grandpa used to tell me old Potawatomi stories about Owasippe. Some folks used to say it was haunted.'

'Oh, yes?' Jack asked him. 'Haunted by what?'

'Oh, not by people or nothing. By this white albino deer, with special powers. It could run so fast that it could catch up with itself. And nobody who saw it ever told the tale, because the deer used to make them cut out their own tongues rather than say that they had seen it, and where it was.'

'That's a pretty gruesome story.'

'My grandpa had a whole lot like that. Do you know what? He said that when he died his spirit was going to go live in a tree, and I should walk around knocking on all of the trees and asking if he was in there. Can you imagine that?'

'Quite a character, your grandpa.'

They drove due north for the next twenty minutes on Russell Road, with scrubby trees and bushes on either side. Sparky start mumbling again and drawing patterns on the window with his fingertip, as if he were drawing an invisible star chart. Jack decided to say nothing. Sparky was obviously stressed and the last thing he wanted to do was upset him even more.

Eventually the taxi driver turned into the scout reservation entrance and pulled up outside the main buildings. Jack handed him fifty dollars in bills, and he licked his thumb and counted them.

'I didn't mean to put you off none, you and your boy. Owasippe is a great spot really, and I don't suppose Manito Sucsee Wabe really exists.'

'What?'

'The white albino deer. Its Potawatomi name is Manito Sucsee Wabe, which means "white deer spirit".'

'Really?' said Jack, looking pointedly at Sparky. 'Manito Sucsee Wabe?'

'That's the one,' said the taxi driver. 'My grandpa used to say that if you shot at it, and missed, you'd get sick. But if you shot at it and you actually hit it, that would be instant death – for *you*, not the deer. But there are all kinds of different stories. Some say that if you even go looking for it, you will go mad and kill yourself. One of my cousins thinks that's what happened to those boy scouts. But then my cousin is pretty fond of his firewater, so we never set much store by what *he* has to say.'

*   *   *

They went inside the scout headquarters. Unlike the last time they had been there, the hallway was deserted and quiet, although from one of the offices they could hear the sound of somebody rattling away on a computer keyboard. It smelled strongly of cedarwood and dust, and all the floors looked gritty, as if they needed sweeping.

'Is that what you were saying, on the plane?' Jack asked Sparky. 'Manito Sucsee Wabe?'

Sparky was looking at the noticeboard, with dozens of photographs of scout troops and camping parties pinned on to it.

'Manito Sucsee Wabe,' Jack repeated, coming up behind him and laying his hands on his shoulders. 'The white deer spirit. How did you know about that?'

'I didn't. I don't. Look – Malcolm's in that picture. That must have been taken on the day that they committed suicide.'

'You distinctly said it, on the plane, just after we landed. Manito Sucsee Wabe.'

'No, I didn't.'

At that moment, an office door opened and out came the bald bespectacled scout leader that Jack had encountered on the day that they had come to identify Malcolm's body.

'Can I help you?' He blinked. It was obvious that he didn't recognize them. 'I'm afraid that we're shut down here for the rest of the season. There won't be any activities until winter camping in November.'

'We were here last week,' Jack told him. 'My son's friend was one of the scouts who died here. We just came back to see where he died and pay our respects.'

'Oh, I'm sorry, sir. I can't let you do that. Owasippe is off limits to members of the public on account of liability insurance. If you and your boy went out there and broke your legs or something, you could sue us from here to Tuesday and we wouldn't be covered.'

'But we have to,' said Sparky.

The scout leader shook his head. 'Sorry, son. There's no chance. The Chicago Area Council owns Owasippe and they won't be budged. No unauthorized hiking, biking, picnicking, cookouts or camping. Especially after what happened here last week.'

'But we *have* to,' Sparky insisted.

The scout leader continued to shake his head. 'Come on, Sparks,' said Jack, laying his hand on his shoulder. 'If they won't let us in, they won't let us in. There's nothing we can do about it.'

'*We have to!*' Sparky shouted. His fists were clenched in frustration and his face was emptied of color. 'Don't you understand how *important* this is? You said it yourself, didn't you?'

'Hey, calm down there, son,' said the scout leader. 'Exactly *what* did I say?'

'You said that there were things in the woods,' said Sparky, and his voice was still trembling with anger. 'You said that there were things in the woods and the things in the woods would fight back.'

'Yes, well I meant it,' said the scout leader. 'Folks don't understand that the woods have their own personality. Their own spirits, if you like to call them that. Anybody who treats a forest badly is going to suffer the consequences. Same with anything else in Nature. Lakes, mountains, oceans.'

'We have to go into the woods,' said Sparky. 'We have to go in the woods and find them.'

Again the scout leader shook his head. 'I'm truly impressed that you believe in such things, son. Most people who don't know the forests think I'm talking out of my ass, if you'll pardon my language. But I've felt them for myself, those spirits, when I've been out alone amongst the trees, and that feeling's been stronger this season than it's ever been before. Well – we've seen the results of that, and they were tragic.'

'So you'll let us go find them?' Sparky asked him.

'No, son. I told you. I can't do that.'

'Supposing we sign a waiver, holding you blameless if we do have an accident?' Jack suggested.

'Sorry, sir. Any smart lawyer can talk his way around a waiver. You hurt yourselves, or you die, then the CAC are going to be held liable. All those suicides . . . they're already a legal nightmare. They could put this reservation out of business altogether, and it's already touch-and-go, financially.'

'You have to let us in,' said Sparky, very quietly.

'No, son. I don't, and I won't.'

'*You have to let us in!*' Sparky screamed at him. '*You have to let us in!*'

'Sparks, for Christ's sake!' said Jack, and tried to grab his arm. But Sparky stalked stiff-legged right up to the scout leader and shouted straight into his face. His voice was an ear-splitting combination of a shriek and a roar, as if two people were shouting at the same time.

'*You have to let us in! You have to let us in! You will die, if you don't!*'

'Sparks! That's enough!' Jack snapped at him.

But Sparky was almost incoherent with rage. He pushed the scout leader so hard that the man lost his balance and fell back against the notice board, and a shower of photographs and news clippings and thumbtacks dropped off it. Then he ran to the doors at the end of the hallway which gave out on to the balcony. He rattled one door, but it was locked, and then he rattled the next one, but that was locked, too.

'*Sparks!*' Jack shouted at him, and went striding after him. But just as he had almost reached him, Sparky opened one of the doors and escaped outside.

Jack went after him, but Sparky was already jumping down the steps three and four at a time, and as soon as he reached the bottom step he started running toward the trees. Jack followed him, holding on to the handrail in case he stumbled.

'Sparks! Come back here! Sparks!'

Now the scout leader was out on the balcony. 'You can't go into the woods!' he called out, his hands cupped around his mouth as if he were making an announcement to a crowd. 'You – cannot – go – into – the – woods!'

White Deer Spirit

Jack ignored the scout leader and went running after Sparky as fast as he could. After a hundred meters, however, he was already gasping for breath, and his chest hurt. He hadn't realized that he was so unfit, but the restaurant took up so much of his time that he had been forced to give up swimming and squash, and even the occasional jog along Montrose Drive, by the lake.

It was a glaringly bright afternoon, with only a thin cloud covering, but Sparky was wearing a dark khaki T-shirt and lighter khaki shorts, and as soon as he reached the tree line he disappeared altogether. Jack glimpsed his blond hair for an instant, but then he was gone. He thought: *shit*. When Sparky threw a tantrum there was no telling what he would do or where he would go.

If he had been mentally normal, Jack would never have given Sparky half so much latitude. Jack's own father had always considered that a sharp smack on the *dupa* was the best way to deal with a young boy's wilful behavior. Either that, or being sent up to bed with no supper. But Sparky was obsessive, and whatever he set out to do, he simply couldn't stop until he had done it. If he couldn't, he was liable to go into a seizure, almost like an epileptic fit.

Jack stopped when he reached the tree line, panting.

'Sparks!' he shouted out. 'Sparky, for Christ's sake come back! I'll fix it for us, so that we can take a look around, I promise!'

By now the scout leader had caught up with him. He must have been in much better shape than Jack, because he wasn't panting at all, although his bald bronze head was beaded with perspiration.

'You'd best get that son of yours out of these woods, sir, or else there's going to be serious trouble. It's going to be my head on the block, for letting you in here, so let's hope and pray that he doesn't run into any trouble.'

'Trouble like what? One of your forest spirits? Or a white deer spirit?'

'Oh, you know about *that*?' said the scout leader. He sounded surprised – and strangely, a little annoyed, as if nobody else should know about the white deer spirit but him. 'That white deer spirit, that's a Native American superstition. According to them, these forests used to be jam-packed with spirits. Standing room only, that's what you'd think, the way they tell it, and the white deer spirit was the one who took care of them all.'

Jack said, 'Listen – my son is kind of different. He has a form of Asperger's syndrome. I don't want to get you into any trouble but please let me go look for him. As soon as I find him, I'll make sure that we leave. I promise.'

The scout leader puffed out his cheeks and wiped the perspiration from his forehead with the back of his hand. 'I don't know,' he said. 'I could lose my job over this.'

'No, you won't. I'll go find him and then we'll leave and nobody else needs to know that we were here.'

The scout leader checked his wristwatch. 'OK . . . I'll give you a half-hour. After that, I'll have to put in a call that I've seen some unauthorized intruders.'

'Thanks,' said Jack, and immediately started walking off into the forest. After a few yards he turned around to give the scout leader a wave of appreciation, but he was already making his way back toward the main building.

The forest seemed unusually silent. No breeze was stirring the upper branches of the pines, no blue jays or finches were chirruping. Jack walked straight ahead until he could no longer see the scout building behind him, and then he stopped and listened. Nothing. Not even a raccoon running furtively through the undergrowth.

'Sparks!' he called out. 'Sparks, can you hear me? Where are you, Sparks?'

Silence. In fact the forest was so noiseless he could have believed that he had gone stone deaf.

'Sparks! You have to come out of there, wherever you are! Come on, Sparks, we can work something out with these scout people!'

There was still no response. Jack carried on walking, but the deeper into the forest he went, the more concerned he became about getting himself lost. He looked up through the trees to see where the sun was, and it was almost directly ahead of him. At this time of the afternoon, he reckoned, he must be heading south-westward.

'Sparks! *Sparks!* For Christ's sake, Sparky, I'm beginning to lose my patience here!'

Still nothing, and so he continued walking. The ground in front of him began to slope downward, quite steeply, with rocky outcroppings on his right-hand side. They reminded Jack of the rocks in the Kampinos Forest, the rocks that resembled a witch, except that these rocks had fibrous tree-roots growing out of them like tendrils. If anything, they looked like some giant squid-creature that was trying to force its way out from under the soil.

'Sparks!' he shouted, yet again. He recognized where he was now, and it wasn't too far from the pool where he had found the headless woman and her drowned companion. It was hard to believe that Sparky couldn't hear him. The forest was so silent, and even if Sparky had been running, he couldn't have run so far that he was out of earshot.

Jack slid down the slope until he was almost at the bottom, and then tripped on a root and stumbled. As he did so, he heard the strange squeaky little laugh of a bald eagle calling, as if it were mocking him. But when he steadied himself, and looked around, and listened, he began to realize why the eagle was calling, and it wasn't because of him. He could distinctly hear a rustling sound in the bushes, and the trees were beginning to creak and whisper. The eagle had been alarmed by the sudden arrival of something else.

Please don't let me start panicking. There's nothing there.

But the rustling continued – about seventy-five feet up ahead of him, he guessed – and the upper branches of the pine trees began to sway. *Tree talk.*

Don't panic. There's nothing there. Sparky had said that there was nothing there. But what was "nothing"? "Nothing" could mean exactly that – no thing, no physical thing, but a spirit, or a ghost. A Waldgeist, *or a* nish-gite, *or a white deer spirit.*

'Sparks!' he shouted, although a warmish breeze was rising,

and it swallowed his shout as soon as it came out of his mouth, as if it fed on shouts. 'Sparks, where the hell are you?'

Off to his left, behind the trees, he thought he saw something white. It was running, or dancing, or maybe it was nothing more than sunlight, playing on the tree trunks. But then he saw it flickering again, farther away, and farther off to his left; and then again. He stood still, uncertain what he ought to do next. Should he go after it? Should he try and corner it, and try to see what it actually was?

He was telling himself to be rational, and calm; but in spite of that he could feel his mouth drying up and a slow crawling sensation up his back. He was starting to panic. He knew that he was starting to panic, even though he had seen nothing more than an indistinct white figure which had probably been nothing more dangerous than a startled white deer.

You are not going to panic. There is nothing here. And even if there is something here, don't you remember what that headless girl told you?

'*It was frightened, Jack. It was* frightened. *It was even more frightened than we were.*'

What if she was right? What if the panic he was feeling was only the spirit's own fear, which he was picking up somehow, like the panic spreads in a nightclub when the stage catches fire, or those hundreds of panicking pilgrims who were crushed underfoot at Mecca?

But thinking it about it rationally didn't seem to help. He began to sweat, and breathe more quickly, and he felt a pain around his chest, like a tight metal band. He began to think, too, that the forest wasn't real, and that he was only imagining that he was here. He even began to think that *he* wasn't real – classic symptoms of panic disorder.

I have to get out of here, he thought. *But what about Sparky? Sparky's in there someplace, amongst the trees. Supposing he's feeling as panicky as I am? I have to control myself. I have to find him, no matter how scared I am.*

He kept on walking forward, although he had no real idea of where he was going, and he found it difficult to keep his balance. It was like being drunk. He heard another sharp rustling amongst the bushes, but this time it was close behind him, not ahead of him. He twisted around, and this time he did lose his balance, and fell awkwardly on to his knees, as if he were praying in church. There was something there, he was sure of it. Something cruel beyond all imagination, which wanted to pull him apart. Something which was going to press its thumbs into his eye sockets until his eyeballs popped, and then split open his chest so that his lungs bulged out. It would plunge its hands into his intestines and heave them out of his pelvis and dump them on to the forest floor. And all the time that it was tearing him apart like this, he would still be conscious – still alive, but screaming in unbearable pain, and knowing, worst of all, that he was far beyond saving, that he was inevitably going to die.

He managed to climb back on to his feet and brush himself down. *You're acting like a fool*, he told himself. *Go find Sparky and then get out of here. Even if there is something hiding itself behind those trees, it hasn't had the nerve to come out and attack you yet, has it? Maybe she was right, that headless girl.*

'The howling angel. The thing that you call the Forest Ghost, the *nish-gite*. It was frightened.'

At that moment, though, he heard a rushing noise, and it was coming closer – fast. For a split-second, he couldn't think what it was – but then a wind suddenly blew through the forest like a bomb blast. Leaves and dust and twigs and pine needles came whirling through the trees like a blizzard, and Jack had to close his eyes tightly to prevent himself from being blinded. The trees began to creak again, in a terrible off-key chorus, and the birds started screeching. He felt as if the entire forest was telling him to get out, and to run for his life.

He panicked, utterly, in exactly the same way that he had panicked in the Kampinos Forest. He started to run, not even knowing which way he was running. He could hear his sneakers crunching on the forest floor, and he could hear himself panting. He could even hear the blood rushing through his ears. But his sense of detachment was extraordinary. If he hadn't left his clasp-knife at home, he would have stopped running and cut his throat here and now, just to get it all over with, and save himself the agony of being dismembered.

There were no cliffs here that he could throw himself from,

and the nearest lake in which he could drown himself was still a good three-quarters of a mile away. All he could do was run, and run, and pray that the white thing didn't catch up with him.

The wind was now blowing so hard against his back that he kept staggering forward and almost fell flat on his face. Three or four times he collided with tree trunks, and he began to wonder if he could beat his head against a tree hard enough to crack his skull, and kill himself. But how long would that take – and would the white thing have caught up with him before he could lose consciousness?

He had no idea which direction he was heading. For all he knew, he was running further and further into the forest, and he could get irrevocably lost, if the white thing didn't tear him apart first. The wind was blowing too strongly for him to stop and try to get his bearings from the sun, and for all he knew the white thing was only a few meters behind him, breathing down his neck.

He collapsed on to his knees again, and crouched there for a moment, his heart thumping, gasping for air. If the white thing jumped on him now, there was nothing he could do about it. After a while, though, he managed to climb up on to his feet again, and continue running, although he was lurching from side to side like a man on the deck of a storm-tossed ship.

Oh God, it's no good. Oh God, it's going to get me. Oh God, please don't let it get me.

He was close to the point at which he could no longer put one leg in front of the other when he suddenly saw the flag flying above the tree tops. The Stars and Stripes, idly curling and uncurling in the afternoon sunlight. It was the flag that flew over the scout headquarters and he knew that he had nearly reached sanctuary.

He hobbled and jogged alternately the rest of the way. As he approached the scout building, he could feel the wind dying down. A few last leaves flew around him, but as the wind dropped they pirouetted down to the ground, as if they were tired of chasing him. Now the forest was quiet again, except for Jack's panting, and the crunch of his trainers on dry pine needles.

He reached the scout building and climbed the steps to the

balcony. This time he didn't use the handrail to steady himself, as he had when he was hurtling down the steps in pursuit of Sparky, but wearily to haul himself up. He opened the glass door and went back into the hallway. There was a row of chairs in a side alcove, and he sat down with his hands on his knees and his head bent, sweating and trembling and trying to get his breath back.

His panic was gradually subsiding. He was already beginning to think how absurd it had been, for him to run away like that. What was it that had terrified him so much he had considered bashing his own brains out against a tree?

Nothing. And yet this *nothing* could create such panic that it was known almost everywhere, all around the world. Some people said it looked like a ghost. Others said it was an angel, or a cougar, or a white albino deer, or the great god Pan, with the body of a man and the legs of a goat. But Jack now believed beyond question that they were all manifestations of one and the same nothing. It was simply the panic people felt in isolated forests, no matter where they were. Here at Owasippe; or in the Kampinos Forest; or the Mato Grosso.

Although his chest was still rising and falling with effort, he stood up and went across to the scout leader's office. He had almost reached it when the door opened and Undersheriff Porter came out, followed by Sally and the scout leader himself.

'Hey, Jack!' Sally smiled. 'I was hoping you would still be here!' But then she frowned at him and said, 'Are you OK? You look terrible! What's happened?'

'It's Sparky,' said Jack. He told them quickly how Sparky had thrown a temper-tantrum and run off into the forest.

'So you couldn't find him? But my God, what have you been doing to *yourself*? You're covered in dirt and pine needles and you look absolutely *bushed*!'

'I had one of those panic attacks, Sal, like I did before. I couldn't find Sparky. I called him and called him but he didn't answer. Then I just lost it. I saw that white figure again, behind the trees, and the wind started to blow, and I panicked. I can't describe it to you. You feel like you'd rather kill yourself than let that thing get you, and that's what happened to all of those scouts, I'm sure of it.'

'We'd better go look for Sparky,' said Sally. 'Dan – if we can't find him directly, will you be able to call for some back-up?'

'I'll come outside with you and take a look-see,' said Undersheriff Porter. 'If it seems like he's genuinely lost I can get in touch with the forest rangers and rustle up a search party. We've done it here before, quite a few times. Don't you worry, sir. We'll find him. We never failed to find anybody yet, even when it took us a little time – and even when they didn't *want* us to find them.'

'I just hope that nothing's happened to him,' the scout leader put in. 'I mean, if he's been injured, the CAC are going to be held liable for it.'

'Let's start worrying about the kid's welfare before we start worrying about the insurance claim, shall we?' said Undersheriff Porter. 'How long ago since he went missing?'

'Thirty, thirty-five minutes,' said Jack. 'But I really think we need to be careful. I mean, I don't think I panicked for nothing.'

'You said you saw something before, the last time you were here. Something white, you said.'

'I saw the same thing today.'

'But you still don't know what it was?'

'No idea, Sheriff. A ghost, a deer, a spirit, a cougar. Jason Voorhees in his hockey mask, who knows? That's what I've been trying to find out. That's the whole reason that Sparky and I came here today.'

'Oh, so that's it!' said the scout leader. 'You didn't come here to pay your respects after all!'

Undersheriff Porter turned to the scout leader and said, 'It doesn't matter two hoots *why* they came, Ambrose. All that matters is that we find this kid before it gets dark. Now, you know this forest better'n any of us. Do you want to make some suggestions as to which way he might have headed?'

'I think he may have headed toward Lake Wolverine,' said Jack. 'That's where his friend killed himself, and that's where we had our first panic attack.'

'OK, let's drive there now and see if we can maybe head him off. You don't have to come with us, sir, if you don't feel up to it.'

'No, I want to come,' Jack told him. 'If anybody can calm
Sparky down, then it's me. But I will say one thing. If any of
the three of us start to feel panicky – even the slightest bit panicky
– we need to do a U-turn and get the hell out of there. I really
mean that. That panic is like a kind of madness. You lose all
sense of what's right and what's wrong.'

Sally took hold of Jack's hand and patted it. 'We'll be fine,
Jack. I promise you. I never panicked in my life. I was kidnapped
by three crack addicts once, and held hostage until their friend
was sprung from jail. I never panicked once. What was the
point? We ended up playing poker together, and I won eleven
bucks.'

'I don't think you understand what this thing is like,' said
Jack. 'Well – I hope you never do.'

They went around to the side of the building, where
Undersheriff Porter's Jeep was parked. The scout leader followed
them, looking deeply unhappy.

'It's OK, Ambrose,' Undersheriff Porter told him. 'You know
and I know that there's no such thing as ghosts.'

The scout leader said nothing, but looked at Jack, and the
expression on his face said it all. *You know and I know that
there may not be ghosts in that forest, not even Chief Owasippe
and his two dead sons. But there are spirits of some kind,
because we've seen them, and they're terrifying – more terrifying
than words can describe.*

'I'm going to have to call this in,' he said, miserably.

'You do that, Ambrose. But we'll be back before you know
it, and we'll have this gentleman's son with us, too.'

Dead Voices Speak

They drove along the forest track toward Lake Wolverine. As he drove, Undersheriff Porter asked Jack to remind him what Sparky looked like, and tell him what he was wearing, and why he had run off into the forest.

Jack said, 'He needs to understand why his best friend killed himself. He's compulsive about it. They were bosom buddies, those two. Sparky's a little off-center, if you know what I mean, and Malcolm was kind of a dweeb, God rest his soul, so both of them found it hard to make any other friends at school.'

'Sure, I see,' said Undersheriff Porter. 'Well – when we find him, I think I may be able to enlighten him. Our crime scene people re-examined the area where the bodies were discovered, and they came up with an explanation for what happened that so far seems the most plausible. That's why I asked Detective Faulkner here to come back and take a look.

'We know that there was no wacky quasi-religious cult thing going on in that particular scout group; and also that there was no sexual exploitation, nor bullying, neither. They were the normalest bunch of kids you could hope to meet, and their group leaders were all straight arrows, too.

'But less than twenty feet away from where their bodies were found, there was a wide charred patch which we had originally assumed was the remains of their campfire. I mean – scouts, campfire, logical conclusion. But one of our deputies pointed out that it was pretty unusual for scouts to light a campfire that early in the day. They were supposed to be out orienteering, so they wouldn't have lit a campfire and left it unattended.

'When our forensics people took a closer look at this so-called campfire site, they found that there was no wood-ash, and that the ground-covering and surrounding vegetation had simply been subjected to intense heat. In fact it had all the characteristics of a major lightning strike.'

'OK,' said Jack, 'they were nearly struck by lightning. But that wouldn't have made them commit suicide, would it?'

'It may well have,' said Undersheriff Porter. 'Even though none of them were hit directly, they may all have received what they call a secondary strike through the ground. Now, I didn't know this myself, but that secondary strike can travel up through the soles of your feet into your body and play all kinds of havoc with your brain function. In some cases your brain will forget to tell your body to go on breathing. In other cases you can get totally disoriented. You no longer know who you are, or even *what* you are, and what the hell you're supposed to be doing.

'When lightning travels through your skin, you get badly burned, but people who only get burned are the lucky ones. If lightning goes right through your body and zaps your brain, you can end up cuckoo for the rest of your life.

'Our forensic people are pretty sure that this is what happened to those scouts. Like, when you think about it, what other explanation could there be?'

As they drove, Jack was looking into the forest on either side to see if he could spot Sparky. Every time he saw sunlight flickering through the trees, he quickly looked twice, just to make sure. 'I don't know,' he said. 'Would it have made them *all* commit suicide?'

'Maybe one started it and the rest copied him. Who knows? Maybe if one of the scout leaders did it, the rest of the group followed him because they thought that they were supposed to.'

'Is there any recorded instance of this happening before?'

'Our people are looking into that. It seems like some pretty detailed studies into the psychological effects of being struck by lightning have been carried out at Chicago University, and at Finch University, too.'

Now they saw Lake Wolverine sparkling up ahead of them. Undersheriff Porter drove past the scout buildings and the jetty, and circled around the left-hand side of the lake until he reached the clearing where the scouts and their leaders had all been found dead. It was surrounded by metal stakes with yellow tape wound around them: SHERIFF LINE DO NOT CROSS.

They climbed out of the Jeep and ducked under the tape. The forest was very hushed, although the blue jays were calling intermittently and the leaves were whispering, unlike before, when Jack had first gone looking for Sparky. The surface of the lake was glittering, and the boats tied up at the jetty were softly knocking against each other.

'It's idyllic here, isn't it?' said Sally. 'At least it would be, if those poor kids hadn't killed themselves here.' But Jack kept turning around and around, looking not only for Sparky but for any sign of something white. He looked up. Were those oak leaves whispering because they were being stirred by the wind that was blowing off the lake? Or were they talking to each other, and passing on a warning to the white deer spirit that intruders had arrived in the forest?

An outline of every scout and scout leader's body had been marked out with white plastic tape and fastened to the ground with skewers. Undersheriff Porter guided them between the outlines and they trod as carefully and as reverently as if the bodies were still here. Beyond the array of outlines, he led them across to a circle of blackened soil about seven feet in diameter. In the center of it, the matted pine needles had been reduced to a fine gray ash, and Jack could see why the sheriff's deputies had originally thought that it was a campfire.

As Undersheriff Porter had said, though, there was no charred firewood here, and there was none of the usual campfire paraphernalia – no logs arranged around it for the Scouts to sit on, or a barbecue pit rotisserie, or long campfire forks for toasting hot dogs and marshmallows.

'We checked with the weather people,' said Undersheriff Porter. 'The skies were mostly clear over Owasippe that day but they recorded two or three thunder bumpers further up north and so there was every likelihood that this was a lightning strike. In any case, the coroners are going to be carrying out brain scans on all of the deceased to see if there's any evidence of severe electric shock.'

'Now we need to find Sparky so that we can tell *him* that,' said Sally.

Jack walked around the scorched patch of soil. It certainly looked as if there had been a lightning strike here, and he could quite understand that the police were feeling hard-pressed to come up with some kind of rational explanation for what had happened, so that they could say that the case was closed. But three times now he had felt that overwhelming compulsion to commit suicide himself – twice here at Owasippe and once at Kampinos – and it certainly hadn't been caused by lightning.

'*Sparks!*' he shouted. '*Sparks, can you hear me?*'

Several blue jays fluttered away in alarm, but otherwise there was no response. Only the trees rustling, and the clanking of the rowboats, like human skulls knocking together.

'Sparks, if you can hear me, please come on out! We think we know what happened to Malcolm!'

'Sparky!' called Sally. 'This is Sal – Detective Sally Faulkner, from Chicago! Don't be afraid, Sparky! You're not in any trouble! We just want to make sure that you're safe!'

'Sparky!' Jack shouted. 'It's going to be getting dark pretty soon, and then what are you going to do? You can't spend all night in the forest!'

They called him a few more times, and then waited, but there was still no reply. The wind was rising, which made the rowboats knock louder and faster, and more erratically, and the water lapped against the shore.

'What do you think?' asked Undersheriff Porter. 'You're his dad – any ideas what's going through his mind? I mean, is he afraid of being punished? Or is he doing this because he's angry with you, for some reason, and he's trying to punish you? Or is he just being ornery?'

Jack shook his head. 'None of those. Not really. He believes there's some kind of spiritual force in the forest, and that's what caused these kids to kill themselves.'

'You mean this white thing you were talking about? This thing that makes you panic?'

'I think there has to be something there, Sheriff. Don't ask me what it is. But I'm not the only person who thinks they've seen it, and I'm not the only person who's panicked in a forest. It's a well-known phenomenon, worldwide.'

Undersheriff Porter took off his amber-tinted sunglasses and peered into the trees. After a while he put them back on, and said, 'Well . . . no phenomenons that I can see. Not disputing what you say, sir, but I have to believe my own eyes.'

Just as he turned away, there was a sharp, furtive rustling in the bushes, about fifty or sixty feet away from them. Immediately he turned back again.

'What was that? Did you hear that, Sally? Where did that come from?'

'Right over there,' said Sally, pointing directly in front of them. 'Just beside that pine. Look – there it goes again!'

The bushes that surrounded the foot of the pine tree had started furiously shaking, as if a large animal were running around inside them.

'Sparky!' called Jack, and started to walk quickly toward them. 'Sparky, is that you?'

'Sir!' said Undersheriff Porter. '*Sir* – you want to wait up for a moment! That could be your son in there but then maybe it's not! Even the foxes around here can get pretty darn snappy if they think you're a threat.'

Jack slowed down and then stopped. The bushes stopped shaking and the forest became eerily quiet. Sally and Undersheriff Porter came up to join Jack and the three of them stood listening for over a minute.

'*Spark-eeee!*' Sally shrilled.

'Jesus, Sal, you scared the living crap out of me then!' said Undersheriff Porter. 'You don't want to do that again without giving me notice!'

'Sorry, Dan.'

They waited and listened a little longer. Undersheriff Porter said, 'That must have been a raccoon, or something. No way your boy wouldn't have answered a scream like that. Goddamned *dead* person would've answered it.'

'So what do we do now?' asked Jack.

'Not a whole lot we can do, just the three of us. You had a hunch he might be here and maybe he is – but if he *is* here he doesn't seem too keen to come out and show himself.'

He paused, and then he said, 'How old did you say he was? Twelve?'

'Twelve, going on thirteen.'

Undersheriff Porter looked at his wristwatch. 'Well, he ran off voluntarily. Like, he wasn't forcibly abducted or nothing like that. And even if he's suffering from Asperger's, from what you've told me about him he seems to be reasonably capable of taking care of himself. I'm reluctant to put together a search party just yet. By the time we get everybody out here to Owasippe there won't be too much daylight left. My suggestion is that we give him a little more time to come to his senses. He's going to be feeling hungry soon, too, and it's my experience that when the stomach calls, the brain listens.'

'I'm still sure that there's something in this forest,' said Jack. 'Whatever it is, I'm really not happy about leaving Sparky out here all alone.'

'I'm not sure we have a whole lot of choice,' said Undersheriff Porter. 'If we had a positive sighting of a cougar, for instance, or a bear, that would be a clear and present danger, and that would be different. But with all respect, sir, all you saw was some kind of white thing. How am I going to justify a full-scale night-time search party because of some kind of white thing?'

He had hardly finished speaking, however, when they heard another rustling noise, about a hundred feet deeper into the forest. This was followed by a scampering sound, like a very large rodent. Then twigs breaking, and a thump.

'What in the name of all that's holy is *that*?' Undersheriff Porter cried.

Sally frowned, and said, 'Dan – I don't like the sound of that at all.'

'Sparky!' Jack shouted. 'Sparky, is that you? Come on, Sparky, you need to come out now! Like Sally says, you're not in any trouble!'

The bushes were shaken again, as violently as they had been shaken in the Kampinos Forest. Jack began to feel short of breath, and his heart started to beat more quickly. *Not again*, he thought. *You're not going to panic again. There are three of us here, and two of us are armed. What can possibly attack us here?*

The bushes seemed to burst apart, with leaves and broken branches flying everywhere. At the same time, the wind started to blow even more strongly, and the trees set up a monotonous chorus of creaking, like a wooden ship at sea, or an old house in which unwelcome visitors were climbing up the stairs.

Off to their right, behind the pines, Jack caught sight of that white flickering thing again. 'There!' he shouted, snatching at the sleeve of Undersheriff Porter's jacket. 'There it is – look!'

'The *fuck*?' said Undersheriff Porter.

'There!' Jack insisted. 'Look, right there!'

Undersheriff Porter unclipped his holster and pulled out his heavy black Sig automatic. Sally reached into her coat and took out her gun, too.

'For Christ's sake, don't start shooting!' Jack appealed to them, waving his hands. The wind was gusting harder and harder, whipping up a blizzard of pine needles and grit and dry leaves, and he had to shout to make himself heard. 'Sparky might be there!'

Sally stared at him wide-eyed. Her hair was blowing wildly, as if she were standing in an updraft, and her face was empty of color. She kept opening and closing her mouth but she wasn't saying anything. She wasn't even screaming.

Jack felt that chilling paralysis of panic coming on, like having ice-water poured slowly all over him. He wanted to grab hold of Sally's arm and pull her away from there, but he couldn't think how to start moving his legs. He could see that she, too, was incapable of running away. She just stood there with her hair flying upward and her gun in her hand, staring at him in utter helplessness.

He turned to Undersheriff Porter and yelled at him, 'We have to get out of here! Can you hear me! We have to get out! It's going to tear us apart, if we don't!'

Undersheriff Porter stared at him in the same way as Sally, his eyes bulging, his face bloodless. He was trying to speak but it was obvious that he was having trouble breathing.

'*We have to get out of here!*' Jack repeated, but he wasn't sure that any words were coming out of his mouth – or, even if they were, that Sally and Undersheriff Porter could hear him. The wind had risen to a deafening, high-pitched whistle, and now the trees were not only groaning but their upper branches were roaring and plunging and showers of debris were falling down on every side.

Jack thought: *If I snatch Sally's gun out of her hand, I'll be able to shoot her, and then myself, if Undersheriff Porter doesn't shoot me first, and if he does he'll be doing me a favor. I don't care what happens to him. I just don't want that thing to get* me.

He managed to take a step toward her, and then another. He was so frightened that he felt numb, as if he had been anesthetized. He could hardly feel his arms and legs, and his face felt like a cardboard mask. Sally was right in front of him, her mouth still opening and closing in slow motion.

'*I can't get away!*' she seemed to be shouting at him, although he may have been reading her lips. '*But I don't* want *to get away!*'

He stretched out his hand to seize her gun, but she wasn't as near to him as he had thought, and he had to take at least another two steps to reach her. As he was doing so, he heard a loud, blurry bang close behind him, and a sharp shower of something coarse and wet struck the back of his neck. It felt as if somebody had scooped up a handful of shingle from the bottom of a fish tank and had thrown it at him, hard.

He turned slowly around to see Undersheriff Porter standing behind him, but there was nothing left of Undersheriff Porter's head except for his chin and the right side of his skull. His face had been blown into bright red feathery shreds, more like plumage than flesh. The smoke from the .40-caliber bullet was already whirling away on the wind, but Undersheriff Porter remained standing for another few seconds, his automatic pointing rigidly at the place where his face had been. Then he pitched sideways on to the ground, with one leg still shuddering. He was immediately half-covered by leaves and forest debris, as if the forest hurriedly wanted to hide what had happened here.

Horrified, Jack turned back to Sally – only to see that she, too, had raised her gun. She was pointing it directly into her right ear, and her eyes were already closed in anticipation of squeezing the trigger.

Jack knew how she felt. Better to kill yourself quickly than let the Forest Ghost get you. He thought that she was lovely, and it was so sad for her to die like this. But what she was doing would save her from so much agony. He actually envied her for killing herself first, and the only saving grace was that he could pick up her gun when she had done it and shoot himself, too, and it would all be done with.

He quickly looked back over his shoulder, and his heart almost stopped when he saw that the Forest Ghost was very much closer, so much closer that it was playing beams of intense white light between the trees. He thought he could hear a howling sound, too, like a distant pack of hounds. What had the headless woman called the Forest Ghost? *A howling angel.*

He looked back at Sally, just in time to see her shoot herself in the ear. He didn't hear the shot, but the left half of her head burst open and sprayed her brains across the forest floor. Her gun was a subcompact Glock which took only 9mm ammunition, compared to the huge bullet that Undersheriff Porter had used to blow his head off. Its entry wound was hardly bigger than the hole in her ear, but it would have bounced around inside her skull and caused devastating damage before it exited.

Sally – oh God, Sally! he thought, but as she collapsed on to the ground he was already diving down to snatch the automatic as it tumbled out of her hand.

Now it's my turn to escape. Now it's my turn to blot everything out.

He knelt down and picked up the gun, which was still warm. He wasn't at all experienced with guns, but his father used to own a Colt automatic which he had bought when some of the local hoods had started to demand protection money from the restaurant, and two or three times he had taken Jack down to the range so that he could fire it.

He suddenly thought of that when he picked up Sally's gun and held it upside-down, butt upward, so that its muzzle was pointing at his mouth. He had now entered that stage of panic in which he was totally composed, and calm, and reflective. He thought of his father, standing outside the kitchen, wreathed in cigarette smoke. He thought of his schooldays, and playing football, and of all those Chicago winters, so cold that people's eyeballs froze up.

Most of all he thought of Agnieszka. He could see her now, looking up from her sewing, but there was so much sunlight flooding into the living room that she looked ethereal, unreal, which of course she now was.

He opened his mouth and placed the muzzle against his front teeth. It smelled bitterly of cordite, and he felt as if he were breathing in Sally's last second of life. If he angled the gun upward, the bullet would go straight through his palate and into his brain, and he wouldn't even feel it.

Here I come, Aggie, he thought to himself, closing his eyes tightly. *No more pain, no more grief, no more panic.*

Forest Ghost

'Jack,' she said, and she sounded as if she were breathing it into his ear. 'Can you hear me, Jack? *Słyszysz mnie?* Don't do that.'

He opened his eyes. Even as he did so, he felt the wind subsiding, and all the leaves that had been dancing in the air began gently to see-saw back to earth. All around him there was a soft hushing sound as the trees stopped frantically waving and the bushes stopped rustling, and the forest became still again.

He lowered the gun. He had heard Aggie's voice, he was sure of it, but when he turned around he saw not Aggie but Sparky. He was standing about thirty feet away, his arms by his sides, not smiling but looking unusually relaxed. The sun was shining on him down through the trees so that he appeared to have a golden aura, the way that Aggie had looked when he had come into the living room and found her sewing.

'Sparks? Are you OK?'

Sparky nodded. 'I'm fine, Dad. Everything's fine.'

Jack stood up, and looked down at both Sally and Undersheriff Porter. They both would have seemed to be sleeping, if their heads had still been intact.

'How can you say that everything's *fine*, Sparks? These two good people have just shot themselves. And *I* would have done, too, if you hadn't stopped me.'

'It was self-defense, Dad. We can't help it. It's the only way that we can protect ourselves.'

'What the hell are you talking about? Who the hell is "we"? And where the hell have you been? I'm going to have to call the sheriff. Jesus.'

He wished he could stop looking at Undersheriff Porter, whose single remaining eye was fixed on a nettle growing right in front of what was left of his face, as if he were studying it for a botany test.

'They're dead, Dad. There's nothing you can do for them.

It's sad, but that's the way of the world. It's a shock when you
find out that the world isn't at all like you thought it was.'

'I thought I heard your mother,' said Jack.

'You did,' said Sparky, in Aggie's voice.

Jack felt a prickling all over. 'That was *you*? How do you
do that? You sound exactly like her.'

'That's because I'm here, Jack,' Sparky continued, still in
Aggie's voice. 'The spirits of the dead stay close to you after
they die. They look out for you, as best they can, to make sure
that you get over your grief at losing them. Of course, sooner
or later, they have to rest. We all have to rest in the end.'

'This is driving me nuts,' said Jack. 'Let's get one thing
sorted at a time. First of all, we have to go tell somebody that
Sally and this deputy have shot themselves. The spirit stuff can
wait until later. Come on. Do you know how to work a police
radio?'

'Yes, but I'm not going to.'

'Come on, Sparks, for Christ's sake. These two law officers
have just killed themselves right in front of us. We have to
report it.'

Sparky made no attempt to come any closer. 'You don't
understand, Dad. It's over. We're not going to take care of you
any more. We started to leave you years ago and now we're the
last few left. By this time next week, we'll all be gone, and
then you'll have to fend for yourselves.'

'Sparks, I don't understand one word of what you're saying.
Now, come on, let's get going.'

Jack suddenly realized that he would need the keys to the
Sheriff Department Jeep. He had to kneel down next to
Undersheriff Porter's body, roll him over, all heavy and soft,
and tug the keys out of his pants pocket on a chain. Glittering
green blowflies were already starting to cluster inside the half-
broken mixing bowl of the undersheriff's head.

He stood up again and said, 'Sparks. Come on.'

Sparky shook his head. 'I told you, Dad. It's over. We tried
to protect you but all you did was show us that you don't value
anything. You don't even value your own souls.'

'*Sparks*,' said Jack, and he was growing angry now. He was
still trembling with shock from having witnessed Sally and

Undersheriff Porter shoot themselves, and he hadn't fully recovered from his own hysterical panic. Now here was Sparky talking in Aggie's voice and spouting meaningless nonsense about leaving. He was seriously beginning to think that at last Sparky had lost it. He should never have brought him here to Owasippe to identify Malcolm's body, and he certainly should never have agreed to take him to Poland, or bring him back here a second time. He would have to make another appointment with his therapist when they got home.

'It's no use, Dad,' said Sparky. 'I'm not coming with you. I *can't* come with you. I'm leaving. We're all leaving. We don't know how you're going to manage on your own, without us, but we really don't have the strength or the will to do this any longer. What do you call it? We've reached the tipping-point.'

The tipping-point? What the hell was he talking about? Jack stood staring at Sparky in bewilderment. His voice sounded like Sparky's, flat and expressionless, and he *looked* like Sparky, with his washed-out face and the sun shining in his fine blond hair. Yet somehow, inexplicably, he wasn't Sparky. His words bore no relation to anything that Sparky had ever said or done before, and Jack simply didn't understand what he was trying to tell him. This wasn't just a symptom of Asperger's syndrome. This was something else altogether. Jack could almost believe that Sparky was hypnotized, or that somebody was using him like a ventriloquist's dummy.

'Sparks,' Jack said, trying to keep his voice steady, 'I'm going to drive back to the scout headquarters and I'm going to get some help. I'd prefer it if you came with me, but if you really don't want to, then I'm asking you to please stay right here. I shouldn't be too long. Just make sure you don't touch anything.'

'It's over, Dad,' said Sparky. 'We'll be going soon.'

'OK, you'll be going soon. I get it. But please wait here until I get back.'

'This was the very last place where people believed in us. The first place, too. Strange, isn't it? No matter how far you travel, no matter what you do, you always come back to the place where you started.'

Jack took two or three steps backward. He was beginning to feel panicky again, and he didn't want to turn his back on

Sparky, not until he had put some distance between them. He had the irrational fear that Sparky would come running up behind him and jump on him.

'You promise to stay here, then?' he repeated, raising one warning finger to show that he really meant it.

'It's over, Dad,' said Sparky, but this time he didn't sound like Sparky at all. He didn't sound like Aggie, either, or the headless girl he had found in the pool. His voice was thick and harsh, with a heavy accent. 'I am sorry for what I did. I apologize. But then I was panicking, and I was not thinking straight. I did not think of the future, or of anybody else. I thought only of that moment, and of myself.'

As he spoke, Sparky began to shine, brighter and brighter. His face became blurry, with only dark smudges to show where his eyes were. Soon he was incandescent, as bright as burning magnesium, and Jack had to raise his hand to shield his eyes. Right in front of him, Sparky had turned into the same dazzling figure that he had seen in the hotel bathroom in Warsaw.

Still shielding his eyes, Jack looked around him in disbelief. The forest was bleached with brilliant white light, like a movie set, even brighter than the sunlight that was still shining through the trees. And here, right in front of him, almost too bright to look at, stood the Forest Ghost, the *nish-gite*, the white deer spirit. Here, right in front of him, was the actual apparition that the Ancient Greeks had called Pan, the god of panic.

'Where's Sparky?' he shouted at it. He couldn't think of anything else to say. 'What have you done with my son?'

Sparky spoke to him again, in his flat Sparky voice, although this time he sounded as if he were right inside his own head. 'It's over, Dad. I told you. We're going now.'

'Where's my son? I want my son back!'

He took a step toward the figure, and then another, and then another. The figure hesitated, but then it appeared to back away from him.

'*It was frightened, Jack. The howling angel. It was* frightened. *It was even more frightened than we were.*'

'Where's my son?' Jack demanded. 'What – the – fuck – have – you – done – with – my – son?'

He suddenly thought: this Forest Ghost is going to hurt me. It's going to rip me apart if I come any closer. But he took another step forward, and yet another, and the figure backed away again.

It *was* frightened. He was sure of it now. As the headless woman had told him, it was much more frightened than he was.

He saw it now. It was like a revelation. Whatever they were, these things protected themselves not by attacking people who ventured into the forests, but by causing them to panic. They made them mad with fear – so terrified that they might be torn apart limb from limb that they would rather kill themselves first. And this is what these things had been doing for centuries, in forests all over the world.

'Who are you?' he said, hoarsely. '*What* are you? What have you done with my son?'

'We needed your son,' said Sparky's voice, still inside his head.

'What? Why? What did you need him for?'

'He was one of many who were promised to us. We began to realize that the time would soon come when we would have to leave. There was only one way for us to gather here, from all the places where we were scattered.'

As the figure spoke, Jack saw more white figures appearing through the trees. None of them were as dazzling as the creature in front of him, but they still had an eerie luminescence. They were approaching from all directions now, at least twenty of them, and maybe more. They came within fifty feet or so but then they stopped, and stayed where they were, utterly silent, watching and waiting. The sun was going down now, and the forest was filling up with shadows, as if hundreds of dark spiders were weaving webs among the branches. As the gloom gathered, the figures looked even more ghostly.

'These are all that remain,' said Sparky's voice. 'You won't try to harm us, will you, Dad? We'll be gone before you bring help.'

'Why should I try to harm you? I just want to know where my son is. I can hear him talking – I saw him – I thought *you* were him. So where is he?'

'We came here many thousands of years ago to protect your

world,' said the figure. 'We came to protect your forests and your oceans and to teach you that you and your world are one. Some of you are beginning to understand that, but far too few of you, and now – well, now it is much too late.

'We tried to stop you from destroying your forests and poisoning your oceans, but now they are beyond saving. There is nothing more that we can do.'

'So what the hell are you?' asked Jack. 'Martians, or what? How can you say that you're protecting us when you make young kids panic so much that they cut their own throats?'

The figure wavered slightly, and began to grow dimmer. Jack sensed by the tone of its voice that it was growing tired, as if it was an effort to stay shining so brightly.

'We hoped . . . we very much hoped . . .'

'Go on. What did you hope?'

'We hoped that you would eventually understand that everything in the universe is connected inextricably to everything else. *Everything*. Plants, animals, people, spirits. Every move you make is dictated by the movement of the planets, and of the stars; and you, in your turn, affect *them*. Some of you began to understand that, but it was only regarded as superstition, or a game.'

'Astrology, you mean? My son understands it.'

'Of course he does. He was always ours, right from the moment he was conceived.'

'Yours? What do you mean, *yours*? He's not yours.'

'We have to go now,' said the figure, sounding even more weary.

'Where's Sparky?' Jack insisted. He walked toward the figure but it just as quickly backed away. 'If you don't tell me where my son is—'

'Your son is here, within me. For the time being, anyway. I will leave him behind when I go, and then . . . then you will find him somewhere in this forest, like so many others.'

'Will you talk sense, for Christ's sake? Where is he? I want him back, *now*!'

'You will find him somewhere in this forest, when I am gone. Where do you think the human spirit goes, when a human dies?'

'How the fuck should I know? Heaven? Hell? Who knows!'

Jack was walking faster now, but the figure was retreating even more quickly.

'*The trees!*' it screamed at him, with its dragged-down mouth, and it sounded just like Sparky when he was angry or frustrated. 'That is why we had to protect your forests! That's where you go, when you die! Into the trees!'

'What?'

'Every time you clear a forest – every time you start a forest fire – you sacrifice hundreds and thousands of human spirits! Why do you think the trees talk when you walk into a forest? They're frightened of what you're going to do, just like we are! *That's* why we make you panic!'

'*What?*'

Jack felt as if he were going mad. This couldn't be real. This had to be a nightmare. But if this figure somehow had Sparky inside him, Jack was determined to get him back. He took three quick strides toward it, and made a lunge for it. The figure tilted away from him, so that he missed it, and then it turned and started to run. Jack went after it. He reached out and managed to grab its shoulder, and even though it seemed to be nothing but dazzling white light, it actually felt like a human shoulder – a cold, bare shoulder. He could even feel its shoulder blade moving.

The figure twisted itself free. Jack tried to grab it again, but it feinted to the left, and then to the right, and carried on running. All of the other figures were running, too, on either side of them, between the trees. They made a soft rustling sound as they ran, like the wind blowing through the leaves. It was a hushed, ghostly marathon – a dreamlike race to nowhere at all.

They ran up a long sloping hill, and then over the top. On the other side, however, the hill fell away steeply, and then even more steeply, until it was almost a vertical drop. The white figure was rushing down it without any difficulty, but it became so precipitous that Jack lost his balance, and careered down out of control, his arms windmilling to stop himself from falling over. He ran down so fast that he collided with the figure and they both hit the ground and rolled over and over in a tangle of arms and legs and blinding white light.

Although the figure was so bright, it felt like wrestling a

naked human being, and Jack was repelled by the feeling of cold, bare skin. In spite of his repulsion, however, he was able to force it face-down on to the leaf mold and sit astride it, twisting its arms behind its back.

'Where's my son?' he panted. 'I want to know what you've done with my son.'

The figure said nothing, although Jack could feel it breathing hard.

'Where's my son?' he shouted at it. 'If you don't tell me where my son is, I'm going to break your fucking arms! Both of them!'

Still the figure remained silent. Jack forced its arms further and further up between its shoulder blades until it made a strange whining sound, more like an animal in pain than a human.

'Where's my son? I'm not letting you go until you tell me!'

At that moment, though, he became aware that the forest around him was growing lighter. He looked up, and saw that twenty or thirty of the other figures were gathering around him. They, too, appeared to be made of nothing but light, as if they were ghosts, except that they were not transparent. They came closer and closer until they were standing all around him.

'I want my son back, that's all!' he told them. He was sure that he could make out faces on them – fogged with light, like faces in an overexposed photograph, but faces all the same. They didn't look angry or aggressive, as he might have expected them to. Instead, they all appeared to be resigned, and weary.

Two of them reached down and took hold of Jack's arms. Although they seemed to be made out of light, their hands felt human. They were strong, too. Another two of them bent down and pried his fingers away from the wrists of the figure he was sitting on, and then between them they lifted him up, until he was standing. During all of this time, not one of them spoke, and the forest was silent. Jack didn't try to struggle, or twist himself free. There were too many of them, and he didn't know what they were capable of doing to him.

Next, five or six of them lifted him up, until they were holding him above their heads, lying on his back with his arms spread wide, as if he were being crucified. They carried him around the hill that he had just run down, and back through the forest.

It was the most extraordinary sensation he had ever experienced in his life. It was like floating on his back on a sea of hands. He looked up and he could see the purplish early-evening sky through the branches of the pines, and even the moon.

At last they carried him back to the place where Sally and Undersheriff Porter were lying. They lowered him down, still without saying a word, until he was standing on his feet again. He turned around and looked at them, and they stood looking back at him.

'I'm coming back for my son,' he warned them, although he couldn't stop his voice from shaking. 'You don't frighten me any more, whatever you are.'

'We will be gone by the time you return, Jack,' said one of them, in Aggie's voice. It spoke quite gently, and sadly. 'There is no point in us staying here any longer. You can never be saved from yourselves.'

'What about Sparky? What about my son?'

'A promise is a promise, Jack. All those souls who sleep in these trees will tell you that.'

'Where is he?' Jack shouted. But none of the figures replied. Instead, they all turned their backs and began walking away. There was nothing that Jack could do but watch them disappear through the pines, until the last of them had gone. He was left on his own, except for the bodies of Sally and Undersheriff Porter, in a forest that was rapidly growing darker and darker.

He was tempted for a moment to pick up Undersheriff Porter's Sig automatic and go running back after those figures. But then he thought: *no – there are still a whole lot more of them than there is of me, and I don't know how many rounds there are in that gun's magazine. Certainly not enough to bring them all down, even if I manage to hit one of them with every single shot – and even supposing that bullets won't just pass right through them. They may feel solid, but they shine like light.*

He skirted around the two bodies and jogged his way out of the trees to Undersheriff Porter's Jeep. As he climbed up into the driver's seat, he looked back at the forest but saw no flickers of light. He started the engine, backed up to the edge of the lake, and then drove back toward the scout headquarters. The Jeep bounced and swayed and jolted into potholes, but he kept his

foot down as hard as he could. This might be his last chance
of saving Sparky from – what? He had no idea. Those figures
could be anything. Ghosts, aliens or angels. Or something that
nobody had ever heard of.

He reached the scout headquarters and slewed to a halt beside
the steps. He ran up to the balcony but when he tried to get
into the hallway he found that all the doors were locked, and
inside, the hallway was in darkness. He hammered on the
window with his fist. Nobody appeared. He hammered again,
and shouted out, 'Anybody there? Anybody there? I have an
emergency!'

He was just about to give up and go back to the Jeep, to see
if he could make radio contact with the sheriff's department.
Suddenly, though, a door opened on the left-hand side of the
hallway and light streamed out. Ambrose, the bald-headed scout
leader, appeared, and frowned in his direction. Jack knocked
on the glass again.

The scout leader came over and unlocked the door. 'What's
wrong?' he said. 'Where's the undersheriff?'

'He panicked. They both panicked. I was standing right next
to them and they shot themselves.'

'Holy cow. What about your boy? Did you manage to find
him?'

Jack shook his head, but he said, 'He's in the forest someplace.
Those white things have got him. Those spirits, or whatever
you want to call them. I saw them. I chased one of them, and
had a tussle with it, but the others pulled me off him. They
were like ghosts, only . . . I don't know . . . they were more
like *people* than ghosts. Only they weren't really people, either.
They were *glowing.*'

He stopped. He realized that the scout leader was looking at
him in a quizzical way, with his head tilted to one side and one
eyebrow lifted.

'You don't believe me, do you?' he said. 'Well, OK – *don't*
believe me. But Detective Faulkner and Undersheriff Porter,
they both shot themselves, and they're lying out there right now.
And my son's still missing, and whether you believe it or not,
those spirits have got him.'

The scout leader said, 'I'll call the Sheriff's Department, and

the forest ranger station, too. As soon as I've done that, you
and me can go looking for your son. If the spirits have got him,
I don't think they'll hurt him.'

'You *do* believe me?'

The scout leader looked almost annoyed. 'Of course I believe
you. I've been taking care of this campsite for fourteen years
and I've seen those things for myself. It's not something that
you can tell to anybody else, though – not without them thinking
that you've gone doolally.'

'They told me they're leaving. The way they said it, it's
like they're leaving right now.'

'They're leaving *now*? I always knew they were going to,
one day soon. But you mean *now* – like, tonight?' For the first
time Jack noticed that the scout leader had one green eye and
one brown eye.

'That's what they said. They used my son's voice to tell me.
And my late wife's voice, too.'

The scout leader nodded and now he looked convinced. 'They
do that. They use voices that you're going to recognize. People
that you love – people that you trust. Listen – let me make
those calls and then we'd better get going. Where did this
happen? Out by Lake Wolverine?'

Jack waited at the scout leader's office door while he called
the Sheriff's Department in Muskegon and then contacted the US
Forest Service ranger station. When he had hung up the phone,
the scout leader said, 'OK. We should have some deputies here
in a little over forty-five minutes, and rangers in maybe an hour.
Meantime, let's go look for your son. My name's Ambrose, by
the way. Ambrose Weld.'

The scout leader led Jack outside, and around to the parking
lot, where they climbed into his tan-colored Chevy Avalanche.
The back of the pick-up was stacked with folded-up tents and
other camping equipment, like folding chairs and pressure
lamps.

'You've really seen these spirits?' Jack asked as they drove
out toward Lake Wolverine.

'Sure, and I've heard them, too. Talking to me, and sounding
just like my late friend Woody, who passed over more than
seven years ago.'

'What did they say to you?'

'They cautioned me to keep my distance, that's about all. I think they knew that I didn't mean the forest any harm, so they didn't make me panic. Just the same, though, they didn't want me trespassing. This was – what – two or three years ago. I've known about them ever since I started working here, but that was the first time I saw them for real.'

'You knew about them before you even saw them?'

The scout leader slowed down to avoid hitting a gray ruffed grouse that was sedately waddling across the track. The bird hopped, hopped again, and then burst into flight.

'When I joined the staff here, I wanted to run this scout camp in a way that safeguarded its environment. I mean, look at it, Owasippe is just beautiful. So I thought I'd best find out everything I could about it. You know – become something of an Owasippe expert.

'I talked to Jim Dunn, this real old forest ranger, and I talked to some of the elders in the Potawatomi tribe, and one or two naturalists, too. Doctor Claude Duval, he was one of them. They didn't just tell me about the wildlife, and the plants. They also told me stories about these legendary spirits who had come here thousands of years ago from God alone knows where to protect the forest from the one thing that threatens it more than any other.'

'Which is?'

'*Homo sapiens*, what else? Or *homo* not-so *sapiens*.'

'But if you knew about these spirits, why didn't you warn those Scouts about them before they went off camping?'

'Because they hadn't made people panic like that for years. I don't know why they suddenly started again now, but maybe it has something to do with them leaving.'

'OK – but why didn't you tell the police about them?'

For a long moment, the scout leader took his eyes off the track ahead, and looked at Jack with a complicated expression on his face – part guilty, part irritated. 'What do you think they would have said to me if I had? They would have thought I was ready for the nuthouse. I probably would have lost my job, too.'

'Oh, great,' said Jack. 'You kept your job. I'm real pleased about that. But maybe if you'd spoken out, two more people wouldn't have killed themselves. One of them was a very good friend of mine. And maybe my son wouldn't have gone missing.'

'Nobody would have believed me, not for a minute, and you know that!' the scout leader retorted. 'In any case, even if they *had* believed me, what could they have done? You can't catch these spirits – they're *spirits*. Even the Potawatomi say that you can't catch the Manito Sucsee Wabe, and even if you could, you couldn't kill it.'

They had almost reached Lake Wolverine. Jack could see it sparkling through the trees, with a moon reflected in it like a broken dinner plate.

'I guess you're right,' he said. 'I'm sorry. It's been such a goddamned trauma, that's all. It's good to find somebody who doesn't think that I'm going crazy.'

'Either that,' said the scout leader, as he pulled the Avalanche in beside the SHERIFF LINE KEEP OUT tape. 'Or somebody who's just as crazy as you are.'

They made their way into the trees.

It may have been quiet before, but now it seemed as if every bird and animal in the forest was screeching and howling and jabbering. It was like a soundtrack from a jungle movie.

'Something's going on,' said the scout leader, shining his flashlight in between the oaks. 'You never normally get as much excitement as this, especially when it gets dark. Listen – hear that drumming sound? That's a grouse, beating its wings together.'

Jack led him to the place where Sally and Undersheriff Porter had shot themselves. He was sure he had exactly the right spot: he remembered the trees and the way the ground had sloped. But there was no trace of either body – not even a dent in the underbrush or a blood spatter to show where they might have been.

'Well – either this isn't the location or else they recovered from their injuries and walked off someplace,' said the scout leader.

'They blew their heads off,' Jack told him. 'There is absolutely no way that anybody could have recovered from that.'

He walked fifty or sixty feet further. There was still no sign of the bodies anywhere.

'The spirits must have carried them away,' he suggested.

'All right, maybe they did,' said the scout leader. 'But exactly what for?'

'Maybe they're curious about the human body, the way we are about them. Maybe they *are* aliens, and they've taken them away to study them.'

'Well, you could be right. But whatever they've done with them, they're dead. It's your son we need to find, before he gets the urge to kill himself, too. That's if he hasn't done it already.'

'Thanks,' said Jack.

'I'm sorry. Just being realistic.'

The cacophony of birds and animals was still going on, relentlessly. If anything, it was growing louder, and every now and then Jack could make out an agonized howling sound, like somebody grieving. Slowly, he and the scout leader made their way further into the forest, with the scout leader probing the beam of his flashlight from left to right, and back again.

'Sparks!' Jack shouted. 'Sparky – where are you? Can you hear me, Sparks?'

The scout leader took a brass whistle out of his shirt pocket and blew several long blasts. Then he too shouted, 'Sparky! Where are you, Sparky? You can come on out now, Sparky! Nobody's going to give you a hard time!'

He blew the whistle again, and called out, 'If you don't know where we are, walk toward the sound of my whistle! OK?'

After that, as they walked slowly forward through the forest, he blew his whistle every thirty seconds or so, two short blasts and one long one. Every time he did so, however, the racket of birds and animals in the forest seemed to grow even louder, as if they were furious at being disturbed.

'Never heard anything like this, ever,' said the scout leader. 'Something's really got them worked up.'

Jack stopped, and shouted out, '*Sparks! Sparky!*' but still there was nothing but the screeching and flapping and drumming and howling.

The scout leader took out a compass and shone his flashlight on it. 'I'm taking us side to side, in semi-circular sweeps,' he said. 'That's what we call the half-moon search, or arc search. It's the classic pattern for underwater searches, especially in swamps and black water, or for anybody lost in the woods, if there's only a couple of you. Takes time, I have to admit – but if anybody's deliberately hiding, or unconscious, you have a much better chance of finding them. Besides, the deputies and the rangers should be here pretty soon, and then we can start to do an extended line search.'

Jack shook his head. 'Jesus, Sparky could be miles away by now. How big is this forest?'

'Five hundred forty thousand acres, give or take.'

'Jesus.'

'We'll find him, don't you worry,' said the scout leader. 'The deputies will bring at least one tracker dog with them, and that'll make all the difference, I promise you.'

As if to punctuate his sentence, he blew his whistle again.

The first arc of their search had taken them almost back to the edge of the lake. Before they turned around to start another arc, the scout leader stopped to check his compass again. As he waited for him, Jack glimpsed pale white lights flickering behind the trees, about two hundred feet ahead of them, and slightly to their left. It was only for a few seconds, but he was sure that he had seen some of the illuminated figures which had carried him out of the forest.

'They're *there!*' he told the scout leader, pointing. 'I saw them, right over there.'

The scout leader frowned into the darkness. 'You're sure about that? I don't see anything.'

'Sure of it. Looked like more than one of them, too.'

'Do you feel anything?' the scout leader asked him. 'Any sense of panic?'

'No, none at all. But maybe it's different now that I know they can't hurt me.'

'I don't know about *can't*. Just because they didn't hurt you, that doesn't necessarily mean that they're not capable of it. All it means is that they didn't want to. I still think we need to be careful. Some of the Potawatomi legends say that the spirits could take a man apart as easy as a chicken.'

Jack kept looking in the direction in which he had seen the lights. 'I'm sure they have Sparky. I can't say that I understand *how*, exactly, but it's like he's been possessed by one of them.'

'Possessed? You mean like in *The Exorcist*?'

'Maybe that's not the right word, but one second he looks like Sparky, the next second he's turned into one of those white things. Maybe they're messing with my head, the same way they can make people panic. But I still think they have him, and he's alive, and I still think we can get him back.'

They were about to set off when they saw jostling headlights approaching from the opposite side of the lake, and heard the whinnying sound of SUVs.

'Well, they sure didn't waste any time,' said the scout leader. He made his way back through the underbrush to the taped-off area where the scouts' bodies had been found, and Jack followed him. They waited as two white patrol vehicles circled around the end of the lake and parked next to the scout leader's Avalanche. Seven deputies climbed out and came across to them, the beams from their flashlights criss-crossing as they walked. One of them was the K-9 officer, Deputy Ridout, with his panting German Shepherd Barrett – the same tracker dog who had sniffed out the headless woman in the pool.

A shaven-headed big-bellied deputy with fiery cheeks and gingery eyebrows held out his hand and said, 'Hi, Ambrose. None of us could believe it when we got your call. Dan Porter, of all people. Most level-headed guy I ever knew.'

'This gentleman was with them when they shot themselves,' said the scout leader. 'Jack, this is Sergeant Jim Truscott. Jim, this is Jack Wallace, father of the missing boy.'

'You actually saw them commit suicide, right in front of you?' asked Sergeant Truscott.

'I had my back turned when Undersheriff Porter shot himself,' said Jack. 'There was a bang, right behind me, and when I turned around I saw that he had blown his head off. Then Detective Faulkner shot herself.'

He lifted two fingers, pistol-like, to his ear, to show him how Sally had done it.

'So you and Undersheriff Porter and this detective were all out looking for your boy?'

'That's correct. But then they just panicked. Well, I panicked, too, but I didn't have a gun.'

'They *panicked*? They were both law officers. What made them panic?'

The scout leader looked at Jack as if to say, *will you tell him, or shall I?* Jack shrugged, and so the scout leader said, 'There are some people in the forest who can have that effect on you.'

'People? What people?'

'We don't know for sure who they are.'

Sergeant Truscott didn't answer at first. He was turning his head around, searching for something. Then he said, 'Where are their bodies? Dan Porter and this detective woman?'

'I think they've been taken away,' Jack told him.

'Taken away? Who by? What in hell's name is going on here?'

'Jim,' said the scout leader, 'I don't think we have a whole lot of time. Jack here has reason to believe that these people are going to be leaving momentarily.'

'Leaving? Where are they going? Do they have vehicles? Who the hell are they?'

'I think they have my son,' said Jack. 'The last time I saw them was about ten minutes ago, in that direction. I think there's about twenty or thirty of them. Please – we have to get after them.'

'OK, sir, we'll get after them,' said Sergeant Truscott. 'But who are they? What do they look like? Did they abduct your son for any particular reason? I really need you to fill me in here a little more. I can't—'

'Jim,' the scout leader interrupted him. 'How long have we known each other? Nearly five years, must be. Can you just trust me on this? Let's just go after these people. After we catch them, *then* we can talk about the whos and the whats and the whys. For now, let's just say that they're a kind of a cult, and they all look kind of shiny.'

'*Shiny*? What the Sam Hill does that mean?'

'You'll see. I promise you. Trust me, Jim, please.'

The rest of the deputies had gathered around them now. Sergeant Truscott hesitated for a moment and then he turned around to them and said, 'Listen up, men! We're looking for

maybe twenty-plus suspects who may or may not have kidnapped
this gentleman's son. How old is your son, sir? Can you tell us
his name, and what he looks like?'

'He's twelve, skinny, with blond hair. He goes by the nick-
name of Sparky.'

'OK, everybody. we're looking for Sparky, who's twelve.
The only description of the suspects that we have is that they're
shiny – and before you ask, I don't have a clue what that means,
either, but apparently you'll know them when you see them.'

He turned to Jack. 'That direction?' he asked.

Jack nodded. 'I'll come with you,' he said.

'Sure you can. But stay well behind us, would you, in case
there's any trouble. You, too, Ambrose. Keep well in back.'

The deputies spread out and began to make their way through the
trees. Three of them were in uniform, including Sergeant Truscott,
but the other four were wearing jeans and casual shirts and
jackets. Jack was surprised how young most of them were.
Sergeant Truscott and one other deputy looked as if they were
in their mid-forties, but the rest of them looked as if they had
just finished high school.

There was no reason for them to walk stealthily. The
cacophony in the forest was still as loud as it had been before,
with birds screeching and whooping and chattering and – somewhere in the distance – that eerie, other-worldly howling.

'Sure *sounds* like something's going on here,' said Sergeant
Truscott, falling back a little to join Jack and the scout leader.
'Last time I heard the forest as noisy as this, the whole
goddamned shebang was on fire.'

'I think the birds and the animals are all feeling anxious that
these people are leaving,' said the scout leader.

'How's that, Ambrose? How would they know?'

'These people have been taking care of them for a long, long
time, that's how.'

'I don't understand a word you're saying to me, Ambrose.
You're talking about these shiny people, right? I mean, have I
ever seen them?'

'No, Jim, you haven't. Not too many people have.'

'But if they've been here a long, long time, Ambrose, like

you say, how can I possibly not have seen them? Muskegon County has a population of only one hundred seventy-one thousand three hundred and two people, and I know almost all of them.'

Just then, Barrett started barking – short, sharp, intermittent barks, followed by a high-pitched howling that sounded almost the same as the howling in the forest.

Deputy Ridout was saying, 'Barrett! Hush up, will you! Barrett! What's wrong with you, boy? Barrett! Quit pulling like that! Barrett!'

'What is it, Eric?' called Sergeant Truscott. 'Has he picked up a scent?'

Deputy Ridout had dropped his flashlight, so two of the other officers shone theirs on him. He was struggling hard to keep control of Barrett, who was leaping and twisting and jerking at his leash.

'Barrett! Sit! I said, sit! I said *sit!*'

But Barrett appeared to be having a seizure. His eyes were bulging and his tongue was hanging out, and he wouldn't stop throwing himself into the air, almost choking himself on his collar. He dropped on to the ground on his back and rolled himself over, and it was then that Deputy Ridout lost his grip on his leash. Barrett immediately ran off into the darkness, and disappeared.

'What the hell was all that about?' said Sergeant Truscott. 'Looked like he was having an epileptic fit!'

'I have no idea,' said Deputy Ridout, panting. 'He had a medical only last week and he was A-one healthy. He never did anything like that before, ever.'

'Well, we'll just have to let him go for now. He'll probably find his way back to you once he's calmed down.'

Deputy Ridout could only shake his head in bewilderment. 'He never did anything like that before, not ever. That dog is the sanest dog I ever handled. That dog is saner than most *people*, for Christ's sake!'

Suddenly – between the trees up ahead of them – Jack saw a white shape running; and then another, and another. He laid his hand on Sergeant Truscott's shoulder and pointed and said, '*There* – that's one of them! Can you see it?'

The white shapes vanished almost immediately, but then they reappeared, and another two or three shapes came flitting between the trees. They were only about three hundred feet away, maybe less.

'See what I mean, Jim?' said the scout leader. '*Shiny!*'

'OK, men!' Sergeant Truscott snapped. 'Let's go get them! But remember they may have a hostage – so if it comes to a firefight, make sure you're clear what you're aiming at!'

He unclipped his holster and hauled out his gun, and all of his deputies did the same. They advanced into the forest with their flashlights pointing in front of them and their weapons held high. Jack and the scout leader followed them, but staying well back. If there was going to be shooting, Jack didn't want to get caught in any crossfire, even if it was friendly.

For the first few hundred feet, the forest was in total darkness, although with every step they took the noise seemed to grow even more deafening. The howling, too, grew louder. Then, directly up ahead of them, Jack saw three or four fluorescent white figures, flickering like neon strip lights. Then more of them, and more.

Here they were: the Forest Ghosts, the white deer spirits, the howling angels. The white things that had caused hundreds of people to kill themselves out of panic. Yet now Jack realized that he wasn't panicking at all. He was desperately anxious about Sparky, but he felt none of that dread that had gripped him before, and it didn't look as if Sergeant Truscott or any of his deputies were panicking, either. Understandably, they all looked tense, but they were showing no signs of the madness that had led Sally and Undersheriff Porter to blow their own heads off.

Cautiously, the deputies stepped out of the trees and into the clearing where the white figures were gathered. Jack and the scout leader followed them. Here, the light was bright but gray, like an overcast day, and the howling was so loud that Jack could hardly hear himself think. They could see now that the figures were standing in a circle, each with their arms intertwined. Their heads were bowed, and their mouths were stretched downward as if they were moaning with grief.

They all seemed to be concentrating hard, like a circle of

people holding a séance, or trying to summon up Satan. They didn't appear to have noticed the arrival of Jack and the scout leader and the deputies – or, if they had, they were ignoring them. *So much for them being frightened of us*, Jack thought.

Sergeant Truscott crossed over to Jack and the scout leader with one hand lifted to shield his eyes. 'What the hell are they?' he shouted, over the howling.

'Spirits, I guess you could call them!' the scout leader shouted back at him.

Sergeant Truscott shook his head in disbelief. '*Spirits?*'

'Forest Ghosts, that's what they're generally known as.'

'Never heard of them. Think they understand English?'

'Oh, yes. They can use the voices of people you know to talk to you.'

'Can't even believe what I'm looking at,' said Sergeant Truscott. Then he turned to Jack and said, 'Do you see your son around here, sir?'

'No,' Jack told him. 'Nowhere. I don't know what they could have done with him.'

'In that case, whatever these people are, I'm going to be breaking up this little gathering. But keep an eye open for your son and shout out if you see him.'

'OK, sure.'

Sergeant Truscott beckoned to his men and they positioned themselves around one side of the circle of white figures, all with their weapons raised high.

'Now listen up!' Sergeant Truscott shouted, trying to make himself heard over the howling. 'This here is unlawful assembly as defined under paragraph seven-five-two subsection five-four-three of the Michigan State penal code! You are trespassing here on private property and I require you to cease this activity as of right now!'

'My God, he has to be joking,' said the scout leader.

The howling continued, and the figures began to flicker even more rapidly. Sergeant Truscott waited for a few seconds, and then he bellowed, 'Break it up! You hear me? Cut out that goddamned racket and lay down flat on the ground! Now!'

Still the white figures took no notice of him, and now they were flashing almost like stroboscopic lights. Jack could sense a tightening in the air all around them, as if some huge electrical charge were beginning to build up.

'*Assume the position!*' roared Sergeant Truscott.

Jack thought he could hear a deep humming, too, underneath the howling. The trees all around them were swaying and rustling, and the birds were literally screaming. He looked at the scout leader and shouted, '*What?* What's happening?'

'I don't know!' the scout leader shouted back. 'But I think we need to get out of here!'

'I can't leave Sparky!'

'You don't even know that he's here!'

'I saw him! He spoke to me!'

'It's all an illusion! These spirits – I think I got them all completely wrong! I don't think they're benign at all!'

At that moment, Sergeant Truscott screamed, '*Shut the fuck up!*' at the circle of luminous white people, and fired his gun into the air.

The response was instantaneous. The howling didn't stop, but the circle suddenly broke apart, and the white figures went for Sergeant Truscott and his deputies as ferociously as two-legged wolves. Two of them seized Sergeant Truscott's arms, while a third one plunged its hands straight through his uniform shirt and into his stomach. It ripped him open with a thick tearing noise that sounded like burlap being torn apart, right up to his ribcage. Jack could see him staring down in shock as his bloody pale intestines tumbled out of his abdomen and dropped down on to the forest floor. He didn't scream as he watched this happen. He could see it, and he must have been able to feel it, and yet by the expression on his face Jack could tell that he couldn't really believe it. *This can't be me, being torn open like this, and all my insides falling out. How can this be me?*

Then, however, one of the white figures twisted his right arm around in its socket, all the way around, so that the sinews crackled. It twisted it around again and then again, and this time Sergeant Truscott let out a shrill, agonized whoop that was almost girlish. His arm was wrenched right off, and tossed away into the underbrush, and then the second figure twisted off his left arm, too.

At the same time, more white figures were swarming all over the other deputies, and were pulling them apart, too. Jack saw blood flying across the clearing, and dismembered arms and legs, and even though the figures kept up their howling, the screams of the deputies were even more penetrating.

He backed away, between the pines, and Ambrose the scout leader came after him. The scout leader kept crossing himself and mumbling, 'Holy Mary Mother of God, Holy Mary Mother of God.'

Jack thought that they had managed to escape from the clearing unnoticed by the white figures. He was just about to turn around and start running when five of them caught sight of them and immediately came rushing toward them.

'No!' screamed the scout leader. 'No! I always took care of you! I always protected the forest! No! I never hurt you! I never told anyone about you! No!'

But four of the white figures took hold of him, and forced him on to his back on the ground. The fifth figure came after Jack.

Jack ran as hard as he could into the darkness, dodging and jinking like a football player as he tried to avoid hitting the trees. But he could hear the white figure catching up with him, its footsteps close behind his back and its pale light shining on the trees up ahead of him.

He bounded down into a hollow, and as he did so the figure leapt on top of him, bringing him crashing down into the bushes. The figure was cold, and strong, and Jack was exhausted. He lay there, with his cheek against the dirt and the leaf mold, gasping for breath and resigned to die. Only two or three hundred yards behind him, he could hear the scout leader screeching as he was torn to pieces.

Jack closed his eyes. *Think of nothing*, he told himself, *and it will soon be over*. The white figure remained sitting on top of him, keeping him pressed down against the ground, but seconds went by and it made no attempt to pull off his arms or to turn him over and disembowel him. He heard the scout leader screaming, 'Jesus! Oh, Jesus!' He was almost singing it, like a hymn.

After that, the forest fell silent, except for an occasional blue jay screeching. Even the howling had died away.

'You should go now, Dad,' said the white figure, in Sparky's voice.

'Sparks? Is that you?'

'It *was* me, Dad. Not any more.'

'Where's Sparky? What have you done with him?'

'We needed him. We needed many. Sparky was just one of them. We had to bring them all here, from wherever they were scattered. This is the place where we first arrived, and this is the only place from which we can leave.'

'I said, where's Sparky? I want to know what the hell you've done with him.'

There was a lengthy pause. A cool breeze was blowing through the forest, and for some reason Jack detected a note of sadness in the white figure's voice.

'Sparky was promised as so many were promised. We had no way of knowing then when one of your family would be needed. For all we knew at that time, it could have been many hundreds of years before we had to leave. But you could not be stopped from wantonly destroying all the beauty and the riches that were given to you, with greater and greater destructiveness, and we have no wish to witness you doing it, or to try to stop you any longer.'

'Is Sparky dead?'

'It depends what you mean by dead. It depends if you understand what happens when you pass from one level of existence to the next. Some of your cultures almost grasped it. But none of you have ever understood it enough to protect it.'

The white figure climbed off Jack's back and stood up. Jack sat up, wiping the dirt from his face with the back of his hand. The white figure was only faintly phosphorescent now, but he could just make out the features of a face, which looked like Sparky, only older.

'So – aren't you going to rip my arms off and tear my guts out, like everybody else? Or make me panic and kill myself?'

The white figure not only sounded sad; it looked sad, too. 'No, Dad. It's too late for that now, and you've given us enough. You should go now. Forget about Sparky. Forget that you ever saw us. You will have to live a new life now. A very different kind of life.'

With that, the figure turned around and began to walk back toward the clearing where the rest of the figures were gathered.

'*Sparks!*' Jack called after it. The white figure hesitated, but didn't look back at him.

'Sparks, I love you!'

Three long seconds went by, and then the white figure continued walking. Jack could have done what it had told him to do, and leave the forest, but he needed to see where Sparky was going, and what all of those figures were going to do next. How could he ever forget him, or forget what had happened here?

He followed the white figure, keeping his distance. As he approached the clearing, however, he looked up into the trees and saw the remains of the scout leader, and for a few moments he had to stop and press his hand over his mouth to stop himself from retching. The scout leader's arms and legs had all been wrenched off, and then his trunk had been split open and suspended from an overhanging branch by loops of intestines. The scout leader was swaying from side to side, and staring down at him with a slightly mystified expression, as if he were thinking, *this wasn't the way I was supposed to die, was it? I was supposed to die in bed, when I was old, with a priest to give me the last rites.*

He stayed well back amongst the trees while the white figure rejoined the rest of the figures, and crouched down behind the bushes. He didn't want to go too close in case the other figures couldn't be trusted to spare his life, and also because he didn't want to see too much of the bloody litter of human bodies that was scattered around.

The figures gathered in their circle again, with their arms linked together, and began to howl. They howled higher and louder, and they flickered faster and faster, until it was like watching the last blank frames of a movie film flapping through a projector.

As their howling reached a crescendo, it sounded as if every bird and animal in the Owasippe forest was joining in. The circle of white figures started to rotate, very slowly at first, but gradually they spun around faster and faster until they were only a blur of light. The light rose up in the air, up to treetop height. It hesitated there, as if the spirits were reluctant to leave the forest which they had guarded for so long.

Beneath them, the matted vegetation on the forest floor began to smolder, and turn black. Acrid smoke drifted across the clearing and through the trees, as gray and silent as ghosts. Jack now saw what had caused the patch of scorched earth beside the lake – not a campfire, not a lightning strike, but the heat created by the first of the white figures rising up into the air, and returning to wherever it was they originally came from.

He walked out into the clearing, with burning pine needles sparkling all around him like the lights of a miniature city. He stood looking up at the white figures and he had never felt such radiant power in his life, such a palpable sense of inspiration, and it moved him to tears that they were going. He had felt desperately lonely ever since Aggie had died, but to see these spirits leaving the world gave him an even deeper feeling of loneliness, as if the whole of mankind was now being abandoned to the cold, dark emptiness of space. Nobody to watch over us any more, nobody to save us from our own ignorance and our own greed and our own blind destructiveness.

Standing beneath that light, as it gradually rose higher and higher, he could understand what angels were; and he could almost understand what God was.

The light kept on rising until it looked as small as a paper lantern. It passed through a high skein of cirrus clouds, and after that, Jack could see only the faintest spot of white light, and then nothing at all. Whatever the Forest Ghosts had been, the white deer spirits, the *nish-gites*, had gone forever.

Jack walked back through the forest. He was beginning to feel very chilly now, and he was in shock. He reached the edge of Lake Wolverine and stood there for a while, breathing slowly and deeply and feeling the breeze that was blowing off the water. On the other side of the lake, he could see more head-lights approaching, and he guessed the forest rangers had arrived. He couldn't even begin to think what he was going to say to them.

He was still standing there when he heard a voice in his ear. 'Jack? Can you hear me?'

It was such a soft whisper that it could have been nothing but the breeze, rustling in the trees behind him.

'Jack, *słyszysz mnie?*'

'Aggie,' he said, but so quietly that nobody else could have heard him, even if they had been standing close.

'You will find him where you left him, Jack.'

'What do you mean, "where I left him"? Where did I leave him?'

'He doesn't blame you, Jack. He always saw it coming, in his stars. He knew what his destiny was.'

'Aggie, I don't know what you mean. Tell me.'

But now the forest rangers' Jeeps were coming around the edge of the lake, and he could no longer hear her. And as they approached, there was an immense bang high in the sky directly above him – more like a sonic boom than a burst of thunder. He looked up just in time to see an intense flash of white light.

He was still staring up at the sky when one of the forest rangers walked up to him, a thin, wiry-looking man in flappy shorts and with a Frank Zappa moustache. The forest ranger looked up, too, and said, 'What in the name of all that's holy was *that?*'

The Promise

And then, two weeks later, at 6.07 in the morning, Krystyna called Jack from Warsaw. He reached out from under the bedcovers and dropped the phone on the floor. After he had leaned over and retrieved it he frowned at his bedside clock and said, 'Krystyna? What time is it?'

'I'm really sorry. It's one p.m. here. I know it's early for you.'

'Well, I'm usually up by now but I had a late night. I've just re-opened the restaurant after closing for a week.'

'I'm sorry. But I have found out something very important concerning your great-grandfather and I thought you would like to know about it as soon as possible.'

'Did you get your permission to dig?'

'Yes, I did. The Kampinos National Park authorities gave me the go-ahead on Friday, so a colleague and I have been excavating the site all weekend.'

'OK. Good. So what did you find?'

'I found the bones of Mrs Koczerska's great-uncle Andrzej.'

'Go on.'

'Nobody else's bones. Only great-uncle Andrzej. It does look, from the damage to his skull, though, that he may well have committed suicide.'

'But what about all that stuff in his diary about them both committing suicide together, him and my great-grandfather?'

'That's why I'm calling. There was a message, left with the bones, in a tobacco pouch. Most of it is still legible. Do you want me to read it to you?'

Jack sat on the end of the bed while she read him the message. It took her only a few minutes, but when she had finished, he sat in silence for a very long time.

'Do you want me to read it again?' she asked him.

'Yes,' he said. 'But you can do it face-to-face. I'm catching the first plane I can get to Warsaw.'

* * *

Jack left Tomasz in charge of the restaurant again, and promised him an even bigger bonus this time. Tomasz said, 'You don't have to pay more, Boss. I know grief, too. I lose baby girl by woman who is not my wife. My heart is broken, but who can I tell?'

Jack said nothing, but gave Tomasz a hug, and slapped his back.

That evening, he took a cab out to O'Hare and caught the direct 9.50 p.m. flight to Warsaw. He tried to sleep on the plane but the message that Krystyna had read to him was rolling over and over in his mind. It was the first hope that he had been given since Sparky had disappeared into the Owasippe forest that he might be able to find out what had happened to him, and not spend the rest of his life wondering if he was still alive – or, if he had died, *how* he had died, and where. At the very least, he might be able to give him a grave.

It was warm and sunny when he arrived at Chopin airport the following afternoon, and Krystyna was there to meet him – wearing the same librarian spectacles that she had worn when she first picked him up. He kissed her and she still smelled as fragrant, too.

As she drove them into the city center, she said, 'Do you believe what your great-grandfather wrote? You don't think it was just an excuse? Maybe he and Andrzej were caught by the Germans before they could commit suicide, and the Germans made him do it, and took him prisoner. He was a very famous person, after all, your great-grandfather. Maybe they just never had the chance to boast that they had caught him – the world-famous violinist who had fought with the Home Army.'

'No,' said Jack. 'I'm sure he was telling the truth.'

He paused, because he found it hard to tell Krystyna what had happened to Sparky without developing a painful catch in his throat. But slowly, and with as little drama as he could, he explained how they had gone back to Owasippe. He told her about Sally and Undersheriff Porter shooting themselves; and how the Forest Ghosts had torn all those sheriff's deputies to pieces; and how they had gathered together and risen into the clouds, like some ascension from the Bible.

Krystyna listened without interrupting him. After all, she had seen for herself what panic could do to people in a forest. When he had finished, she said, 'What did your police say, when they found all of this massacre?'

'They questioned me for twenty-three hours straight, but it was obvious that I hadn't done it. They found Undersheriff Porter and my friend Detective Faulkner in a shallow grave, covered with pine needles and leaves. That was the Forest Ghosts for you . . . I think they loved us, and cared for us. Well, they must have done to stay here for so many thousands of years. But I think they were just like parents when their teenage kids go bad. There comes a time when they wash their hands of them, and say, like, you made your bed, you damn well lie in it.'

'So how did they explain all of those officers being torn to pieces?'

'Cougars.'

'*Cougars?*'

'Yes, we still have a few big wild cats in our forests, just like you have lynxes in Poland. I don't think the medical examiners really believed it, not for a moment. Even the most dexterous cougar couldn't twist a man's arms and legs off like that. But the media were satisfied, and that was all that mattered.'

Krystyna drove Jack to her apartment in Sadyba. It was on the fifth floor of a quiet brown-brick block in a gated community, surrounded by trees. The apartment itself was furnished in a modern, minimalist style, with a white leather couch and a large abstract mural in gray and white, and a tall rough-textured sculpture of a sad-looking nude.

'Beer?' asked Krystyna.

'You read my mind.'

She poured him a beer and a glass of chilled white wine for herself, and sat down on the couch next to him with her legs tucked up under her. On the glass-topped table in front of them lay a red folder, and two or three books, and a worn, dark-brown pouch made of oilskin, of the kind used by sailors and soldiers to keep their tobacco dry.

She opened the pouch and took out two folded sheets of paper. One had been torn from a notepad, and was crowded with scrawly writing in green ink. It was stained and faded, but most of it looked legible. The other was a music score, with five or six lines of crotchets and quavers.

She held up the sheet from the notepad and said, 'This was signed by "Grzegorz Walach" and dated April 17, 1946, so it must have been buried with Maria Koczerska's great-uncle Andrzej's remains after the war was over. Whoever put it there must have known exactly where his remains were located, and there was only one person who could have known that.'

'My late wife Aggie knew,' said Jack. 'Otherwise *we* never would have found them, would we?'

'Come on, Jack. It was somebody who *sounded* like her. But you told me yourself that the spirits always talk to you in the voices of people you care for. I suppose that's how they get your attention, and your trust.'

'So read me this letter again,' Jack asked her.

Krystyna took off her spectacles. '"To any of my descendants whom I have hurt and betrayed, I address this message, and pray that the time never comes when any of them read it. I beg your forgiveness with all of my heart. On November twenty-ninth, 1940, Andrzej buried his diary and his notes for safekeeping, and then we walked deeper into the forest to take our own lives.

'"Once we had found a quiet place, poor Andrzej shot himself. I then knelt down to follow his example, praying to the Lord to receive my soul. As I knelt there, however, I heard the voice of my dead sister Danuta speaking to me, so close that I could have believed that she was standing next to me. She said that if I made a solemn promise to the Forest Ghost, it would not harm me, and that I would no longer feel that the only way to stop feeling such terror was to take my own life.

'"I opened my eyes but there was nobody visible. I continued to listen, though, because I had loved Danuta dearly. She died of pneumonia when she was only nine years old, and after all those years I still missed her sorely. She said that it was possible that, many years in the future, the Forest Ghost would have to leave this forest and journey to another forest in another part of the world. There were spirits in every forest, and they had been here for thousands of years, but the time might come when they had to leave this Earth, which they could only do from the first place where they had arrived.

"'In order to accomplish this journey, said Danuta, the Forest Ghost would need to possess the shape of a living human being. It would spare my life and relieve me of my panic if I promised that one day in the future it could take the shape of one of my descendants. She said that this would probably never happen, and that even if it did, it would be many hundreds of years from now. It was, however, a binding promise, and one day it was possible that a descendant of mine, not yet born, perhaps, would pay the price for it.

"'I agreed to make such a promise. It was cruel and it was craven of me to do so, but it is hard to describe to you the abject terror that I was feeling, and quite simply I wanted to live, and not to die. I do not know if any of my descendants will ever pay the price for it, but if they do, I can only tell you that I will be ashamed of my promise for the rest of my life.

"'I am now working as a teacher and accountant in Wrocław, under the name of Feliks Wasilewski. I have picked up a violin only once since I made my promise, and that was to compose these few lines of music, which I have written as a requiem for whichever descendant of mine might have paid the price for my cowardice.'"

'It's signed Grzegorz Walach,' she said finally.

Jack sat for a long time in silence once Krystyna had finished reading. She reached across to him and held his hand.

'Well,' he said at last, looking at her. 'I think we know where Sparky is now, don't we?'

Along with Komisarz Pocztarek, three police officers with a Labrador tracker dog and two forest rangers, they returned to the part of the Kampinos Forest where they had searched for Krystyna's colleague Robert.

They started by finding the place where Jack and Krystyna had stopped to consider killing themselves and Sparky had run away from them. Jack gave the tracker dog one of Sparky's T-shirts to sniff. It had rained several times since they were here, but the overhanging trees had protected the scent from being totally washed away. The tracker dog hesitated and wuffled two or three times, but it managed to follow the trail deeper and deeper into the forest.

Before long, they reached a long downhill slope where the pine trees grew so close together that it was difficult for them to shoulder their way through. The forest was utterly silent, and dark, and claustrophobic, and Jack began to feel that they would never be able to find their way out of it.

'If your son is here, this dog will find him,' said Komisarz Pocztarek, trying to be reassuring. 'The nose of this breed is so sensitive, they can even smell cadavers under running water.'

Jack said nothing. He wanted to find Sparky, but not like this.

After about ten minutes of struggling through the trees, however, the Labrador let out three sharp barks and began to scuffle with its paws at the brown matted pine needles. Its handler pulled it away, and the other two officers pulled on blue latex gloves before they hunkered down and started to brush aside the vegetation with their hands.

Jack stayed well back, and Krystyna held his hand. Neither of them spoke.

After a few minutes, the officers exposed the pale blotchy flank of a body. Komisarz Pocztarek walked over and took off his cap. 'I'm sorry for this, sir, but it looks like your son. Could you please identify him for us?'

Jack let go of Krystyna's hand and went up to the edge of the shallow grave. At least the Forest Ghost had respected Sparky enough to bury him, so that he hadn't been lying here naked on the forest floor, prey to any passing animal. The body's face was so puffy that he didn't look like Sparky at all, but Jack instantly recognized his blond hair, and the metal pendant that he was wearing around his neck – the pendant that used to belong to his mother.

'– *dependant* . . .' That's what Jack thought she had whispered to him on the plane. But in reality she had been telling him where he was, and how he could identify him when he found him.

'– *the pendant* . . .'

Komisarz Pocztarek said, 'I am very sorry for your loss, sir. But I still do not understand. I saw your son leave the forest and I presume that he flew back to America with you. How did he return here?'

Jack turned away from the grave. 'I'm just beginning to find out how little any of us understand about anything, Komisarz. And now we never will.'

Requiem

Two weeks later, Sparky was buried next to his mother at Saint Boniface Cemetery. It was a dry day, but very gusty, and black hats and funeral scarves blew away in the wind.

As the casket was lowered, a single violinist played the requiem that Grzegorz Walach had written for the descendant whose life he had given away, even though he had never known who he was. Jack had wondered whether to have this music played or not, but then he decided that even if it was not yet time to forget, it was time to forgive. He had experienced the same panic for himself, and it wasn't easy to judge his great-grandfather for the terrible promise that he had made.

The notes of the requiem were sad beyond description. They summed up all of the pain and despair that so many people had suffered over so many years, and the deep uncertainty about tomorrow. Only Jack and Krystyna knew what they really meant. They meant loss, and abandonment, and betrayal. They meant that the spirits who had protected us for so many millennia had now left us to survive on our own.

When the violinist had finished, Jack threw a clod of earth onto Sparky's casket, and then turned away from the grave, pulling out his handkerchief to wipe his eyes. Krystyna gave him a sympathetic smile.

'Looks like I'm on my own now,' he told her.

She shook her head, although she didn't say anything. She linked arms with him and they walked together toward the cemetery gates, with angels watching them on either side.